"I think I've been burned."

Sunny didn't bother to lie to her superior. "I'm going to be in the tabloids tomorrow...as Jock Prentiss's latest lover."

"Pictures?" asked Bosey.

"Yup."

"Who's Jock Prentiss?"

"He lives next door. As far as I can make out, he's a television cop. His real claim to fame, at the moment, is an alleged love affair with a peer's wife."

"And you got caught outside his place wearing close to nothing while trying to chase after your friend's cat, so the paparazzi think you're involved with him?"

"Yes."

"It doesn't matter. Our *friend* likes famous people. So now you're famous. And maybe this Jock already knows him and can get you an introduction. Any problems you foresee in working up an acquaintance with Prentiss?"

Sunny thought of the heated way Jock Prentiss had looked at her that morning. "No," she said. "Probably not."

Dear Reader,

Once again, Silhouette Intimate Moments is breaking new ground. In our constant search to bring you the best romance fiction in the world, we have found a book that's very different from the usual, and yet it's so appealing and romantic that we just had to publish it. I'm talking about *Angel on my Shoulder,* by Ann Williams. Ann isn't a new author, of course, but the heroine of this book definitely *is* something new. In fact, she's an absolute angel—and I mean that literally! Her name is Cassandra, and she comes to Earth on a mission. Her assignment is to save the soul of one very special man, but she gets a lot more than she bargained for when she takes on an earthly shape—and starts to experience earthly emotions. I don't want to tell you any more for fear of spoiling the magic, so I hope you'll start reading right away and discover for yourself the special nature of this book.

Another book is special to me this month, too, though for a more personal reason. In *The Man Next Door,* author Alexandra Sellers not only creates some very appealing human characters, she introduces some precocious felines, as well. And if you think Lorna Doone and Beetle are too good to be true, I feel honor bound to tell you that they're actually very real. In fact, they're both living in my house, where they're more than willing to cause all sorts of trouble. But now, through the vividness of Alexandra's writing, you can get to know them, too. I hope you like them—as well as *The Man Next Door.*

Marilyn Pappano and Lucy Hamilton, two more of your favorite authors, finish off the month in fine style. And in coming months, look for Kathleen Eagle (back after a long absence), Emilie Richards, Heather Graham Pozzessere, Kathleen Korbel, Jennifer Greene and more of the top-notch writers who have made Silhouette Intimate Moments such a reader favorite.

Enjoy!

Leslie Wainger
Senior Editor and Editorial Coordinator

ALEXANDRA SELLERS

The Man Next Door

SILHOUETTE·INTIMATE·MOMENTS®

Published by Silhouette Books New York

America's Publisher of Contemporary Romance

SILHOUETTE BOOKS
300 East 42nd St., New York, N.Y. 10017

THE MAN NEXT DOOR

ISBN: 0-373-07406-9

First Silhouette Books printing November 1991

Printed in the U.S.A.

ALEXANDRA SELLERS

used to force her mother to read to her for hours. She wrote her first short story at ten, but as an adult got sidetracked and didn't get published until she was twenty-seven. She also loves travel; she wrote one book in Israel, and began another in Greece. She is currently living in London, but that could change at any time.

This book is dedicated to my editor's cat

Chapter 1

The perp was poking her with the barrel of his gun, all up and down her body, *jab, jab, jab,* and all the while Bosey was screaming incomprehensibly. Sunny pushed the gun away, more irritated than frightened, and suddenly Bosey stopped screaming and started to purr loudly in her ear. "Bosey, cut that out!" she said, pushing at him; and then, opening her eyes, she stared into the bright amber eyes staring into hers from point-blank range and laughed in relief.

"Cat, what are you doing?" she demanded weakly. The sun was shining brightly through the bedroom curtains, but as far as Sunny's body-clock was concerned, it could be any time. She rolled over and read her watch. "Five-thirty-eight?" she asked incredulously. "A.M.? Do you make a habit of this?"

The cat smiled encouragingly at her and kneaded her deltoid muscle through the duvet. It trilled happily in its throat. Clearly it wanted something, probably food. Sunny calculated briefly. She'd been asleep last night by eight-

thirty; that meant nine hours. Probably if she got up now
and went to bed at a reasonable time tonight her body-clock
would be perfectly in sync with English time by tomorrow
morning.

"All right." She signalled her capitulation to the cat by
flinging the duvet back and burying her under it. The cat
screamed delightedly. On her feet in her red T-shirt, Sunny
glanced around for a bathrobe. There wasn't one handy, and
her own clothes were all still packed, but the house already
had the warmth of the summer morning. Outside in the
street she could hear an odd jangling noise, which her brain
tried but failed to label. It didn't push any warning buttons, and Sunny let it go. "All right," she said to the owner
of the slightly demented amber eyes gazing at her from under the duvet. "All right, let's go."

The cat bounded off the bed and rushed out the door
ahead of her. At the top of the stairs they were met by a
second cat, an entirely ordinary black ex-tom, as though,
Sunny thought, Emma were compensating for the oddness
of one cat with the commonness of the other. Both cats tried
to trip her on the way downstairs. "You realize this is at-
tempted homicide," Sunny informed them conversationally, though she didn't normally talk to animals. "I could
book you both." The cats quite properly ignored the warning, since it wasn't true. "Vot sacrifices I mike forr my
cahntree," Sunny moaned, clutching the balustrade for
support. "Do I really have to put up with you two for the
duration?"

A few minutes later, sitting at the breakfast table, the
door open onto a still-shaded garden, a fresh wind rapidly
blowing away her mental cobwebs, and a cup of black tea in
front of her, she read Emma's note of instructions. "How
did you get a name like Lorna Doone?" Sunny asked mildly,
tilting her head to look at the tortoiseshell cat weaving excitedly around her ankles under the table. She had put
tinned food in the cats' bowls last night, but this morning

they weren't getting anything till she had read Emma's note headlined, "CATS: CARE AND FEEDING OF."

The cat burst into voluble explanations in the same squeaky but effective voice that had been used to wake Sunny up. Sunny gazed at her. It was a cute cat, all right, if you didn't mind the boxer's body and the cauliflower ears, but that this was a "designer" cat—as Emma insisted—surprised her. With its thick, bunchy body, and those weird ears, and its almost geometric patterns of cream, grey and amber fur, she would have called it a souped-up alley cat herself. Sunny grinned suddenly. "I suppose that's what makes you a designer cat," she told Lorna Doone. "You look so down-market you have to be up." She bent down and extended a hand, and the cat instantly fell on its back in sensuous expectation, its miaow becoming the strange, trilling sound in its throat she had heard before. "What a repertoire you have," Sunny said admiringly.

She rubbed the cat's stomach absently for a moment while she sipped her tea, then straightened up and reached out to pick up Emma's letter again.

"Lorna Doone is in heat," said point number two, heavily underlined. "She is not to be allowed outside on any pretext whatever. Beware. She is very persuasive."

Sunny leapt up and rushed to the garden door. Beetle, the black cat, was already out in the garden, stalking something invisible. Sunny closed the door and leaned against it, gazing at the cat named Lorna Doone, who was watching her curiously. "I don't know," said Sunny, in a tone of heavy resignation. "Why do I get the funny feeling you guys are going to be more trouble than you're worth?"

"Something I thought you'd like to know," she had said to Bosey.

He was bent over his desk. Wasting no energy, as usual, he only raised his eyes. "What's that?"

"You know this address, where the partner lives in London?"

"22 Banbury Square," said Bosey.

"Yes, sir. I thought you'd want to know that my best friend from university has a house in the same square. Number 40. I'll bet she knows the guy. She was married to a really rich Egyptian and when—"

She broke off when Bosey sat back in his chair and gazed at her, one eye narrowed, the other eyebrow raised. Slowly the focus of his eyes left her, and his heavy forefinger tapped the edge of his desk. She waited while the finger slowed and stopped, and Bosey, without moving a muscle, focussed his eyes on her again. "The Brits have been trying to infiltrate that operation for six months," he said softly at last, and then he said what she hadn't allowed herself to hope to hear. "This friend," Bosey had said. "Any chance she might invite you for a visit?"

She yawned suddenly, in spite of the nine hours' solid sleep. Her flight had been badly delayed yesterday, first because of a late takeoff from Toronto, and then, in London, a bomb scare at Heathrow had meant that the plane had sat at the end of a runway for hours before being allowed to approach the terminal and unload its passengers. Sunny hadn't slept at all on the flight, and as soon as she was through passport control someone had whisked her off for a meeting. It had been eight o'clock last night before she actually got to Emma's beautiful house, where the cats were awaiting her. The cats had been in an absolute fury of hunger, loneliness and—Sunny supposed now—sexual frustration, at least on Lorna Doone's part, but Sunny had been too exhausted to do more than scrape some food into their bowls, pour out the last of a pint of milk, get undressed and fall into bed.

Sunny sipped her tea and made another face at Lorna Doone. "I wish I hadn't given you all the milk last night," she muttered. Sunny could drink anything, she'd had to learn to, but when she had her druthers she preferred her tea with milk. And she would have bet any money that the posh neighbourhood around Emma's house didn't boast any twenty-four-hour milk stores. If there was such a thing in London.

Sunny continued reading:

They get dry food in the morning and tinned—1/2 tin each—at night, mixed with any leftover dry food. The cats each have their own dishes, but if Lorna decides to gobble Beetle's, I give him extra later.

The house is all theirs. They sleep on the bed, and if that bothers you, you'll have to sleep in the guest room, but I shouldn't bother, because I expect they'd follow you. Anyway, the guest room bed is feeling its age.

There are about two dozen cat toys around the place, and at least six or seven should be available at all times. Look under the sofas and the kitchen hutch for the missing.

Sunny rolled her eyes unbelievingly. "Oh, what I do for my country!" she told the cat again. Taking this for an invitation, Lorna Doone leapt up into her lap and pushed her head against the letter, making little throaty sounds of encouragement and pleasure. Sunny scratched behind one peculiarly flattened ear and went back to the note.

Along with Spidey—bright blue, eight legs—Lorna particularly loves her catnip carrot, while Beetle is partial to his catnip panda. Try to see that these don't get lost for very long.

Give them lots of attention. They will sometimes respond to their names, but will always—if awake—come running if you yell "Mousers!" in a very excited tone. This means you're going to feed them a treat, and you

have to make them sit first—say 'sit'—and then feed
them. They are used to getting a treat last thing at
night, at the very least.

Sunny eyed the cat in her lap with mammoth disfavour.
"Catch me yelling 'Mousers' in a very excited tone," she
warned it. "I doubt it. You come when you're called, or you
don't eat." Sunny had not had a great deal of experience
with cats and really believed what she was saying. Lorna
Doone, of course, did not trouble to contradict her, cats always having time on their side.

They can't go out the front door, *ever,* and as long as
Lorna's in heat, only Beetle goes out into the garden. I
live in fear of the day they find a way over the garden
wall, and I've got into the habit of shouting if I see
them get very enterprising in that direction. It would
help if you could keep this up.
I've left orders for a pint of milk a day. You can have
half, and the cats get the other half. If that's not
enough, just leave a note for the milkman.

"Of course!" Sunny exclaimed, setting down her cup.
"Milkmen! The milk's delivered to the door!" Now that she
had a concept to attach the noises to, she had no difficulty
working out that the jangling noises she had heard earlier
meant there was a pint of milk on the front doorstep now.
With Lorna inside, she pulled the kitchen door almost
closed, then went lightly across the hall towards the front
door. After undoing the chain and the dead bolt she paused.
She was wearing nothing but the T-shirt she had slept in. It
fell not quite to midthigh, only barely keeping her decent.
On the other hand, her bathrobe was still packed, it was six
in the morning, and who would be out there to see? She
twisted the lock and opened the door. There were two more,
a bolt at top and bottom, but last night she hadn't bothered

with them. She sighed. London hadn't used to require five locks.

It was a windy but beautiful and sunny London morning, and Sunny took a deep, happy lungful of memories before carefully bending to pick up the milk bottle. There were two newspapers on the mat, as well, which the wind had just begun to get to. They were out of reach of where she stood, but in another five minutes they would be blown all over the front walk, if not the neighbourhood. She stepped out of the doorway and crouched to pick them up one by one. *The Independent* and one of London's awful tabloids, she noted.

The Independent was headlining the oil rig explosion that had happened yesterday while Sunny was in the air, but of course *The Daily Blatt* had no time for such picayunity when the love life of an English peeress was at stake. Sunny glanced down at the appalling photo of a rather beautiful young woman with her face contorted in what might have been rage, but could just as easily have been a sneeze. "'MY SEX LIFE IS MY BUSINESS!' says Lady Caro," the headline screamed in thick black letters.

Sunny laughed as she stood up, folding the paper under her arm. "Oh, Emma," she apostrophized with a grin. "This taste for the crude!"

As she turned back inside the doorway, a fat grey-and-amber bullet shot out of it, nearly overbalancing her, and then Lorna Doone looked wickedly over her shoulder at Sunny from her position in the middle of the walk.

"Oh, my God!" breathed Sunny. "That's all we need! Cat!" she commanded.

Lorna Doone smiled an enigmatic smile and twitched her tail as she raised her nose to the wind.

"Come here," Sunny ordered firmly. "Now, come on, cat! Lorna!"

It was entirely the wrong sort of voice to use, but then, Sunny didn't live with a cat. She was used to that tone of authority in her voice producing exact results, and it was with something like horror that she realized it was having no effect.

Suddenly she remembered Emma's note. "Mousers!" she called, trying to inject excitement into her tone, as Lorna Doone took another few steps down the walk towards the gate. *"Mousers, mousers!"* she screeched. Oh, how the mighty are fallen. It was the first time Sunny had ever submitted her will to that of a cat, and it was unlikely to be the last; yet she scarcely noticed her own capitulation. "Mousers!" she tried again.

It was going to wake the neighbours, but Lorna Doone had gone deaf. With what Sunny saw as fiendish glee, the cat ignored her to sit up on its hind legs and examine a drooping blossom that hung over the walk.

Sunny glanced around the square of beautiful white terraced houses. It was asleep. The trees in the tiny park that formed the centre of the square rustled and swayed in the wind, but nothing else moved. Hitching the papers and the milk firmly under her left arm to free her right, she stepped down the walk towards the cat.

The cat maintained the otterlike position she had adopted to examine the rose, right up to the instant that Sunny made a sudden swoop for the back of her neck. Then she dropped to all fours and hopped two paces away. With a grunt of annoyance Sunny straightened up and adjusted the papers and the bottle of milk under her arm again; and just at that moment there was a gust of wind through her tousled hair and she heard a very ominous bang behind her.

Nothing like as loud as a gunshot, but a lot more frightening to Sunny just at that moment: the front door had blown shut. She whirled and stared at it in horror. Of course she had pushed the safety on the lock before stepping out. Of course she had. Sunny marched calmly back up the walk to the door, the cat, perversely, choosing to follow at her heels. She was too well-trained to have come out the door without securing...

The door was locked. Sunny closed her eyes. "Lorna Doone," she said conversationally to the cat, "why doesn't Emma get you fixed?"

Chapter 2

"The people at Number 22!" Emma had repeated in surprise. "Do you mean Farid?"

Sunny had raised a fist into the air and jerked it downwards to signal victory to Bosey and Wayne, who were standing over her. "You know him, then?" she said into the phone.

"He gives a lot of parties. I've been to quite a few. What—"

"But he's not a particular friend?"

"Rafiq knew him better than I did. I don't think he even sees him now. At least, he's never there when I go. But maybe that's just Farid being politic."

"I want to meet him, Emma. If I came for a visit, could you introduce me?"

There was a pause. Then Emma said in a low, theatrical voice, "This sounds *fascinating*, Sunny. What's going on? Drugs? Conspiracy? Has someone been trying to steal the Canadian identity?"

"Emma . . ."

"Sorry. Do tell me, what's it about?"

"Nothing," Sunny said flatly. "And that's all you know, and all you get to know. Can I come?"

"All I get to know?" Emma laughed softly. "Now, Sunny, in the past ten years, when has either of us ever had an adventure without involving the other?"

"Well, I don't know, your marriage was pretty adventurous, from what I heard." They both laughed. "And you missed my entire year in Rabbit Falls, Saskatchewan."

Of course Emma couldn't resist the bait. "Oh, was that adventurous? Funny, from your letters I always got the idea that Rabbit Falls was just a wee bit slow. In fact, I think I remember a line to the effect that its middle name was Tedium."

"I didn't want you to be jealous," said Sunny. "I mean, once a guy hit a moose with his station wagon, Emma. Stove the front of the car in, and there was blood everywhere."

Emma shuddered audibly. "*Ooooh,* how thrilling. Was it moose blood?"

"Yeah, but it's the same colour as human, you know."

"You should have told me. I would have come."

"Actually I think we were snowed in that winter."

"I'd have chartered a snowmobile, Sunny."

Bosey's eyebrows were going up and down, and Sunny nodded at him. "Yes, well, I'm using the people's money here, Emma, so I have to be quick. Can I come for a visit?"

"You know I'm going back out to the dig shortly?"

"Oh, hell, I forgot. How long are you staying?"

"The whole season, I guess. How long are you?"

"As long as it takes," Sunny replied. "Damn! What can—"

"I don't suppose you'd care to catsit for me? I mean, I hate sending them to a kennel, especially as I've only had Lorna a few months, and it would be good cover for you, wouldn't it? I do have the term correctly, I hope?"

Sunny had frowned dubiously into the phone. "I don't know much about looking after cats, Emma."

"Oh, cats are independent creatures. They look after themselves, really," Emma had said.

Famous last words.

The cat was struggling in her arms and Sunny knew she was deep in raw sewage. She didn't have to glance along the frontage of impassive white stone to know that there was no way into the back gardens down a side lane or driveway; there would be no lanes and no driveways in this area. On each side of the square, the elegant Georgian terraced houses extended around four small streets, and they all backed up to an area of private, walled gardens inaccessible except through the houses. She had three choices: break in through Emma's front door, stay in the street, or wake up the nearest neighbour and ask permission to walk through their house to the back garden, climb over the wall into Emma's garden and get into the house through the kitchen door.

And all that without benefit of what the English called "knickers." Terrific. If Bosey and Wayne heard about this one, they would never let her live it down. Well, Sunny would just make damn sure they never heard about it.

For a moment she glanced over her shoulder wistfully at the other side of the square, where behind the trees Number 22 must be. If only Emma lived at Number 20! What a way of getting an introduction this would have been!

She would have liked to put down the milk and papers, but she couldn't do that now without putting down the cat, who, once she had caused catastrophe, had been willing enough to be picked up. But she might not be amenable again, Sunny knew, and if the cat ran away and got pregnant Emma would be deeply upset. Sunny took a breath and hoped that the neighbour's housekeeper lived in. She emphatically did not want to meet any of her new neighbours this way.

"Forty-two, or thirty-eight?" she asked Lorna Doone in a roughly crooning voice that soothed the cat's nerves so that it jerked up its head and slowly closed its eyes at her.

"I'm sure you're right," she said, and went through the gate and turned left, and in a few steps had reached the front door of Number 42. If only she had arrived a week ago, as planned, she would have had time to get Emma's rundown on all her neighbours in the square, Sunny reflected as she nervously pressed the bell. She might even have met some of them. But the Brits, in their wisdom, had delayed giving permission for this invasion of their turf till Sunny's advantage seemed pretty well wiped out, to everyone's irritation.

"Do they want to get in there at all?" Wayne had asked, as yet another fax message had delayed giving final approval for Sunny's visit.

"Sure they do," Bosey had said imperturbably. He was the only one not letting his emotions show. "But they'd rather do it themselves."

"Why don't I just take my holidays?" Sunny had offered. "I could go over and stay with Emma and wait for their permission there."

"Because it would offend them, and they wouldn't give it. Don't worry, they're going to let you in. We just have to wait this out."

"Just as long as Emma's cats don't starve," Sunny had murmured, although the brutal truth was, she wasn't thinking of the cats at all. She was thinking of the job, and how suited to it she was, as though she'd been carved out of life for this exact moment in time. If she was kept off this assignment by a bunch of paper pushers, she would never forgive them as long as she lived.

"Oh, *please* wake up!" she pleaded aloud when there was no response to her ringing. Maybe the bell was broken.

Sunny began to knock loudly. She no longer cared whether it was the housekeeper or the residents who came to the door. All she wanted was to get off the street before it started to wake up, which she supposed would be soon. Behind her, in confirmation of her fears, she heard the sound of a car door closing, but she kept her eyes resolutely away from the sound. If she didn't turn her attention on whoever it was, they would be less likely to notice her. She began to hammer with her knuckles in the authoritative rap she had learned was most likely to get results.

Now she heard footsteps on the pavement on the far side of the square. She pressed the bell and held it for five long seconds, then resumed rapping, and at last she heard the sound of turning locks and the door opened to the extent of the safety chain.

"Well, this is a new one," she heard before she could speak. A man stood in the six-inch opening of the doorway, eyeing her up and down without offering to let her in. Short and stocky, with dark hair and a broad chest under a red-trimmed navy bathrobe, he seemed vaguely familiar to Sunny, but she was beyond being able to place him at the moment. It would be surprising if some of Emma's neighbours *weren't* famous, but at the moment the square was waking up and Sunny didn't care if it was Paul McCartney himself, as long as he let her and the cat in off the street.

His eyes were black, his voice had been cold, and he looked furious. Either he hated being awakened so early, or he was something like the latest thing in rock music and didn't appreciate strangers at the door. Either way, she had some fast talking to do.

"Please excuse me," she began, smiling. "I'm—ah..." God, she hadn't realized how awkward the explanation was going to be. "I'm staying with a friend of your—I mean, I'm a friend of your neighbour—Emma York—and I'm staying in her house and I've locked myself out." She seemed to have lost her presence of mind under his angry gaze. She was babbling, and it was an unfamiliar, and most uncomfortable sensation. "With the cat. She's in heat and I can't—I wonder if you'd mind if I—you see, the back door's unlocked—"

He was looking at her as if he hardly heard her. "You got any clothes on under that, matey?" Sunny blinked in a sudden access of anger. Whoever he was, it didn't excuse him being so rude. She felt enough of a fool as it was.

"What do you—" she began irritably, but his look cut her off. He shook his head once. "Well, that's dedication." He looked at her in contempt. "How much are you getting for this? I hope it's enough to support you for a long time, because believe me, you're not going to find work again soon!" He looked over her shoulder and swore. "And here comes your backup team, just in time."

She felt completely stunned, and grabbed at the only comprehensible thing he'd said. "My backup team?" She threw a half look over her shoulder, but in her confusion her attention quickly refocussed on him. "But . . . that's impossible!" She hadn't been assigned one yet, as far as she knew. If the Brits weren't being obstructionist, they sure weren't eager. Anyway, how could he know? "Who are you?" she asked in amazement.

He laughed in real amusement. "They didn't tell you?" He shook his head. "Matey, I think you got done. I'll leave you to it."

He closed the door on her gaping face, and then Sunny heard the sound of shouts and running footsteps behind her. She whirled. At least a dozen men and women were running towards her from various points around the square. In the otherwise silent square it seemed an army. Lorna Doone panicked. Her agile body twisted and heaved in Sunny's hold, and she clawed Sunny's bare arms ruthlessly for purchase as she tried to escape. The milk bottle and newspapers fell from her grasp as Sunny made a futile attempt to hold on to the cat.

The bottle exploded with a loud popping noise, spraying her liberally with milk and drenching the cat, who landed in time to get the full burst. Lorna Doone howled in bewildered terror and froze against Sunny's ankles. Sunny immediately put her bare foot on a piece of broken glass, lost her balance and fell backwards against the door of Number 42, staring in amazement as the army, shouting and calling, raced across the road towards her.

"What did he say?"

"Who are you?"

"How do you feel about Caro? Is she poaching on your territory?" The last two questions were from a small, thin woman who was leading the way with a strange, gazellelike leap, waving a notebook gracefully over her head as though to gain Sunny's attention across a busy railroad platform.

But their shouts were gibberish to her, not least because her attention was taken up by one dreadful, central fact: some of them were pointing cameras at her. It wasn't possible. Sunny pressed against the door behind her and flung her hands up to hide her face, staring at the advancing horde in increasing shock. *Pictures!* she thought frantically, wildly. *They mustn't take pictures!*

The small mob arrived together at the front gate and all charged it at once, creating a bottleneck, so that they bounced off it and each other for a few seconds. First through was the gazelle woman, who, close up, looked as though she might eat cats alive for breakfast. From her station behind Sunny's feet, Lorna Doone howled piteously.

"Does she know about this?"

"Who had him first?"

"How did you meet?" The lunatics shouted, sometimes severally, sometimes in concert, as they rushed up the walk.

Somewhere during those few moments, Sunny's reason deserted her. Nothing made sense; nothing added up. It was as though she'd walked into the fifth dimension through a hole in the real world. They wanted to burn her before she even began, but why? There was no understanding them. "Stop!" she cried helplessly, and flung her arms across her face, elbows out, frankly cowering. Blood was dripping down her arm, and she glanced at it in distant surprise, not knowing how it got there. She wiped at it, then stared uselessly at her bloody hand.

They saw it, too. "My God, she's bleeding! She's bleeding! Steve, get a shot of the arms!"

"Terrific!"

"Why are you bleeding? Did Prentiss cut you up?"

"Did you try to kill yourself?"

"Did you threaten Mr. Prentiss?" They were around her like animals now, like dogs, some snarling, some baying, as though something—the scent of blood, perhaps—excited them almost sexually.

Her blood. Sunny looked at the greedy faces surrounding her and felt her stomach heave with a horror of her fellow human creatures, which, with all her experience of the darker side of human nature, she had never felt before, and it was this, at last, that broke her nerve. She whirled and beat against the wood of the beautifully painted door in an absolute frenzy. *"Let me in!"* she screamed. *"Help, help, let me in!"*

"Have you known him long?"

"You must be terribly—"

"Why did he—?"

"Why did you—"

"Where did you—?" They called at her, as though they did not notice her panic, did not, she thought, notice her *humanity*. And all the time there was the whirr and whine and click of cameras.

"Can you look this way?"

"What's your name?"

"If you'd like to tell—"

The door opened so abruptly that she fell through the opening, and as quickly shut behind her. Outside, the roar of voices rose to a shriek, and there was the sound of palms and fists like a sudden squall against the door.

The strong hand that had grabbed her arm and kept her upright as abruptly released her, and she fell against the wall, sobbing in reaction.

"If you're one of them," said the man who had opened the door, in a cold voice that shocked her back to sanity, "I'll strip you naked and throw you back out to the wolves. And don't think they wouldn't accept the sacrifice of one of their own. That bunch out there would drink a toast in your blood if it meant a good story."

Chapter 3

He was about five-nine, Sunny noted automatically, square-set and solidly built, with a craggy, attractive face, hair mid to dark brown, heavy eyebrows, large nose, brown eyes. Small scar above right eyebrow. Skin medium tan. Somewhere near thirty.

"Right," he said, after a long moment of mutual sizing up. "You're not hiding much under that, are you? No camera, no bug?" He almost seemed disappointed in her.

Sunny's brain had calmed down faster than her body. The dry heaves in her stomach stopped now, but she still couldn't catch her breath. She leaned against the wall to support herself and stared at him, her breath coming in involuntary gasps. "What th-*unh*—what th-*unh*—what the hell is happening?" she panted. "Who are those—" she swallowed "—those people out—*unh*—there?"

Whoever they were, they were still hammering on the door. Sunny glanced over her shoulder as though the sight of it might tell her something. The stranger reached up beside her and fastened the chain.

"Never mind them, matey," he said, gazing into her eyes without warmth. "Who are you?"

"I'm—*unh*—your—*unh*—neighbour." Sunny wished her breathing would calm down. She sounded near hysteria. She had seen many people in this state, their breath entirely beyond their control, but she had never before experienced it. She was taking in air in jerky pants, as though she were about to cry, or sneeze, or had a strange kind of hiccups. She wished he would slap her. "Nu-*unh*-umber for-*unh*-ty."

His eyes narrowed. "No, you're not, matey," he said steadily, "I've met my neighbour. Tall, thin sheila, long blond hair." He looked her up and down, as though to emphasize how far from tall and thin she was. Around the department they called Sunny "the pocket Venus," though never in her hearing. A few inches over five foot, she had the kind of figure that the ancients used to mold in clay and worship, and it wasn't being disguised at the moment by the red T-shirt. And though her taupe-coloured hair could be mistaken for blond in some lights, its medium length was tousled all over her head and neck in a ragged cut that could never be classed with Emma's long, smooth ash-blond cut.

"And English," the man finished his catalogue in a tone of finality, when his eyes reached Sunny's again. "You're not even English."

Neither was he, Sunny realized with a jolt. "Australian," she noted, glad to find her brain functioning. She should have picked that up with the first word out of his mouth.

"Nah, you're not that, either." His eyes and voice were getting progressively harder. He gestured briefly towards his broad chest with a strong thumb. *"I'm* Australian."

"Yes, I meant you," Sunny explained. "I'm Canadian." Her breathing recovered suddenly. "And I am your neighbour—Emma's gone out of town and I'm looking after her cats for a while." She closed her eyes. "Oh, that wretched cat!'' She shook her head and looked at him again. "Do you mind telling me what is going on?''

The banging and shouting outside swelled in intensity, and the man looked at the door in a sudden burst of annoyance and cursed. "Right, come in here,'' he ordered, and reached out to take her arm. "Hell, you're dripping blood!'' he exclaimed sharply, and looking down, Sunny saw drops of blood on the white marble floor and a smear of red under her feet.

The stranger grasped her arms, not very gently, and turned them up to expose her inner elbows. Three long gashes on her right arm and two on her left were welling red, and her hand was smeared with the blood she had tried to wipe away. It almost looked like a razor job, Sunny noted absently.

Now he fixed her with a look that was full of suspicion again. "Who hired you? Bloody hell!'' he said in exasperation.

"Are you crazy?'' she demanded. "You think someone hired me to slash my wrists and die on your doorstep?''

"Someone's crazy,'' he agreed. "But it's not me.''

Whoever they were, they were still pounding on the door. He had a point. "Yes, well, it isn't me, either,'' she said. "The cat clawed me to get away when those people—are they *journalists?*'' she interjected in dismay, "—came after me. She's not supposed to be out, and that's why—oh, God, oh, *God,* what have I done? That damned cat, she's ruined everything!''

"Nah, she hasn't,'' said the Aussie firmly. "Cat's over there.'' He nodded to a large potted plant sitting on the black-and-white marble. Lorna Doone, wet and miserable, her amber eyes stretched with fear, was crouched behind it, her sides heaving with every breath. Her coat was matted with milk, and there was blood on her ear.

He thought she was making all that fuss over the sex life of a cat! He must think her a total bean-brain, and she'd

better reinforce the idea. "Cat!" Sunny exclaimed in simulated relief. "You came in, too!" She *was* relieved, up to a
point. She really would not have relished the task of explaining to Emma how it was that Lorna Doone had got
pregnant by some unknown mongrel on Sunny's first day as
catsitter. But beside her own catastrophe, half a dozen
mongrel kittens just didn't stack up. "She looks sick," she
added to the Aussie. "Do you think she's all right?"

"She'll get over it," said the Aussie. "You're the one
who's bleeding. Come on." He turned away towards the
back of the house.

"I'll get blood all over everything," Sunny warned him.

He turned to look at her over his shoulder. Sunny was
struck again by the feeling that she should know him.
"Don't walk on any carpets," he ordered simply. "The
marble won't stain." With a shrug she followed him. Her
left foot was leaving a trail of blood on the marble; she must
have cut it on the broken bottle.

"Sit down," he ordered again, as they reached the
kitchen. "Let's have a look at you." He closed the door,
shutting the sound of banging down to a distant drumming. Sunny didn't move. "Why don't you sit down?" he
asked as he turned, indicating the chair behind her with a
nod.

Sunny shook her head. The kitchen was very different
from Emma's, with a brick-tile floor and antique pine table
and cupboards. "I can't," she said, and in spite of everything her lips twitched.

He looked at her, trying to work it out. "Why not?"

She said, "Do you think you could lend me something to
put on? This thing only keeps me decent while I'm standing."

He laughed outright at that. "Matey, it doesn't even do
that! I've already seen all you've got, and so's that bunch
out there. You'll be lucky if the whole city doesn't get it off
the front page tomorrow."

Sunny blushed to the roots of her hair, not that she believed him. If she thought they would publish pictures of her butt rather than her face, in fact, it would be a relief. "They were journalists, then?" she asked, although by this time it was obvious to her. Damn, damn, damn, what a piece of luck. Over before she began, and no one to blame but herself. You can't blame a cat for your failure to secure a door, after all.

"Reckon that's what they call themselves." His tone suggested he had a more accurately descriptive word for them.

"Why are they interested in you?" she asked lightly.

He stood looking at her a moment. "Matey," he said, "you've got a nice line in casual questions. I wonder why you're so interested?"

Sunny allowed herself to get hot. "You've just told me they're going to print pictures of me half-naked! I'm interested to know who they'll say I am, that's all!"

He grinned, but it was not friendly. "I guess you must be my new girlfriend, my old girlfriend—or someone trying to get some cheap publicity," he finished, in a voice heavy with innuendo.

He turned and went out of the kitchen then, leaving her to mutter unhappily to the empty air, "Publicity is the *last* thing I want."

When he came back, he was dressed in ragged denim shorts and a polo shirt, and carried a pair of jeans and a belt in one hand. "Here you are," he said.

They were obviously men's—his own, perhaps—clean, but well-worn and soft from repeated use. "They'll get blood on them," Sunny said dubiously.

"Don't worry about it," he said. He turned away to the sink, where he busied himself with running water into a bowl, and while his back was turned Sunny kicked her legs into the jeans. They were far too big for her, but the belt had decorative holes all around, and she pulled it tight around her waist and rolled up the legs, and she was at least covered.

"All right," she said, sitting down by the pine table, and there was a little whiff of antiseptic, and then the man turned to her with some cloths in one hand and the bowl in the other and set it on the table beside her.

His arms were brown, well shaped and very muscular, and so were his legs. "Let's have a look," he said, reaching for her arm. This time when he turned up the underside to expose the scratches, his touch was gentler, but his hands were strong and firm, and it crossed Sunny's mind just at the edge of consciousness that he was a man who would keep a firm grip on anything he cared to take hold of, and for some reason that thought seemed to send a little expectant shiver through her.

The antiseptic burned in the wounds as he deftly washed the blood from her arms. The scratches were deep, from the cat's hind claws, and the Aussie glanced speculatively at her face as Sunny accepted the pain without protest.

"You're not soft," he observed mildly when he had covered the scratches with antiseptic cream and adhesive bandages. "What do you do for a living?"

"I'm a writer," Sunny said, adding, before he could say anything, "with no ambitions whatsoever to be a journalist." She watched his face covertly to see if he believed her.

His eyes went a little opaque. "Yeah?" he grunted. "What sort of thing do you write?"

"Fiction," she said.

She opened her mouth to change the subject when something else did it for her. The banging on the front door had stopped at last, a fact they only noticed when the rattling of the kitchen door suddenly became audible. For a moment it seemed as if the people on the front step had got through the door. Sunny gasped, but the Aussie just went still, and she glanced at him, wondering again who he was.

Lorna Doone's paw was visible under the door. She had reached through the broad gap at the bottom of the antique pine door, and was clawing alternately at the floor and the door, and crying, with all a cat's desperate dislike of being shut out or in, making it rattle.

Sunny and the Aussie both expelled their breath on laughter, and he strode to the door and opened it. Lorna Doone burst into the kitchen, looking more demented than ever, her wide eyes nearly black. In the middle of the floor she abruptly halted, sat down and began to wash her fur, so that the Aussie, coming up behind, needed a little fast footwork to avoid being tripped.

"That's an awful cat, matey," he observed mildly. "What happened to its ears?"

Sunny uncharacteristically giggled; she was more given to raucous laughter. She supposed it was the unusual nature of this morning's stress. "According to Emma it's a Scottish fold. It was born like that."

"Looks like someone took an iron to its head." Having negotiated his way around the intent body of the cat, he crouched down in front of Sunny. "Now, let's have a look at that foot," he said.

"Actually she looks a bit like you," Sunny said, holding out her bloody foot.

He raised his head. "What, the cat?"

"Yeah," Sunny said musingly. "Something to do with the shape of the body. She's kind of square and bunchy, like you, and she has those heavy paws."

He had both his strong, square hands around her foot now, turning it this way and that to examine the cut. She supposed her feet had got a bit chilled out there on the pavement, because the heat from his hands was noticeable on her flesh. "Must be the Scottish blood," the Aussie said. "I was born in Scotland myself. Shard of glass in here, matey. Gonna have to get it out."

She'd been imagining that it was just the pain of the cut. But now that he mentioned it, she could feel that it was more than that. "Can you do it?" she asked.

He nodded once. "It's deep," he said. "You need a painkiller?"

Sunny shook her head. "No, I'll be all right."

He set her foot down, stood up and went and rooted in another cupboard. When he came back he was carrying a pair of needle-nose pliers. "Let's see if these'll do the trick," he said. He knelt in front of her again and she lifted her foot. But the angle was awkward for him, and he said at once, "Be easier if you lie on the floor."

The foot was throbbing now, and without a word Sunny slipped off the chair and down onto her face on the floor. She set her foot carefully on his thighs, but he lifted it again behind her, pushed the leg of the jeans she was wearing up towards the knee, then lowered her foot again to his knees. She felt them part, and he set her foot between his thighs, as though into a vise, and gripped firmly.

His thighs were bare and hairy and warm, and there suddenly seemed to be an erotic charge to everything, as though her yielding posture, his firm command of the situation and the touch of flesh on flesh had mistakenly summoned up some half-attentive angel to breathe sensual fire on the scene. An unexpected shiver rushed up Sunny's body from where his hand touched her tender sole all the way to her scalp.

At that moment Lorna Doone jerked her head up from her flank as if she had been called, staring in their direction, her hind leg extended, motionless, as if her feline affinity for the sensual angels had been triggered by the presence of one of them. After a moment the cat drew her leg in, stood, marched over and carefully touched noses with Sunny, her nostrils twitching curiously.

Sunny laughed, grateful for the chance to do so. "I've only been at this cat's mercy for about ten hours so far," she said over her shoulder, "and look at the mess I'm in. What'll my life be like after a few weeks?"

"Don't think that far ahead," the Aussie said. "Tomorrow will be bad enough, believe me. Now, don't talk," he commanded. "I want to concentrate."

His hands were firm and certain, with none of the false gentleness that can be so irritating to people with wounds. It was comforting to be in such capable hands, and Sunny set her face on the cool brick floor and gave herself up to his ministering.

The pain she endured in silence, as he found the glass shard with the needle-nose pliers and pulled it out, though it was sharp enough to be slightly sickening; but when he lifted her foot and she felt his mouth wet against the inner arch she gasped audibly. "What are you doing?" she protested, though she could feel perfectly well that he was sucking the wound.

Behind her the Aussie stopped sucking her foot and spat into the bowl. "Making sure there's no glass left behind," he said briefly, before he fell to sucking again. "You wouldn't want any working its way through your system."

The angel was dancing over her thighs, brushing her flesh with his delicate fire. Sunny groped for something to say to dispel the mood, but as long as the stranger's mouth was on her flesh she couldn't think. At last he seemed satisfied, and stood up and rinsed his mouth at the sink, making sure that he swallowed no glass himself.

Sunny rolled over and sat up, drawing her foot up onto her right thigh to examine the wound. "Thank you," she said. "I'm sure that's dangerous and you shouldn't have done it, and I—thanks a lot."

He wiped his mouth on a towel and stepped over to give her a hand up. "That's all right," he said, pulling her smoothly to her feet. He stood over her, his feet apart, so that, standing, she was between his legs and very close. He steadied her with a hand against the small of her back.

"Tell you what," he said softly, and one hand moved to grasp her upper arm. "Why don't I give you a real story to sell? They're going to write it anyway, and it'll bankroll you a bit, if you play your cards right."

Sunny frowned. His breath was against her cheek and ear, and he was slowly drawing her into his hold. She felt as though the angel's fire was melting her entire body, bone and flesh. "Say what?" she asked, struggling for control.

" 'How I Seduced Jock Prentiss on His Own Kitchen Floor,' " he explained softly. "You can sell it as an exclusive, and I won't be able to sue if it's true, will I?"

Chapter 4

Afterward Sunny did wonder how she might have reacted if circumstances had been different. But two factors contributed very materially to her being able to hang on to common sense through the sensual smog that was enveloping them. The first was, of course, that it was unpleasant to be accused of slyness and perfidy by a man who was simultaneously trying to seduce her. The second was Bosey. A mental image of his face was all it took to drive the overzealous angel back to the regions beyond human awareness.

So, immune now to his nearness and the heat of his hands on her upper arm and the small of her back, she looked the stranger firmly and prosaically in the eye. "Jock Prentiss," she repeated, without inflexion, taking it in. "That's you, is it?"

He seemed to come to his senses, too. He let go of her and stepped back, straight onto the tail of the cat, who was busy examining the bowl of antiseptic. Lorna Doone screamed and took a punitive swipe at his bare calf, and Jock Prentiss's foot automatically shifted and went down again just on the edge of the bowl. It bounced crazily up, emitting a spray of liquid, and the cat, taking extreme exception to this, leapt high into the air, clawing wildly. Since she was between Jock Prentiss's legs at the time, and since, in her panic, she was extending her claws to lethal length, this assault took Jock Prentiss by storm. He lost his balance completely and, arms flailing, went down with an almighty thud, taking Sunny with him by dint of knocking her feet out from under her as he went. He ended up flat on his back on the floor with Sunny on his chest, completely winded. The cat, wisely, had gone for the hills.

Jock Prentiss had a very impressive vocabulary of curses, even granting that they lost impact through the breathlessness of the delivery. "Sorry," Sunny said, struggling to get up, her words losing the ring of truth insofar as she was trying to stifle laughter. "I'm really sorry."

"What is it with you?" he gasped incredulously. "You're a walking disaster zone! Get off me, woman, I can't bloody breathe," he ordered, pushing her up.

She manoeuvred herself off his chest and, ignoring the fact that there was a spreading puddle of antiseptic around them, she looked down at him. Trying not to laugh, she nodded apologetically, because he was right about what he'd accused her of, though it generally took people longer to work out the connection if they weren't told. "Things just seem to happen around me," she admitted. Bosey and the others called her Little Cat Feet—or, if they were really annoyed, Blunder Woman—when such things happened.

The Aussie sat up. "For a minute there I thought I was going to be disembowelled." He gently eased himself. He had been startled rather than hurt—the cat's soft body had lost velocity by the time it reached his groin and her claws hadn't made contact, but he was no less irritated for that.

Sunny snickered. "I bet you did!" she said, losing the battle suddenly. "Oh, boy, your face! Your feet! Do you dance the merengue, too?'' She went off in a peal of laughter.

It was not every man who would have enjoyed being laughed at in such circumstances, and Sunny did have the failing of finding her own jokes amusing. It was also difficult for her to stop laughing once she had begun. After a few moments the storm felled her, so that she lay on the floor shaking with uncontrollable laughter.

If Sunny's jokes didn't make you laugh—and they rarely did—people said her laughter would. She could make a roomful of people laugh at a joke that no one but she herself could see the humour of. Jock Prentiss was no exception. At first a few unwilling, rather bemused chuckles were drawn from him—he found it not entirely pleasant, perhaps, to be laughed at by someone he didn't trust—but in the end he couldn't resist. He found himself laughing as raucously as Sunny, which at least had the virtue of easing the tension that had been building up in him since he'd been awakened by the knocking at his door.

Of course, shared laughter can be a very sexy thing, and Sunny in a thin T-shirt and jeans lying on her back laughing was a sight to stir anyone's loins, even if they *had* just taken a direct hit from a cannonballing cat. But Jock wasn't falling into that particular trap twice. His laughter subsided, and he got lightly to his feet, grinning down at her.

He was attractive when he smiled, his dark eyes full of humour, and Sunny abruptly stopped laughing, too, and sat up as he offered her a hand.

She accepted the hand without putting much weight on it, and when she was on her feet the Aussie bent to pick up the empty bowl. ''We'd better finish what we started,'' he said. ''That cut on your foot needs to be bandaged. Ugh, it smells like a hospital in here.''

He stepped across the floor to the garden door and opened it wide. ''Is your garden enclosed?'' Sunny asked, ever mindful of Lorna Doone.

Jock Prentiss nodded. "Yeah, it is, but it would serve that cat right if it got pronged by the mangiest stray in the city, matey, and I'm not gonna worry too much if it tries."

That made her laugh again. "Emma would kill me," she said.

"Sit up on the table" was all he said. He pulled a mop from a tall cupboard and made a very workmanlike job of wiping the floor while she watched. When he had finished that, he refilled the bowl with water and a stronger concentration of the antiseptic, then knelt in front of her to wash her foot.

The antiseptic stung badly, but again she made no sound, only breathing deeply and relaxing against the instinctive impulse to tense up with the pain. "Your name is Jock Prentiss?" she asked again. He had seemed to expect her to recognize it—or at least, he had said the name as though it were something of a household word. But it wasn't to her.

"You didn't know that?" he asked, his head bent over his work, only faintly sounding as though he didn't believe her.

"No, why—who are you? Are you famous?"

Kneeling at her feet by the table where she was sitting, he looked a long way up into her eyes. "How long did you say you've been my neighbour?" he asked. His voice when he asked such questions was very flat, giving nothing away.

"What time is it?" asked Sunny.

His eyes narrowed. "About seven, seven-thirty, I reckon."

"Well, then, I've been your neighbour for about eleven hours," said Sunny. "And if you're famous, I guess I've missed it." She remembered her earlier idea, when he'd closed the front door on her. "Are you a musician? I don't listen to rock music much. Ahh!" she gasped, as pain unexpectedly shot through her foot.

"Sorry, just making sure there's no more glass in there. Do you feel anything?"

"No," said Sunny. "I think it's clean. Feels clean." She paused as he spread ointment on the wound. "Does that mean you're not a rock musician?" She grinned. Maybe she'd insulted him. Maybe he was a concert violinist, though she couldn't see the gutter press spending the night in the open to interview Paganini himself. Unless he'd been reincarnated into a parrot, of course. "Opera singer?" she hazarded. After Pavarotti and Placido Domingo, she supposed opera singers were good press.

He competently bound her foot with gauze and fixed it with adhesive tape, then looked up. "Matey," he said, "if you're faking, you're doing a very good job. If you're trying to convince me you're a good actress, I have to admit you might be. But don't get excited, because I wouldn't put you in the film now if you were the last sheila in the city, see? Not after a trick like that one out there on my doorstep this morning."

Sunny looked at him, entirely unfazed this time by the unjust accusation. If he wanted to imagine her as a hustling actress she couldn't have cared less. Her brain was focussed on absorbing the information inherent in what he said. "Actor or director?" she said, almost to herself. He merely gazed at her.

"Look," said Sunny. "I'm sorry if you think I've given them fuel for whatever fire they're building for you, but if you really think I'm going to end up in tomorrow's papers on the strength of it, I wish you'd tell me what it's about so I'll know what to expect. I've never been in the public eye, and I don't want to be, and if there's anything that can be done to stop it, I'd like to try. So could you just relax and tell me what's going on?"

He looked at her for a long moment. "You can't do anything to stop it, believe me, unless you've got the kind of friends who can hand out D-notices to the press. What's your friend Emma's last name?"

"York. But if you know her husband, his name's Rafiq Abdulhaqq. She never took his name, but some people called her by it anyway."

"And where do you normally live?"

"Toronto. But I'm hoping to move here, and this is a kind of reconnaissance trip. I get to stay in Emma's house while I decide if I really want to live in London, and she gets someone to look after the cats while she's away."

She was volunteering a little too much information, perhaps, but it was her first chance to give her story an airing in the field, and she wanted to hear how it hung together.

"And you're a writer." She nodded. "What sort of things do you write?"

"Novels," she said slowly. "Well, that's what I want to do. I'm not published as a novelist yet, but I have published one or two little things. I've just started a novel, and that's what I'll be working on if I move to England." She gazed into his eyes with deliberate frankness. "And I promise you that the one or two little things I've published have not been exposés of public figures in the gutter press and never will be. Now—who are you and what are they going to say about us tomorrow?" she finished. Somewhere in her heart she was still faintly hoping it wasn't a complete disaster, that something could be done to fix it, that it could not possibly be all over within twenty-four hours of her arrival. "Blunder Woman" indeed. And the Brits weren't used to her. They'd think she was out of her mind.

Jock Prentiss was assessing her through narrowed eyes. "Matey," he said at last, "you're lying to me. I don't know what, and I don't know why, but somewhere in there was at least one lie."

Sunny smiled and shook her head as though to say, "There's no way to convince a doubting Thomas." But underneath she was shocked. She'd thought the story hung together well. It had sounded good, and she thought she'd sounded good telling it.

"So what does that mean?" she asked drily. "You're not going to tell me anything in case I go out there and sell them some story about what you said about whatever it is that's got them hot for you?" She suddenly wondered why she was bothering. Obviously if he was front-page news all she had to do was go have a look at some recent newspapers.

"You're pretty sharp, aren't you?"

"You're pretty obvious, aren't you?" she countered.

"What's your name?"

"I don't think I want to tell you. You might go out there and sell it to that bunch on your doorstep to pay me back, mightn't you?"

They were actually getting a little steamed, both of them. *Don't get mad!* Sunny commanded herself silently. Nothing would put her at risk faster than losing control of her temper.

"What are you so concerned about keeping out of the papers?" he asked suddenly.

She looked at him in affected amazement. "Are you crazy?" she demanded, though her heart was sinking to think she'd played it badly. "You've done nothing but tell me how awful it's going to be, you've said they'll run pictures of me nearly naked, and you wonder why that bothers me? I'm a human being, that's why! And if you don't mind, I think I'll go home now. Forget I asked. I guess you're not exactly privileged information. I'll wait and read about it in the paper tomorrow."

He was looking intently at her, his eyes very dark and assessing. Just my luck to run up against someone in the acting profession, she thought. Of course he can sense when someone is playing a role. Well, thank God it's not him I'll be up against, assuming they don't decide I've been burned and the operation goes ahead.

But as soon as the thought crossed her mind, she realized it was premature. Jock Prentiss, for all she knew, might very well be her enemy, and she had better keep her guard well up around him. It wouldn't be difficult. She was angry enough now to take a swing at him.

"You do that, matey," he said flatly. He was referring to her finding out about him in the papers, not to what she was thinking, but his timing was remarkable nonetheless. "You do that."

Chapter 5

There was a longish pause, too much tinted with hostility to be awkward, while they sized each other up again. For Sunny, it seemed a little odd to be facing a stranger with so much feeling in her blood. For years now, she had schooled herself to remain aloof from violent emotions in any confrontation with strangers. Furthermore, she knew there was no reason for her to be angry with him—why *should* he trust her?—but angry she certainly was.

That made two of them. Jock Prentiss was angry with Jock Prentiss, too. His irritation with the woman in front of him only fueled his irritation with himself. Trust him to get the uncontrollable hots for a sheila who was looking to ride to fame on his coattails! Just look at that body. She reminded him of berries or melons ripening in the sun—her skin fresh and tightly packed and full of juice. She thought she was tough; he could tell she thought she was tough. Look at her, straightening her spine as if she were in military college. Man, he'd like to show her how far from tough she was. He was sorry he'd given her the jeans. She was

pretty annoyed with him now, but let him once get his
mouth between her legs and she'd fall into his hands like the
ripe fruit she was.

And then she would sell her damned experiences to the
barracudas of Fleet Street, Jock reminded himself coldly.
The pressure in his groin eased, and he followed the thought
up, groping for control along its thin thread. They would
run a picture of her in some frilly gear that barely covered
her nipples, and then every actress in the country with gi-
ant knockers would throw herself at him, thinking she was
just his type. Everybody knew the film still wasn't cast.

He wished he hadn't thought of her in frilly gear that
barely covered her nipples. He was actually beginning to
hope that she *was* an actress. He could offer her the sidekick's part and tell her that if one word about him got into
the papers from her he would throw her out of the film.

She would make a cute little cop, too. He could just see
her strutting around with a gun looking tough. "Pint-size."
Just like the sidekicks in the old Westerns. Yes, and he could
add some competition between the society bitch and the
tough sidekick for his favours—why hadn't he thought of
that before? Well, it had been done. But so had every—

"I said, have you got a ladder?" she was saying impatiently.

Jock blinked. "What?"

"The garden wall. You got a ladder, or do I have to
scramble over?"

"What do you want to climb over the garden wall for?"
he asked, amazed.

She took a deep breath. He wished she wouldn't. "To get
back to my friend Emma's house. It's hard for you to believe, I know, but I do live there. And so does..." She
glanced around her. "Where's that stupid cat got to?"

"I haven't got a ladder," Jock lied quickly. "Come on,
I'll give you a leg up."

"Yes, well, I have to find the cat first. *Mousers!*" she called suddenly, so that he jumped. "Mousers!"

"Cats don't come when you call their names, matey," Jock informed her. "They're like women, they get contrary when they know they're wanted."

She looked at him witheringly. "It's not her name. It's a signal she's going to get some kind of damned cat treat. *Mousers!*"

Lorna Doone raced excitedly into the kitchen. She had used her time well, washing her fur until it was almost clean, but it was sticking up in bunches as it dried, giving her a startled look. Before she had time to realize that no treats were on offer, Sunny swooped and grabbed her, getting one hand firmly around both of her lethal back paws, the other arm around her middle. "We're going home," she announced. It was getting to be a habit, talking to this cat. She would be a senile old woman before she knew it.

Jock followed her out into the garden, where she unceremoniously tossed the cat up onto the six-foot-high wall and shoved her over into Emma's garden. She supposed she'd now fed the cat exactly the information Emma didn't want it to have: that if you climbed up on the wall you got Out. Too bad, Sunny thought grimly. The whole entire episode was the cat's fault in the first place.

"You want a leg up?" Jock asked, bending and offering his clasped hands. Her bare foot had rich black garden dirt adhering to it, which ground sensuously into his palm as she tested her weight. She was heavier than she looked, and very agile; most of that body must be muscle. The zipper of the jeans pressed briefly against his face, and then her weight was gone. "Thanks for everything," Sunny called from the top of the wall. "I won't forget your jeans."

"Neither will I," said Jock feelingly, and watched as she pushed off and disappeared from his sight.

Sunny landed lightly in a crouch in Emma's nasturtium bed, Beetle and Lorna Doone, sitting side by side, watching her curiously.

"Well, thank goodness we never have to see *him* again!" she told them. Rather foolishly, perhaps, but then, it had been a morning for famous last words.

Jock Prentiss, it appeared, was an Australian actor, well-known in England for his role as streetwise cop Matt Patten in the Aussie series *Sydney Streets,* the latest of the Downunder imports to make a hit in England. On the strength of this, he had come to England to make a feature film with the same character, a joint English/Australian project. One of the London actresses rumoured to be up for the female lead was Caro Deane, otherwise known as Lady Carola Isham, wife of Lord Isham. Caro Deane had previously guest-starred in an episode of *Sydney Streets* while she'd been on tour with an acting company in Australia.

That much seemed to be fact. On this, the tabloids had built quite an edifice of speculation. According to the *Daily Blatt* and the *Sunday News,* which jointly seemed to be Emma's pipeline into the world of scandal, Jock Prentiss had fallen violently in love with "Lady Caro" while working on that episode with her. She had refused his advances and clung to her peer husband—"I LOVE HIS LORD-SHIP" SAYS CARO—or had fallen violently in love and had a torrid affair with him but had refused to get divorced—"I WON'T BREAK MY SACRED VOW"—LADY CARO—depending on your choice of paper.

Everybody agreed on what had happened next: Jock Prentiss had followed Caro to England, had dreamed up a film project just for her, and was laying siege to the castle. The metaphorical castle that was Lady Caro, of course. The peer lived in a house in Belgravia, his family having lost the ancestral home two generations ago. Either Jock Prentiss and Lady Caro were having the affair of the decade—

CUCKOLD PEER SWEARS REVENGE—or else Lady Caro was furious with her ex-lover for not accepting his dismissal when he got it—"STOP FOLLOWING ME, JOCK!"

It had been feeding the gutter press on and off for several weeks, and Emma, for no reason that was readily apparent to Sunny, had saved all the relevant copies of both the *News* and the *Blatt* since then.

Sunny, surrounded by the back copies of what seemed to her appallingly tasteless publications, but which she was pretty sure were only somewhere in the middle range of London's numerous yellow papers, was for the moment sunk in depression. What a mess to have walked into! How would they bill her tomorrow? As a "Mystery Woman"? As a starving actress storming the citadel? She knew the gutter press was rough, not to say ugly, in England. Her imagination just wasn't up to what they would come up with to cover a half-naked woman with slit wrists on Jock Prentiss's doorstep at six in the morning with a bottle of milk, two newspapers and a cat with cauliflower ears.

But *how* they would bill her was nothing compared to the simple, shocking, *ruinous* fact that tomorrow her picture would almost certainly appear in the pages of at least one London paper. Sunny could have wept.

She woke Bosey from deep sleep, of course. She had forgotten the five-hour time difference. "Bosey," she said, "you won't believe what's happened."

"Aw, hell, already?" he remarked. He knew that tone in Sunny's voice: it meant trouble. "What?"

"I think I've been burned." Bosey started softly swearing. "I'm going to be in the cheap tabloids here tomorrow, either as an actress doing a razor job on herself to get a part in a movie, or else as Jock Prentiss's latest lover."

"Pictures?" he asked.

There was no point trying to dress it up. "Yup."

"Who's Jock Prentiss?" he asked. Bosey woke up faster than most people, she thought. She felt him taking charge, and already it seemed less of a disaster.

"As far as I can make out, he's a television cop. His real claim to fame, at the moment, is an alleged love affair with a peer's wife."

"Ahh," breathed Bosey, as though he were in pain. "And the paparazzi think you're involved with him."

"They can hardly think it, but I guess they'll *say* it."

"What time is it over there?"

"I don't know, around about eight, I guess."

"Sunny, you haven't been in the country one day yet."

"I know, I know. I'm sorry, Bosey. What should I do?"

"Does your team know what's going on?"

"No. I haven't met the team yet. No one here seems to think there's much reason to hurry. I guess this'll put the kibosh on the whole operation, eh?" she asked, in the tone of one hoping to be told she was wrong.

Bosey didn't answer that. "You'd better tell me exactly what happened."

He didn't do more than grunt through the entire recital, not when she confessed to not securing the lock before going out, not when she told him they probably had pictures of her without underwear, nor when she described the cat scratches that looked like a razor job.

When she was finished, he said, "All right, let's think about damage control for a minute here. You're still the best chance we've got at the moment, and I'm not calling it quits unless I have to. What are the chances they got a shot of your face?"

"From a distance, before I knew what was going on, probably," she said bluntly. "I don't think they got a clear close-up, because I put up my hands and kept them up."

"How many people you know in London?"

"Dozens, Bosey. I went to university here, remember?"

"Yeah," he said in dissatisfaction. "All right, tomorrow's Sunday, and whatever they've got will come out in the Sundays. We'll pretty well know the worst. When's your first meeting?"

"Monday morning, ten o'clock." Sunny was beginning to feel hopeful in spite of herself. She *had* covered her face, after all. She had had that much presence of mind. And if she wasn't recognizable, what did she care what other part of her anatomy got onto the front pages?

"Good. Have you talked to Jacques?"

"Not yet. Want me to call him?"

"Yeah, tell him about this and get him to call me. We'll have to decide how to take on the Brits so they don't get cold feet and pull you out before they've considered. Jacques is going in there with you Monday, eh?" Sunny grunted. "So long as you're not recognizable, I think we might still pull this off. But you and Jacques will have to do some fancy talking."

Sunny said sadly, "But I'll almost certainly be recognized here in the Square. All the residents must know Jock Prentiss is a neighbour."

"Yeah, sure they do. That doesn't matter. Our friend likes famous people, doesn't he? So now you're famous. And maybe your new friend, the actor, already knows him."

"Oh, my God," Sunny breathed thankfully. "Bosey, that's . . . that's . . ."

"Any problems you foresee working up that acquaintance?"

She thought of what she'd said to the cats an hour ago—"We never have to see him again"—and then she thought of the way Jock Prentiss had looked at her when he pulled her to her feet, and then of Bosey's oft-stated belief that in police work more than any other, you should always try to turn a disadvantage into an advantage. "No," she said. "Probably not. Unless—well, time'll tell."

"Probably be a good idea to push it a little now."

"Do I go around to 22 with him if I get the chance?" she asked. In fact, she would rather have gained entrance some other way. Jock Prentiss made her nervous. But personal feelings didn't matter in this.

He hesitated. "That's gonna be a tough one to call from here. If the press is on his tail, you might do better to lie low till the thing blows over. On the other hand, if you got a chance like that, you might think it too good an opportunity to miss. Use your judgement here, Sunny. And you can always consult Jacques."

"Right," she said.

"Anything else?" he asked after another few minutes of discussion.

"I think I'm okay."

"All right. You better get some pants on and get on to Jacques for a powwow. Oh, and, Delancey—"

"Yes?"

"Try to keep them on after this, will you? I can pull your butt out of the fire only so many times."

"Low blow, Bosey," said Sunny firmly. "Very low blow. Goodbye."

Chapter 6

Sunny Delancey had decided to be a police officer—specifically, she had decided to be a Royal Canadian Mounted Police officer—when she was nine years old, on the day her father had been killed in the line of duty. Of course, the inclination had begun earlier than that. She was the oldest of three children and she had been her father's favourite from the moment he had seen her; and as for Sunny, her heart had never beat faster than on the day they had gone to Ottawa to see her father in his bright uniform high on a horse in a parade at the Parliament Buildings. But it was only after his death that becoming a Mountie herself had become a clear, conscious purpose.

Of course, when Sunny was nine years old, there were no women in the RCMP, but that hadn't fazed her. Even then, she'd been the sort of personality who figured if she just made up her mind, nothing could stand in her way. And as though to confirm her new dedication, it happened that within a year of her father's death the RCMP announced that it was admitting women to its ranks for the first time.

If Sunny got the idea from that that history would be made just for her, who could blame her?

By the time she graduated from high school, she was still a little short of the regulation five foot four that the force required for women, but that didn't bother Sunny, either. She had always intended to go to university first, and the obvious solution to the problem was to gain some knowledge there that the force simply couldn't resist.

She had a knack for, and a love of, languages. "Get fluent in French," she'd been advised by the man who had been her father's closest friend on the force, but Sunny was already pretty good in French. In four years she might discover that a hundred other, taller women had also become fluent in French. She had looked around the world to see what skill or language would be both rare in applicants to the force in four years, and at the same time very marketable.

She had taken a degree in Arabic and Hebrew at the School of Middle Eastern Studies at the University of London, then gone home and, in spite of lots of advice from friends that with such skills she ought to be applying for a post in External Affairs, sailed through the RCMP recruitment procedure with hardly a word being said about the deficiency of three-quarters of an inch in stature.

In Rabbit Falls, Saskatchewan, and most of the other backwaters where she served her obligatory early service, there hadn't been much call for French, never mind the more exotic languages she had to offer, but Sunny had been happy to bide her time. If nothing else, her time in the sticks allowed her to get proficient on horseback, and it had always been her ambition, too, to take part in the Musical Ride. It was something her father had never done, but of course in his day every Mountie could ride, and Sunny had never forgotten that image of him on a horse. She still carried the picture in her wallet.

But the Musical Ride was one ambition that had been doomed to failure. After nearly a year of training, Sunny had developed an allergy, not to horses, but to the leather polish she used on her saddle. That, coupled with her by now famed ability to cause minor disaster wherever she went, had sealed her doom. One day, while executing a tight and difficult manoeuvre, Sunny had sneezed, loudly and uninhibitedly. The horses, excellently trained beasts that they were, would have been fine. But the rider closest to Sunny, deep in concentration, had been startled and involuntarily jerked the rein.

In the end, three horses had fallen down, one officer had a broken leg, two lances were broken, chaos reigned over the practice field, and the entire body of Musical Riders was helpless with laughter. The next day Sunny had offered to give up the Musical Ride, and to her great disappointment, the offer had been accepted.

Her next move was to undercover training school, however, and nothing had interfered with her progress there. Whatever strange force field was in operation around her, it wasn't the sort of thing that caused watches to break, guns to misfire, or radios to malfunction. It was simply that minor disasters had a way of taking place in her vicinity, and that might even be an advantage to an undercover officer. Knocking someone down, after all, could be a good way to meet them.

She had never regretted the move to undercover. And now, with this important operation, even the choice of Arabic was paying off. Sunny was very junior for an international assignment, but Bosey had overlooked that because of her language skills. She had the feeling that her whole life had led up to this moment, where her skills and talents, and the necessities of a vitally important job, were entirely and perfectly matched.

It would almost kill her to be pulled off the assignment now. But Bosey had given her hope, and she was determined that she would not be taken off this case because of public interest in some actor's sex life. If her pictures in the paper tomorrow weren't clearly recognizable, she would convince the Brits somehow that she should be allowed to carry on.

She was convincing herself as she went. After all, they didn't call her "Little Cat Feet" for nothing. They called her Little Cat Feet, Sunny told herself—with some justification—because she had a way of landing on her feet, no matter how hopeless the chaos she caused might seem.

She forgot, in the heat of the moment, that they also called her "Blunder Woman," and not for nothing.

Sunny bathed and dressed and got Jock Prentiss's jeans soaking in a biological presoak, then lay on the bed planning a little strategy. Lorna Doone and Beetle determinedly kept her company. "The best thing," Sunny told them as she tried to keep Lorna Doone from an evident determination to suffocate her, "would be for me to get an introduction over there at Number 22 this weekend. Then they couldn't afford to pull me off the job unless the pictures in the paper were absolutely recognizable, because that contact would be invaluable. The next best thing, perhaps, would be for me to be able to assure them that I haven't given those photographers, if they came back, a second photo opportunity. And that means finding out exactly when they do come back, and staying inside for the duration." She paused and absently pushed at Lorna, who was attempting yet again to sit on her head. "No, that's too risky—until I get a backup team, if I do, I'll never be sure there isn't one photographer lurking out there in the trees or under a car. I wonder what Emma's got around that would serve as a disguise, because I'm going to need to go out for food, if nothing else."

Sensing that Sunny was about to get up, Lorna Doone got up on Sunny's stomach, kneaded briefly, settled down and prepared to fall asleep, purring gently. For good measure she opened her eyes at Sunny, slitted them and smiled at her in loving pleasure. Only a monster of the first order would have been able to dislodge her now. Sunny lay there in guilty frustration, wanting to get up, but inadequate to the task, screwing up her courage. "You did this deliberately," she muttered. Lorna kneaded her gently and purred a little louder. Beetle, meanwhile, came and sat by her ear, carefully extending a loving paw to touch her. "Blackmail!" Sunny protested. "You guys don't love me at all! You're just pretending!"

The sound of the doorbell prevented the engagement from becoming any bloodier. The cats were off the bed like booster rockets, dashing excitedly downstairs ahead of her without even bothering to try to trip her up.

Making sure the chain was fastened, and holding Lorna firmly off with her foot, Sunny spread one hand over her face, opened the door and peered around it with one eye.

"Hi. Sunny?" said the young man standing on the step.

Sunny eyed him keenly from behind her spread hand. "Who are you?"

"My name's Mark. I'm a friend of Emma's. I've been feeding the cats for the past couple of days. I couldn't make it last night, and I wasn't sure if you'd arrived or not. I figured they'd be starving if you hadn't. Sorry to bother you so early, but..." He faded off.

Sunny said, "That's all right, come on in," closed the door and slid the chain open. If he was a reporter, he knew so much she was already burned. "Would you like a cup of something?" she asked, leading the way to the kitchen.

"Sure, yes," said Mark. "So, you're going to be staying at Emma's place for a while?"

"Yes, I hope so. Are you an archaeologist, too?"

"I'm a student. I was supposed to go out on this dig with her, but things intervened. I live just around the corner, so when she goes anywhere I'm usually called upon to feed her cats," he said, settling himself at the table.

"Coffee?" Sunny pushed the button on the kettle.

"Yes, thanks. And what about you? Emma says you're an old friend," Mark said.

"Yes, I'm planning to move to London, and I'm trying it out to see if I really want to."

"She would have sent the cats to a kennel this time, because I can't be sure of being around the whole time, but she really hates to do that. She was so thrilled you were coming. She gave me a whole bunch of instructions for what to do if you didn't make it. You had some problems, I take it?"

Sunny made instant coffee and put out milk and sugar. Mark absently stirred three spoonfuls of sugar into his and sipped, eyeing her over the rim.

"Some family difficulties, but they all cleared up at last," Sunny ad libbed. It wasn't exactly a lie, if you considered that the force was her second family.

"Oh, don't talk to me about family difficulties!" he said good-humouredly. "It really ticks me off to be missing this summer on the dig. And it won't do my university career any good, either."

"That's too bad," said Sunny absently. "Mark, did you say you live just around the corner?"

"On Banbury Place. First street on the right. Why?"

"Well, I thought if you wouldn't mind giving me your phone number, it would be nice to have someone to call if there's something..." She meant, if I can't go out, at least you can come in, but she didn't want to explain about the journalists just yet.

"Oh, sure." He slipped a pen from his pocket, reached out to pull Emma's note, which was still on the table, towards him, and wrote down a number. "If you want to go away for a day or two, I'll be happy to take over the feeding. If I'm here, that is. I'm still hoping to get away for a few weeks, anyway.''

"That's great," said Sunny.

"Actually I'm surprised Emma didn't leave it for you. She asked me if she could."

Sunny opened her mouth and closed it again. "She might have. I realize now that I never finished reading her note." She was stunned to think it was only a couple of hours since she had read the note about the milk! She felt as though she'd been here a week.

"Well," said Mark, when he'd finished his coffee, "I'll just toddle off home. My mother will be wondering where I've been all night. Well, she'll know where I've been, but she'll pretend to wonder. It comforts my mother not to face what she calls unpleasant truths."

There was nothing much you could say to that, so Sunny merely smiled. Chatting idly, they moved down the hall, and as soon as she had closed the door on him, Sunny returned to the kitchen and Emma's note.

That's it for the cats—bet you thought I'd never finish—now for the world news... I thought you'd like to know there's a party at Farid's on Saturday. If I'd seen him, I could have mentioned you casually, but actually ringing him up to mention you would have been extreme. I don't know him that well. I thought you'd prefer me to keep out of it. I don't advise gatecrashing. He's casual, but not that casual. It would look odd, even if you said I'd told you to go. Well, maybe you'd like to look odd, in which case, make free use of my name.

My young friend Mark Snell lives just around the corner at 17 Banbury Place. He usually comes in to feed the cats for me when I'm away. If you have any problems, he says you can call him. He's going through rather a difficult time at the moment, and he may want to cry on a stranger's shoulder. Suit yourself whether you offer yours, but he's a nice kid.

There followed the same phone number Mark had just written.

Next door on your left is my new neighbour, the dishiest man in the country, and before you even look at him I want you to know that he is *mine, all mine,* and you are not to go near him. I will donate the temporary use of my house to the scourges of international crime, but not my entire future love life. His name is Jock Prentiss, by the way, and you can catch him Thursday nights at nine on Channel Four. A programme called *Sydney Streets*. He plays a cop, and no, you are not allowed to go and compare notes with him. As luck would have it, he moved in while I was abroad, and he hasn't been the easiest person to meet. Apparently he's all wrapped up in an actress. I did my best at a party at Farid's one night, but he wasn't having any. If you meet him there, you are deaf and blind to masculine charm for the duration. He is absolutely the most virile man I have ever seen, but I'm going to stop raving for fear of making you interested. Remember—You Have Been Warned.

There was a little more, about minor household matters. Sunny finished it all, then sat back and thought. What amazingly bad timing she had! If only she had taken two minutes to finish reading Emma's note this morning before dashing out for the milk, the whole mess would have been avoided! She would have turned the other way, and the press would have ignored her.

But Sunny was always one for looking on the bright side. It was now confirmed that Jock Prentiss was a visitor at Number 22. He might even be planning to go to the party tonight! All she had to do was work out a way to get him to take her.

And as for Emma's warning, she was sorry to have to ignore it, but it would only be for the short-term. As soon as Sunny had finished with him, Emma could have Jock Prentiss back, and welcome. And she intended to be finished with him very, very soon.

Chapter 7

Emma was one of those people who always seemed to have whatever you needed and she didn't fail Sunny now. Inside a captain's trunk in her bedroom, Sunny found a costume Cleopatra wig in thick corkscrew wool that covered her forehead to below her eyebrows and fell all around her shoulders but was hardly any weight at all. Trying it on in front of the wall mirror in Emma's bedroom, she laughed to think of Emma going to a fancy dress party as Cleopatra. No doubt Rafiq had gone as Mark Antony. It was the sort of joke that most people probably wouldn't have noticed, but though Sunny's jokes tended to be incomprehensible or unfunny to the rest of the population, she generally managed to enjoy other people's humour—and Emma's in particular.

Emma wouldn't have been Emma without a different pair of sunglasses for every day of the week, if not the month, and out of the collection Sunny chose the most usefully outrageous pair. Shaped like welders' goggles, they were black and mirrored and curved around the entire upper part of her face. She looked like an insect—all eyes and no chin. No one would recognize a picture of her in these.

There was a knock on the door. Sunny froze for a moment. Then she adjusted the wig and glasses and ran downstairs. There was no one at the door when she opened it, and she shut it hastily, in case this was some kind of press trick, and stood for a nervous moment before the knock sounded again. It was coming from the back of the house. Her heart kicked in anticipation. That could only be one person.

"Good God!" said Jock with a grin as she opened the kitchen door. "What's that lot for?"

The hostility between them had gone up in smoke. Sunny smiled and preened. Between the wig and the glasses, there was hardly any face visible. "It's my disguise," she informed him. "I have to go out for food today, and just in case..."

"Beaut," Jock Prentiss said. "That's why I'm here. You got any bread? I'm all out, and it's not worth fighting through that bunch out there for a loaf of bread. I'm offering breakfast in exchange." This was only half a lie. The fact was, as with most human action, he'd been prompted by a mixture of motivations, and he knew it. He'd told himself he'd better see if his mysterious visitor actually was living in his neighbour's house, but that was by no means his only reason, or the most powerful—just the easiest to give in to.

Sunny blinked. "You mean they're all still *there?*"

"Of course they're still there. Why wouldn't they be?"

She shrugged. "I don't know. I was hoping they might have taken a break—you said they'd put those pictures of me in tomorrow's paper."

"And they will." He grinned at her. "They send the film down by courier and they phone in the story. They don't leave their posts and run into their editors' offices shouting 'Hold the front page,' you know."

"So what do *you* do, then? Just run the gauntlet every time?" She couldn't afford to do that. One photographer hiding behind a tree she would risk. But she couldn't face the whole lot of them, even in disguise, very often. There was too much at stake.

"I go out when I have to. As you saw yourself this morning, it's more comfortable if you don't try too often. They'll get tired eventually. Some other story will come up."

"I feel like a *prisoner,*" she said angrily. "How dare they treat people like that? How am I supposed to get food?"

"As I said, I'm offering breakfast in exchange for bread, if you have any."

"Oh, great!" Her temper recovered instantly. Maybe the press were doing her a favour after all. Getting friendly with Jock Prentiss was a priority at the moment, after all. "I don't know if there's any bread, though. Emma wasn't sure when I'd arrive, and she didn't stock up for me." Sunny moved to the bread box on the counter and discovered a hardened heel of granary bread. She held it up. "Sorry," she began, then, remembering something the note had said, "Wait a minute, though—the freezer might have something."

The freezer had a bag of bake-them-yourself rolls, and as she pulled them out, Sunny's stomach audibly growled. "You haven't eaten, have you?" Jock asked.

"No, and I'm near starvation. I didn't even eat dinner last night."

He reached over and took the bag of rolls out of her hand. "Come on," he said, leading the way out. "I'll cook."

He had a way of taking over that was difficult to resist. It was exactly what Sunny wanted—to be in contact with him—but she didn't much like it, all the same. She wished she'd arrived before Emma left and been introduced to Farid Abul Hassan by her. Jock Prentiss made her nervous.

But Sunny wanted to do this job and she wanted to do it well, and, she reflected as she allowed Jock Prentiss to give her a leg-up onto the wall again, he might easily be her only chance.

He was a good cook, too. She had to admit that—and not just in the ordinary line. Jock Prentiss threw things into the frying pan entirely at random, as far as she could see: potatoes and peppers and corn and sliced leftover steak, spices and herbs and ketchup, all went in under her bemused gaze, while he talked to her about nothing in particular and hardly seemed to notice what he was doing.

But the resultant mess was very tasty. "This is good," said Sunny in surprise, eating quickly. "What do you call it?"

He watched her wolfing it down for a moment, grinning. "Fry-up," he said. "You don't waste any time, do you, matey?"

"I told you, I'm starving. Did you bake the rolls?" she asked, not seeing them on the table.

He laughed and got up and opened the oven. The rich odour of fresh bread filled the kitchen. Jock Prentiss snatched the rolls one by one out of the oven and tossed them into a small basket, shaking his fingers after each one. "There you are," he said.

When she had taken the edge off her appetite, Sunny relaxed and poured a cup of coffee. "Emma never told me about you," she lied gently. "Weren't you on speaking terms?"

"I haven't been here all that long," he said.

"Yeah, but you're famous, aren't you? Funny she didn't mention it when you moved in."

"She's big on fame, is she?"

"Fame excites most people, doesn't it?"

He shrugged.

"We're not getting your show in Canada yet—at least, not as far as I know. Maybe she thought I wouldn't know who you were."

He was looking bored, and she thought in panic that it would be fatal to bore him. She'd thought he would like talking about himself—in her experience actors did—but perhaps he was different. "She did mention someone across the square that she thought I'd like to meet—Farid somebody. She said he threw terrific parties and invited everybody who was anybody. She wanted to introduce me, but I didn't arrive in time."

"In time for what?"

"Oh—I was supposed to get here a week before Emma went back to Egypt, but I didn't."

"What's she doing in Egypt?"

"Emma's an archaeologist. She's on a dig out there."

"Gonna find another pyramid?"

"No, Emma's interest is post-Islamic. She's on a dig that may go back to the first Muslim rulers of Egypt—the Fatimids," Sunny told him. She was dismayed to find that they had slipped over the subject of Farid Abul Hassan so quickly. "Emma was married to an Egyptian," she rattled on, looking for a way back. "It broke up about six months ago, unfortunately. I suppose Farid was a friend of her husband's, but she said he kept up the acquaintance with her after the breakup."

"Probably wanted to put the weights on her," Jock observed cynically.

"What?"

He chewed for a moment. "Make a pass," he translated. "She's a good-looking sheila, your friend. Blond, too. I think our friend over there likes 'em blond."

"Oh." Sunny chewed on another mouthful of fry-up, absorbing that. "Well, I don't think he ever did. Make a pass at her, I mean. You know him, then?"

"Yeah, I know him, if you mean, have I been to his house. Good parties, mostly. He knows how to get the people he wants, anyway."

She sighed in exaggerated regret. "What a pity I'm going to miss them. I wish I'd asked Emma for a letter of introduction. She says you meet a lot of actors and writers there." Emma, in fact, had never said any such thing. It was the intelligence reports that had given them the information.

"You want to meet a lot of actors and writers?" he asked drily.

She really didn't. One of Sunny's virtues was that neither wealth nor fame made much impact on her. She took people as she found them. And one of her failings was that she faintly despised people who *were* impressed by wealth and fame. It was difficult for her to pretend to have stars in her eyes, because she felt she looked like a fool.

But in undercover work you'd better be willing to look like a fool, or anything else that was necessary to the task at hand. "Well, I wouldn't mind meeting some fellow writers," she told him, a little lamely.

It came across as reluctance to admit she just wanted to meet rich, famous people, but Jock was too knowing to let that bother him. Most people had unworthy motives, in his experience, and this was something he could easily give her.

"Well," he said, as she'd been hoping he would, "there's a party or something around there tonight. I can take you if you really want to go."

As soon as the words were out of his mouth, he was sorry. Farid might not be famous, but he was very damned rich. Probably about a hundred times richer than Jock. And it was Jock's considered opinion that he really did like blondes. He could just see Farid making a play for this one and cutting him out of the running before *he* had even made a move.

Jacques Fallon was an RCMP officer attached to the Canadian High Commission in London as liaison, and he would be Sunny's backup and supervisor and support system—on the RCMP side—in London. She did not know him personally, but he had known her father in the early days, a fact that he reminded her of when she phoned him later.

She was glad he did. It wasn't easy telling her story for the second time, and to a complete stranger, and it was Fallon who was going to have to go in with her on Monday and explain her to the Brits, something she would bet he wasn't relishing. It made it marginally easier that he had known her father, though she noticed he didn't say they'd been friends.

But her father had been killed in the line of duty, and that created a bond with brother officers after death, even if there hadn't been one before.

She wasn't surprised when he passed over the recital of her morning's fiasco with minimal comment. He was far more interested in her proposed actions.

"All right, what time are you going in?" he asked her when she had explained about the party.

"He's picking me up at nine-thirty."

"And then what—you're walking across the square?"

"Well, I—no, he said something about driving around for a bit to throw off the paparazzi, so I guess he means to take a car."

"Does the team know that yet? Where are they going to be?"

"I haven't met the British team yet. I met the S.I.O.—his name is Alex Fairchild—Friday afternoon, but not much happened. There's another meeting scheduled for Monday morning at ten—but I guess you know that. They told me I'd meet the team then."

There was a short silence. "So the position is, you're going to be going in without cover tonight."

"That's the position."

"And you think you might be burned tomorrow morning when the papers come out."

"It's possible."

"This guy Prentiss. How much do you know about him?"

"What I read in the papers. He's a fairly well-known actor."

"Any chance that he's involved?"

Of course, anything was possible, and Jacques Fallon knew it. What he meant by his question was whether, in her best estimate, it was a reasonable possibility.

She thought back to that moment when the cat had suddenly started rattling the kitchen door. Jock hadn't jumped as an ordinary civilian might, he'd gone still, like someone with training. Training the nerves was as essential to criminals as it was to undercover officers. "But for all we know, he was raised in the bush, and trained by aboriginal hunters," she suggested to Jacques as she related the incident to him.

"For all we know," Jacques repeated absently. "All right, look—I'm going to let you do this, Sunny." She heaved a sigh of relief. "I'm sure you know these are not ideal circumstances, but I don't see that it's particularly dangerous tonight. If you're burned in the papers tomorrow, we'll have to pull you out of there immediately, but I don't see anything happening before then. And if you're not burned, this represents the best chance we've got to get into Abul Hassan's organization. I think you're right—the Brits are going to get cold feet when they hear about this, and the only thing that will save the operation is the fact that you've already made contact. Even then they may not like it. Quite justifiably," he added, before she could say anything.

"Won't that depend on how strong a contact I've made?"

"It might. It might. Now, I understand you're under your own name, is that right?"

"Mmm-hmm," grunted Sunny.

"You don't feel this newspaper business leaves you more vulnerable in that regard?"

"Well, I do, but it's a bit late now, isn't it? The thing was, there was going to be the problem of either a false passport or a passport that didn't match my cover name, and Bosey didn't want to ask for a false passport, you know?"

"Right," said Jacques. Undercover police officers weren't spies, after all. Bosey would have had to ask a favour somewhere to get the passport. "We could probably get you everything except a passport, though, within a day or two."

It was tempting. If the press got her name and printed it, even under a blurred photo, she was dead in the water. "But what if I got into the organization and they asked me to go abroad?" Sunny asked. "There might not be time to get another passport...."

"All right," said Jacques. "I leave it up to you. Now, I'll cover you tonight. Do you know what kind of car Prentiss drives?"

"No. But he'll be trying to shake off anyone who follows him."

He didn't reply to that. "I'll be in a black cab. You're familiar with black London cabs?" He hardly waited for her grunt of acknowledgement. "If there's any trouble at the party, you come out and flag me. The licence plate is CDN 8."

An incredulous crow of laughter escaped her. "Does that stand for what I think it stands for?" she demanded. Because if it hadn't been deliberately chosen—it must surely be an attempt at "Canadian, eh?"—it was quite a coincidence.

"I guess so," said Jacques. "It's been here since before my time. Now you can phone me on this number in the car, if necessary." He gave her a number. "All right?"

"Yup," said Sunny, her heart beginning to pound with the equivalent of opening-night nerves.

"If you change your mind about the safety of your situation before you go in, you let me know at once."

"Yes."

"Good luck," he said. For some reason it sounded like a line from a war movie.

Chapter 8

"**Y**ou don't think you're going to fool them with that, do you?" Jock laughed, when, coming over the back wall to collect her later that night, he found her wearing the wig and goggles again.

"No, but at least if they take my picture I won't be recognizable."

He looked at her for a moment. "Who you running away from, matey?"

Any attempt at denial would give credence to the implication. So Sunny merely grinned and shrugged. "You, of course, enjoy being splashed all over the front pages," she said.

"No, I don't," he corrected her matter-of-factly. "In fact, I'd bloody rather give this party a miss tonight. You sure you want to go?"

"Oh, *please!*" Sunny begged. "I've spent hours dressing, and anyway, I may never get another chance."

He raised sceptical eyebrows. "Why not? Your friend goes there. I've met her there." Sunny just looked at him.

"I can't figure you out," he said. "What's your game, matey?"

"We're all ready for a party" was all Sunny could say. She didn't have to fake the disappointment. "Please let's go. Please, Jock."

He looked at her. "I tell you what," he said. "I really want to hear you say that in the bedroom. All right, you win. But don't say I didn't warn you."

With the help of Emma's stepladder this time, they climbed back over the wall to Jock's house and went out the front door there, because Sunny didn't want Jock seen coming out of Emma's house. The paparazzi were on to them before they'd gone three feet down the front walk.

Jock's chauffeur-driven limousine was standing by the curb with the door open, but it was two minutes before they could fight their way through the screaming paparazzi and get inside.

"Is it all over with you and Caro Deane?"

"Have you got a word for your public?"

"Mrs. Abdulhaqq, could you look this way, please?"

"How long have you known each other?"

"Will you look this way?"

Sunny was trembling by the time they got the door shut and the car pulled away from the mob on the pavement. Had she made a mistake, trying to outwit them? "Did you hear that?" she moaned.

"Hard to miss," said Jock.

"Yes, but—they called me—Mrs. Abdulhaqq. So they must have seen me come out of Emma's door this morning!"

Jock shrugged. "Well?"

Impossible to explain how much worse that made things. Until now, she'd been hoping that they hadn't noticed her till she was at Jock's door. "Well, then, they knew I was only a neighbour this morning. So why were they asking

those ridiculous questions and taking my picture?'' she said
instead.

He laughed. ''Because they want a story.''

''But it isn't a story!''

''It will be when they're through with it,'' he said flatly.
''Anyway, whatever it was this morning, it's a story now.''

''What do you mean?''

He looked at her. ''Sunny, at six this morning they saw
you enter my house. As far as they know, you've been there
ever since.''

She gazed at him in dawning horror. ''Oh, no!'' she
whispered. ''Oh, God, what have I done?''

He was a little disconcerted by the force of her emotion.
''I warned you,'' he reminded her.

''Yes, but I never thought...how stupid of me! But—
Jock, how did they find out Rafiq's name so quickly?''

''They go and look up the public records. I guess your
friend's husband is listed as the owner. Then they operate on
trial and error and guesswork. If you look up when they call
a name, they figure they've got you.''

Sunny took a slow breath. Had she looked when they
called ''Mrs. Abdulhaqq''? It had surprised her, though
she'd thought she was prepared for anything.

The paparazzi didn't give chase as the limousine drove out
of the square, and so the driver took no evasive action,
merely leaving the square at one side, driving around the
block and back into the square at the other side. A taxi was
behind them for part of the way, but it didn't follow as the
limousine turned into the square again. Here the narrow
entry street was jammed with cars parked on both sides, and
two cars that had pulled up to disgorge people. A foursome
was climbing up the steps to the front door of Number 22.
The houses here were larger than on Emma's side of the
square, with two additional stories, marble steps up to a
columned portico and an areaway below.

"We'll get out right here," Jock Prentiss said to the driver. Around to the left a taxi drove into the square via another street, pulled up and sat waiting for its fare, its engine running.

Jock suddenly took her arm and held her back as the foursome entered the house ahead of them. Then he said softly, "You better tell me your last name if I'm going to be introducing you as my friend."

In spite of what she'd said earlier to Jacques, Sunny was struck with the sudden, unmistakable conviction that to go into this house under her own name would be fatal to the operation. Rationally there wasn't much reason for it. Maybe she'd just been spooked by their calling out Rafiq's name. And yet, even if no one she knew saw any pictures, for the press to have the combination of her name and Emma's husband's name might be lethal. All they'd have to do would be track her to the School of Middle Eastern Studies, and then her whole life would be open to them. And she could just imagine what a play the press would make out of Jock Prentiss being under surveillance by an undercover cop.

All good police officers not only operated on, but actively cultivated, their intuition, and Sunny was a good police officer. But to take a decision like this on the spur of the moment would have ramifications that she could not expect to foresee.

She would have given anything to have worked it out with Jacques when he offered, but she would get nowhere worrying about that now. Her brain began hastily reading the situation.

Of course it might be dangerous; she might be found out if she just pulled a name out of a hat. Her brain was nudging her, as though there were something obvious here.

And suddenly she saw it: the perfect name, the name that would cover, if need be, the fact that all her I.D. was under another name. Her decision was made in that moment. Sunny looked up at Jock in the summer twilight and smiled.

"Isn't that moon wonderful?" she said absently, starting up the steps. "York," she added softly over her shoulder. "My name's Sunny York."

It wasn't going to slide by Jock Prentiss. He stared at her. "What's the game?" he demanded angrily. "Who the hell are you, and what the hell are you after?"

"Don't shout," Sunny commanded flatly. "You'll get them going on the other side of the square. What's your problem? I was married to Emma's brother for a while, all right? I still use his name. Is there anything else about my past that you'd like to get sorted out before we go in?" She rang the bell. She was going to make it as difficult as possible for him to back out.

Jock shook his head. "Matey, you're some fine liar," he said. He looked her up and down, and his eyes took on a speculative, cynical look. "How far are you willing to go, I wonder, to get your story?"

She felt like slugging him. "I am not after a story, and I'm not in the least interested in you," she told him flatly. "I just want a chance to meet people in London, and Emma isn't here, and I can't ask Pip. That's my ex-husband, in case you haven't met him. All right? God, what an ego!" She didn't have to fake the irritation; she was furious with him. How dare he challenge her word?

Very opportunely, the door opened in front of them, and another couple were coming through the gate behind them. Still Jock looked as though he might decide not to go in.

"Good evening," said Sunny aggressively to the butler, and stepped through the door. She didn't turn to see if Jock followed her. She was amazed at how outraged it made her to be accused of lying by him, when he was merely accusing her of the wrong lie.

"May I take your wrap?" asked a woman in a neat black dress standing inside the large hall, and Sunny pulled off

Emma's light evening jacket, then lifted a hand and dragged off her wig and the welder's goggles and handed those to the woman also.

"Thank you," she said with aplomb. "Is there a ladies' handy?"

"The powder room is just through that door," said the young woman, who had accepted the wig and glasses calmly, but with a light in her eyes that meant she would have a laugh with the butler the moment they were alone.

The powder room had a little vanity with a three-sided mirror and a stool, as well as a full-length mirror. A young woman was sitting examining her reflection intently. Sunny smiled in her direction and turned to her own appearance in the tall mirror.

A figure that causes men to call a woman a "pocket Venus" is wonderful to look at but difficult to dress, as Sunny had long since learned. Anything frilly or tight-fitting, she often said, made her look like a poor man's Dolly Parton; anything loose made her look like a house. Tonight she was wearing a patterned vest that showed off the tanned skin of her arms and neck without revealing too much cleavage, and a soft, pleated skirt that was tight over her hips and then flared, in an olive-green fabric that matched her eyes. Her bare arms, of course, meant that the bandages were visible, but Jock had put on flesh-coloured plasters, and they weren't too obvious.

Sunny was not a woman who took a great deal of interest in her own appearance. The heart-shaped face reflected in the mirror had little make-up on it, and her hair wasn't much improved from what it had been when she'd got out of bed that morning. She took out a comb, pulled it through the disorder, then slipped it back into her bag.

The other woman was prinking a lock of her new-wave hair upright as her eyes met Sunny's in the mirror. Her skin was dead white, her hair bleached to an unhealthy shade of blond, and her black, skimpy dress was encircled with a steel chain for a belt. She wore thin black socks inside clumsy, rather ugly black boots. Her eyes were heavily made up, but only with black. She wore a silver and zircon—or possibly diamond and platinum, Sunny reflected—stud in her nose as her only jewellery. She was looking at Sunny as though Sunny might have come from a planet a long way off and she was wondering why.

Heavy metal, Sunny told herself with an inner smile. Either that, or Abul Hassan had taken to inviting bag children to his parties.

Jock was waiting for her when she emerged. He wordlessly put a hand under her arm and led her up the rather narrow staircase and into a room at the top.

The room was long and beautifully decorated, stretching through an archway and running the length of the house to glass doors that led to a balcony. It was not very heavily populated. They were early, as Jock had warned her they would be, but Sunny was glad of it.

He stood looking around for a moment. "No one here yet, matey," he said regretfully. "Unless you want to meet London's most pretentious art critic, and if you do, you're on your own."

She looked across the room to where a slightly seedy man was holding forth in an appalling voice to a couple who looked glassy-eyed with incomprehension. "To my mind he's always had a rather springlike quality," she heard.

"No thanks," she said hastily, grinning. "Don't you know anyone else here?"

"I know some of 'em," he said drily, as though it were a misfortune. "Here, come and look at this," he said suddenly in a louder voice, taking her arm and leading her across to the far wall. Out of the corner of her eye she saw the woman he was avoiding turn disappointedly away.

He stopped in front of an extremely beautiful example of Arabic calligraphy, which she recognized at once as the *Fatihah*, the opening verse of the Qur'an, which had been written in the shape of a bird. *Bism'Allah arrahman arrakhim*... "In the name of the One God, the Compassionate, the Merciful..."

She resisted the temptation to recite it aloud. "It's very beautiful," she said. "What about our host? Doesn't he appear at these things?"

"Jock!" she heard, as if she had cued it. The voice was deep and heavily accented, and the face, when she turned, was very familiar, though she had seen it only in photos and on video. "How very pleasant to see you."

"Hello, Farid, *salaam aleikum,*" said Jock Prentiss.

"W'aleikum salaam!" said the dark man, and then he turned and smiled down at Sunny, the man she had come three thousand five hundred miles to meet.

Chapter 9

He was smaller than she had expected, although she had read the statistics often enough: five foot six and a half, one hundred and thirty-five to one hundred and forty pounds, dark hair, skin fair rather than swarthy. He had eyes like an angel, dark brown and liquid, with turbulent depths, the lashes long and thick and starry. He was very attractive, which the films she had watched had shown, and deeply charismatic, which they had not. He turned his charm onto Sunny with a casual, almost negligent air—without seeming to be aware of it. Sunny smiled and steeled herself. It was the first few moments of charm that were the deadliest. Once you were captured you had the devil's own work getting free again, and it might colour her every action without her being aware of it if she got caught in the net he was so casually casting now.

But of course she had, at the same time, to allow herself to be charmed. Liking is a two-way street. If she resisted Farid Abul Hassan too successfully, she would lose her chance of charming *him*.

"Yes, how are you? I am very pleased to meet you," said Farid Abul Hassan, with the Arabic-speaker's typical over-pronunciation of all the consonants that Sunny always liked hearing. "I am sure you want something to drink." He snapped his fingers in the air, and a young man in white shirt and black trousers strode over to them. "What would you like to drink?"

"Mineral water, please," she said. Jock Prentiss ordered whiskey, and the waiter nodded and went off. Abul Hassan tilted his head at her in close attention.

"You don't drink?"

"Not very much."

"Ah, that is good. A beautiful woman spoils her beauty when she drinks. I also do not drink. Holy Qur'an says wine is an abomination. You would make a good Muslim."

He was trying to exclude Jock, but Jock wasn't taking the message. "Maybe she likes the harder stuff, Farid, did you think of that?" he observed cynically, keeping right with them as Abul Hassan put an arm out to shepherd Sunny towards the tall windows opening onto a balcony at the back of the room.

Farid instantly looked apologetic. "Oh, of course! But this is in a room upstairs. Shall I show you the way?"

Sunny laughed and shook her head. If she were on the drug squad, she would have been thrilled to get on the scent so quickly, but she only asked, "And what does the Qur'an say about cocaine?"

"Ah. There is no mention of drugs except alcohol in Qur'an. But *shari'a*—holy law—has extended the verses on alcohol to all intoxicants."

She smiled bemusedly at him. The last thing she'd expected to have with Farid Abul Hassan was a discussion of the Qur'an and Islamic law. She wondered how much of her own knowledge and interest she should show. She had originally intended to be as ignorant as any westerner about Islamic matters, but then she hadn't expected Abul Hassan to be—or pretend to be, perhaps—so devout a Muslim. None of their intelligence had reported, for example, that he didn't drink. But then, no one had managed to get very close to him. Farid Abul Hassan seemed to have an instinctive genius for evading spies.

She decided that a little learning on her part might be provocative. So as they moved through the doorway and out into the deepening summer night, she said, "And does that include the verse that indicates that a little can be beneficial?"

He looked at her in astonishment. "Ah, you have studied Qur'an?" he asked.

Jock Prentiss was leaning against the railing on her other side, looking decidedly cynical. She wished he would go away, but not by the flicker of an eyelash did she betray the feeling.

"Just a little," she said. It was only a lie depending on your point of view. By comparison with an ordinary westerner, she had studied Islam far more than a little. By comparison with an educated Muslim, however, she was not far from ignorant.

"I am interested," said Farid Abul Hassan, giving each syllable its full value, "in why you have studied my religion. This is most uncommon in the West."

"I like to know things." Sunny shrugged.

"What is your occupation, Miss York?"

"Actually," Jock Prentiss interposed, "it's Mrs., isn't it? Sunny is married, Farid."

She didn't show irritation, not by a flicker. She smiled at Jock in the friendliest way. "It is Mrs.," she agreed. "But we're not—well, we've split up."

"Ah, this is very sad," said Abul Hassan.

"And have you come back to England to try for a reconciliation?" Jock asked drily. She wondered why he was being so bloody-minded. It was almost as though he were deliberately sabotaging her attempts to interest Abul Hassan. But the suggestion might have merit. It certainly gave her a good unconscious motivation for being back in London. Sunny paused as though she had been caught out.

"No, not really," she said hesitantly, as though she were reluctant to admit the possibility even to herself. "Anyway, he's not here at the moment. Really, I just like England and want to come back and live here if I can."

"Ah, you do not live here in London, Mrs. York? Are you an American?"

"No, I'm Canadian."

"I am so sorry. It is hard to tell the difference, but I know that Canadians do not like to be mistaken for their American cousins."

Sunny laughed again. This was not the turn she wanted the conversation to take. In her experience, nothing bored a stranger faster than a Canadian on the subject of Canadian-American relations. "Just a little sibling rivalry," she admitted. "And where are you from, Mr. Abul Hassan?"

"I am from Iraq," he said. "But I have lived in London many years now, six, seven."

"It's a very attractive city, isn't it? I've been wanting to come back for a long time." That wasn't a sentiment that was hard to fake—Canada had always seemed a little flat after her years in London, and not just Rabbit Falls, Saskatchewan.

"And now you are here. *Ma'shAllah!* Do you know what that means?"

"'As God wills,'" she said softly. "I hope it is."

"But of course. If Allah had not willed it, you would not be here."

It was a very comfortable philosophy, you had to admit. "Now if only He wills that I stay!" she said with a laugh.

"And what is needed for you to stay?"

Sunny shrugged. "Oh, I don't know. Home Office approval, I guess. And a job of some kind."

"What is your profession?" They were moving very quickly. Sunny wouldn't have dreamed of their going so fast. But she would take advantage of it if she could.

"I'm a writer, but I don't make my living at it yet. The first thing I need is some ordinary job to keep me going. Everybody says London is so expensive now."

Abul Hassan raised his eyebrows and smiled. "You are a writer—this means you can type?"

"Oh, yes. Why do you ask?" Sunny was calm and smiling on the outside. On the inside, she was pretty sure, her heart had given up beating.

"My secretary has—"

"I can find you a job." They were the words she had been hoping to hear, but they came from the wrong source. Jock knocked back his whiskey and smiled down at her rather challengingly. "We can always use gofers on the set."

She wanted to punch his head. Why in the hell didn't he go away and leave her alone? She smiled brilliantly at him. "That's terrific!" she said. "When could I start?" She didn't believe for a moment that he meant it, and she had to call his bluff right now. There wasn't much to choose between running the risk that he meant it and running the risk that Abul Hassan would see that what she really wanted was a job with *him*. From there it would be a short step to wondering why.

"Jock, why have you not offered this before?" Abul Hassan asked bemusedly. He'd been effectively sidetracked. Sunny's heart was beating again, so loudly she thought she might explode. She was unbelievably angry, *furious*.

"This is the first I've heard of it," Jock told him with a grin. Sunny could have *killed* him. "We haven't known each other very long. Sunny's staying with my neighbour, Emma York."

"Ah, my friend Emma! I know her very well! She comes here to my parties. So I am even more happy to meet you! Have you known Emma a long time, Mrs. York?"

"Yes, a long time. Since our school days. Emma's father was in the diplomatic corps, you know, and she and Phillip spent time in Canada as children." It was perfectly true, but Sunny hadn't met them then. She hadn't met Emma till university days in London. But she didn't want to tell him that. Emma had studied Arabic along with her archaeology at university, and it was no part of Sunny's design to let Abul Hassan suspect *she* had studied Arabic at the same time as Emma.

"And then you married Phillip. I have not had the good fortune to meet Phillip."

"He's not around much," Sunny said drily, in the secretly angry voice she had heard ex-wives use. "I think he's in India just now, but of course I may be out-of-date." In fact, her secret anger was all directed at Jock, who had so effectively derailed the conversation.

"So many broken marriages," said Farid. "It is most unfortunate, isn't it? My friend Raf is very unhappy over what has happened. Is Emma happy now? I don't believe it, but she is always smiling, she never says to me that she is unhappy. If she did, her friends could arrange a meeting with her husband. What do you think?"

Sunny blinked. It was a little shocking to realize she had actually never thought of it. She had accepted Emma's account of her feelings.... "Well, thank God that's over!" she'd said to Sunny—without even attempting to look under the surface.

"I don't know," she admitted, not without guilt. Her problem was, she'd never been married, never even been in love. She supposed she didn't understand such things. "I suppose—she's very bright and witty at the moment."

"Ah, but wives are brightest and wittiest when they are most unhappy," said Abul Hassan with a wise air. "Isn't that so?"

"I wasn't," Sunny said, wanting to get the conversation back on track before it was too late. "I was just furious." She sounded as though she still was, and for the first time Jock felt she might be telling the truth. "But all this talk is changing the subject. I was about to be offered a job!" she said with a smile.

It was Jock who took her up on it, damn him. "You're serious, are you?" he asked.

She let her face fall. "Yes, weren't you?"

Jock nodded. "Sure, it's no problem. As soon as we start shooting there'll be a dozen jobs. You can have your pick."

"Is there nothing now?" she asked rather dismally.

"Not unless you fancy your chances in the casting department."

"Oh," she said. "Okay, sorry, I didn't mean to press you. I wouldn't have asked, but you volunteered."

She managed to look both angry and humiliated, as though she thought Jock were deliberately playing with her. Her eyes, normally a rather slaty green, were suddenly grey, and wet with suppressed tears of embarrassment.

"What kind of work are you looking for, Mrs. York?" asked Abul Hassan, as if to protect her.

"Oh, anything, really. I've been an office manager mostly, but there are a lot of other things I can do."

"But it will not be difficult for you to find a job with such skills as this, will it?" He didn't mention his secretary again, and instinct told her not to push it.

"Oh, it'll be no problem as soon as I get Home Office approval for work status. At the moment what I need is a black market job. I can work in a pub or something. It's just a case of getting out and looking around."

Behind them the room had been steadily filling up with people, and Abul Hassan, hearing his name called, seemed suddenly aware that he had spent too much time with them. "I am neglecting my other guests," he said. "Your company has been too pleasant, I become a poor host."

When he was gone, Sunny stood looking out over the garden, fighting for composure. So close! She was sure he had been on the point of offering her a job. Under other circumstances, she would have thought this a wonderfully successful encounter. But under other circumstances she wouldn't have been worried about the Brits throwing her off the job on Monday. Oh, if only Jock had shut up! If only she could have gone in there Monday able to tell them that Farid Abul Hassan had offered her a job!

Chapter 10

"Come on," said Jock. He set his glass down on the edge of the balcony and took hers out of her hand and put it down, too, before leading her towards the flight of stairs that led down into the garden. Still furious, Sunny followed him.

"Why did you do that?" she demanded, though she knew she shouldn't. She was angry, and in no fit state to discuss anything. In any case, there was no reason to discuss this with Jock. No valid reason. But at the moment her temper seemed enough reason.

"Do what?"

"Offer me a job when you have no intention of giving me one. He might have offered me something if you hadn't butted in!"

"And is that what you're after? I wonder why?"

She began hotly, "What business is it of yours what I—" then broke off and took a steadying breath. She found it difficult to be guarded with Jock. His presence itself seemed to unbalance her, so that she was always struggling for control. And because no one had ever got inside her guard so quickly before, she had to keep reminding herself to put it up again, though she was not quite conscious that this was what was going on.

Sunny didn't trust many people, though she herself scarcely knew it, and those she did trust she often trusted only in a limited way. She trusted Bosey in the job; she trusted her father's friend for advice, without always following it; she trusted her brothers usually and her mother sometimes. Though she didn't realize it, it was this central lack of trust that made her good material for an undercover officer, and it was her unconscious desire to trust and confide in Jock Prentiss—and the feeling that she *could* trust him—that now made him dangerous to her.

The latter fact she did understand, though only dimly, so that over everything was a sense of threat. The threat she could feel, and the hostility that arose because of it. But Sunny was at a loss over why she felt so emotionally off balance around Jock.

If she had met him in civilian life, perhaps, he might have knocked out her guard before she knew it. But the necessities of the job kept coming to her aid and helping her resist the powerful connection that seemed to exist between them. Instant empathy was a dangerous commodity—a double-edged sword—when you were living a life of lies. It could work for you, or turn drastically against you. She knew she had to be careful. What she hadn't realized before was how difficult that was going to be.

"I've got to start earning some money if I'm going to be staying. That's partly what my decision will rest on," she lied flatly. The irritation still colouring her tone was true, even if the words were not.

Jock shrugged. "What makes you think I didn't mean what I said?"

"A film!" she said disagreeably. "What can I do on a film? Anyway, who's to say when it'll start, if ever?"

He raised an eyebrow. "I am," he said. "There'll be a fair bit of work for special bit extras if you don't want to be a gofer. That's pretty good money."

She had to look somewhat mollified at this, though she couldn't resist saying, "A few days' work is better than nothing, I suppose, but what I'm going to need is a regular job, and I could use it right now."

"And what makes you think Farid was going to offer you one?"

"You heard what he said as well as I did." She'd been relying on the spur of the moment, the quick, unplanned suggestion that she could trade on, that might have made him feel responsible for keeping his thoughtless word. As Jock, in fact, was starting to feel right now. Sunny shook her head resignedly. "He's got enough businesses," she said. "Why shouldn't he hire me, if he can get me cheap because I'm black market? I'm pretty efficient."

He narrowed his eyes at her. "Does he? What kind of businesses? And how do you know about it?"

They had reached the bottom of the garden now, and the darkness covered her consciousness of having made a misstep. Sunny took a deep breath and blew it forcefully out, willing her confusion and anger away. It was weird around Jock. If she relaxed for a minute, she seemed to operate as though she knew him well and he knew all about her. She had to keep reminding herself that she didn't.

"I don't know what kind of businesses." Not much, she didn't. "Emma suggested that he might offer me something," she said.

Jock's eyes glinted in the starlight. "Your friend Emma married an Egyptian, did she?"

"Yes, she—"

"And then they separated, and now she has a house in Banbury to show for her troubles. Was she thinking of helping you along the same road?" He grinned.

"What?" asked Sunny.

"You're after something, matey, and it isn't a job."

"What are you talking about?"

She felt his hands on her bare arms in the darkness. "If it were a job you were after, matey, you'd have been more interested in my offer, wouldn't you? You were turning a lot of charm on Farid, but you don't seem to fancy your chances with me. Why not?"

"Jock, what—"

"Your friend did, though. What's the matter—she warn you off the territory?"

This was so true, and at the same time so false, that Sunny couldn't think of an answer. "You're being ridiculous," she said finally.

"Or maybe you just think I won't fall for it as easily as someone like Farid, eh?"

He was conscious that he was stabbing in the dark, looking for the weakness that would expose her lie to him. It irritated him to think he was being made a fool of so easily, but nevertheless, he couldn't seem to get a grip on himself.

"Fall for what?" she demanded irritably.

"All the charms on offer," said Jock. "You might be mistaken, matey. Farid pretends, but he's got a very cool head underneath that innocent face."

Well, she knew that. "I'm not offering Farid—" she began.

"But me, now, I'd be putty in your hands," Jock said, conscious that it was no lie. Her perfume seemed stronger in the darkness, and he thought that, like an animal, he might have found her through scent alone, if necessary. "What kind of perfume are you wearing?" he asked, putting his face close to her neck.

"I'm not wearing any," Sunny said, shivering as his mouth and nose just barely brushed her skin.

"That's just you, is it?" Jock inhaled again. Terrific. He thought he'd discovered a sure-fire aphrodisiac and it turned out to be Sunny herself. Man, he was looking at trouble, and the worst of it was, he didn't much care.

Sunny felt herself being drawn into his hold, his strong, muscular arms encircling her back with a possessiveness that made her heart thud. In a black polo shirt and black trousers Jock was scarcely visible in the darkness of the bushes that shrouded the wall at the bottom of the garden, but she felt her breasts touch against his chest, felt the heat of his bare arms under her hands and against her back. She pushed against him.

"Let me go," she said. It was a purely artificial response; she didn't really want him to let her go, though she hardly knew it.

"You could push me off forever, and it still wouldn't mean you'd get Farid," he said. It was a lie; he figured there wasn't a man in the world she couldn't have. He bent his head, and she felt his mouth press more firmly against the spot where neck met shoulder, felt the zing of feeling run through her body as though she'd touched an electric wire.

"Aw, *hell!*" exclaimed Sunny, suddenly recognizing her own deep sexual excitement. This was a complication she didn't need.

Jock drew back. "How's that?" he asked. His teeth flashed in a smile, and he sounded amused rather than affronted.

She pushed him off. "Jock, would you leave me alone? I really don't need this," she said, not unkindly, but rather in the tone of a friend asking for a favour.

"I bet you do," he countered softly, still holding her. "Feel like letting me prove it to you?" His hand stroked her cheek and the side of her neck, and that proved it to her then and there, but she wasn't going to admit anything to him.

"No...no," she muttered worriedly.

"All right," said Jock, dropping his arms, and she felt a sense of loss so strong that for a moment she didn't move. She felt as though her body needed to be near him without any participation via her head, and she was amazed she hadn't recognized it before. He was far too dangerous to mess with, and she must avoid him totally from now on. The thought made her feel almost bereaved, as though she were turning back on the threshold of immense possibility.

"You lose, matey," said Jock, while she was still summoning the determination to step away from him, and took her back into his hold, very tightly, and bent his head down and kissed her softly on the mouth.

The actual physical touch was only a prelude to the sudden flooding of her system with an emotional sweetness that knocked her completely off balance. At that moment it seemed to her as though the only thing in the world of any importance was that Jock should hold her and kiss her like this, and like a child she was afraid to move, lest any action on her part should break the spell. So she stood motionless, her hands against his chest, her head back, while his mouth moved against hers, softly and erotically, and his arms tightened around her, and one strong hand moved up to cup her neck.

Sunny didn't notice the little moan she made, but Jock did, and between one second and the next his body was hard against her. That melted her, and she pushed her arms up and around his neck, so that her breasts pressed against his chest, and their bodies were tight against each other. She opened her mouth under his, and his teeth nibbled her lip, then sucked, and when his tongue delicately flicked between her lips she caught it gently in her teeth and sucked on it, almost involuntarily.

Jock grunted, and his hand dropped to pull her body more tightly against him. He began to rub her back and forth against him, then pulled his mouth away and pressed his face against her throat and bit her where her waistcoat top left an inch of shoulder bare.

They were both lost to their surroundings. Jock pulled up her skirt and stroked her bare thigh, pulling her legs apart and pressing her more tightly against him, and Sunny complied with all his physical demands without a thought. When his hand slipped up over her cotton briefs to the bare flesh of her back, she gasped, dropped her head back and pulled his face down to hers, kissing him with furious and demanding abandon.

He was actually relaxing himself for a fall backwards to the ground when the sound of voices nearby jerked them back to awareness. They froze where they stood, and then simultaneously released their breath. *"Hell!"* exploded Jock in amazement. He carefully dropped the fabric of her skirt and stood back, his arms loosely around her. He smiled, and Sunny laughed softly.

She suddenly smelled roses, so strongly it was as though all her senses had become magnified, or she had been thrust into a river of attar of roses.

"Woman," said Jock softly, "what are you packing?"

At the same time she said, "Do you smell those *roses?*" and they both laughed a little.

"Let's go," said Jock, dropping one arm and sliding the other around her as he turned towards the house. Sunny didn't reply, merely complied, walking beside him up the length of the garden into the light that spilled over the balcony and up the steps.

It was, at last, the sight of Farid Abul Hassan that impinged on her feeling of the perfect rightness of things. "You are not leaving already?" he complained, when he became aware of their intention.

"Yeah, sorry, Farid, Sunny's still got jet lag, you know?" said Jock, rather absently.

Farid looked from one to the other and smiled. "Of course," he said. "It was very kind of you to come, Mrs. York. I hope to see you again."

It was the name *Mrs. York* that really did it. Sunny thought dimly, Is that my name? Have I forgotten my own name? Then she remembered everything. "Thank you," she said, as reality returned. "It's been a pleasure to meet you."

"I hope my friend has found you a job. Has he? And you must pay her well, Jock. Or she will have to look elsewhere. I am sure she will have no trouble finding a job if you do not offer something good."

"I'll find her something, Farid," Jock said drily. "Don't you worry about it." He really didn't know why he said it. It wasn't any part of his design to fight Farid for Sunny—or any man for any woman—but that was what he seemed to be doing. And he knew he was infuriating Sunny. She wanted a job with the guy, and Jock knew any work *he* gave her would only be temporary. Furthermore, she would probably be better off in the damned carpet shop, or whatever it was Farid owned, than mixing with film people, though he was perfectly willing to give her an introduction to the life. In his experience young women were always "writers" if they weren't actresses; probably Sunny was no more talented than the next one, and the sooner she stopped imagining otherwise, the better. In short, he was doing her no favours with his offer. It had been a purely selfish move.

"If he doesn't come up with something, I'll come back and ask your advice," Sunny said to Abul Hassan, with a rather flirtatious smile.

"Of course," he said graciously. "My work is less exciting, but more permanent, Mrs. York. You must tell me when you tire of the film world."

Sunny laughed in appreciation of this self-denigration. "It's not a question of tiring of the film world, it's waiting around for it to happen." Then, as though it were a change of subject, "What sort of work do you do, Mr. Abul Hassan?"

"I have an Oriental carpet and antiques shop."

And a few other shops I could mention, Sunny thought. Aloud, she said, "I love Middle Eastern art. I'd love to come into the shop one day and look around. Not that I can buy anything."

Abul Hassan said abruptly, "Come tomorrow. My secretary left two weeks ago. I have not had time to replace her, but I cannot do without a secretary. Maybe if you like the shop you will come to work for me, even for a week or two, until Jock needs you." He pulled out a card case and offered her an embossed card.

She was vaguely aware that there was some masculine game going on here, and she could take advantage of it. Abul Hassan would not have offered her work if he hadn't thought that in doing so he would score a point off Jock. For that, she should be grateful to Jock, and she was sorry to be the means of his loss of face, if that was what it was. She felt like a peahen in the presence of two peacocks who were strutting their stuff, and she had to choose the one she didn't want. But she wasn't going to let personal feeling get in the way of the job. Jock's ego would have to take care of itself.

"Absolutely," she said, accepting the card. "I can start whenever you like." And then she carefully, but with seeming casualness, firmed up her visit to the shop tomorrow and made sure Abul Hassan would be there himself. In the course of this, she was careful to let him establish first-name terms. "Well," she said then, with a happy smile that was in no way false, "two jobs offered on my first day in town. Maybe it's all going to work out, after all!"

"But of course we wish to keep you in London now that you are here, don't we, Jock?"

"Oh, yeah, we do," said Jock. But the spell was broken. He could see that Sunny had forgotten him and everything that had happened at the bottom of the garden. She was pretending to be calm, but he still had his hand on her. She was trembling with excitement; he could feel it, a very different excitement than what he had inspired in her.

He guessed money turned her on even more than fame.

Chapter 11

"LET ME IN, JOCK!" shrieked the *Sunday News* headline. Under it, running down half the page, was a full-length view of Sunny standing in front of Jock's half-open front door with Lorna Doone and a bottle of milk in her arms. She was looking over her shoulder towards the camera, but her face was distorted and unrecognizable, and the picture had the faint blurriness that gave it the scent of something illicitly discovered. It also looked stunningly domestic: woman in cute night gear bringing in cat and milk in the early morning.

Jock Prentiss's Downunder girlfriend arrived in London recently to visit him. At first Jock was thrilled to see her. But early yesterday morning an argument over Jock's attention to actress peeress Caro Deane broke out, and Jock threw her out of the house. She had to plead to be let back in. More pictures, Page 16.

"Oh, no!" moaned Sunny, flipping frantically through

the tabloid to find Page 16. "Oh, cat, I could kill you for this!" She was in bed with both cats and three Sunday newspapers: *The Observer, The Independent* and *The Sunday News,* which she had managed to get from the doorstep without bringing the paparazzi down on herself. To be on the safe side she had worn a balaclava with a blond wig over it, and if they got pictures of that, they were welcome to them.

Beetle, whose brain synapses seemed a little slow, heard the word "cat" and assumed she was making love to him. He got to his feet and approached her over the paper; Lorna Doone was catching at the pages as Sunny turned them, her claws ribboning the fragile newsprint, as though this were a game. "Get off!" Sunny commanded futilely. She pushed at Lorna, who immediately rolled over to play with her hand. "Cats!" shouted Sunny, and everybody froze. Beetle's ears went flat, and Lorna, whose ears were of course already flat, got a slightly demented look in her eyes. Sunny immediately repented; if she hurt their feelings, they might go away and leave her. That she might actually have preferred such a state of affairs didn't cross her consciousness threshold. "You have to let me read the paper," she scolded softly. After a moment the cats forgave her.

Pages 16 and 17 carried a huge colour spread: a series of carefully doctored photographs that proved that the photographer of this paper, at least, had been alert from the moment Sunny opened her door Saturday morning. According to this photo story, Sunny had spent the night with Jock, then been deliberately locked out by him when she went to get the papers. She gazed at the pictures in amazement.

Photo one was a picture of Emma's partially open door with the street number carefully airbrushed out, Sunny's head, and her arm reaching for the milk bottle—"Getting the milk for morning tea," read the caption. Photo two was a shot of her outside the door, gathering the newspapers—

"Jock likes the papers with his breakfast." Photo three had the cat on the front walk, Sunny in the background, calling. Her T-shirt was hiked up on one side—"Pussy, pussy!" Photo four was a back view of her as she turned to look at the closed door—"Why has Jock shut the door?" Photo five had Sunny, now actually in front of Jock's door, whose number was invisible behind her head, her arms full of cat and milk and paper, knocking—"Jock, Jock!" It would have needed a very close observation indeed to notice that it was not the same front door. The sixth shot, of course, had captured the moment when Jock, only a shadowy figure in the photograph, had opened the door six inches— "Are you going to shut up about Caro?" The seventh was a close-up of the back of Sunny's head, fist upraised as she hammered on the closed door—"JOCK, LET ME IN!" The eighth was a blurred, badly angled close-up of the moment when Jock had opened the door and dragged her inside—"Forgive me, darling!"

It was the most extraordinary feeling to see pictures of yourself in the newspaper, Sunny discovered. There seemed to be a cloud of impossibility between her perception and the fact. This could not be real. Sunny gazed at the part of the photo spread she could see after Lorna Doone had settled herself comfortably, trying to believe that this really was her and that this newspaper had a circulation of half a million.

All of the pictures of her face were in full-length shots that had been taken with a telephoto lens and were correspondingly blurry. The close-ups were all of her back. In none of them was she clearly recognizable, and she heaved a sigh of relief.

The phone rang. "Hi, Sunny?" said a voice she didn't quite recognize. "This is Mark Snell. Emma's friend. Is this *your* picture I see spread all over the newspaper?"

"Aw, *hell!*" Sunny cried. "How did you recognize me?"

There was a pause. "Ahhh..." breathed Mark delicately. "Could it be your green eyes?"

Her heart sank. "Which paper are you reading, Mark?"

"The *Sunday News.*"

She exhaled with relief. "So am I, Mark. I don't see green eyes."

"I'm sorry my wit is so feeble."

"You should be," she said without mercy.

"God, how I love it when women savage me. You're almost as much fun as Emma."

"That's great, Mark. Look, are you doing anything at the moment?"

"Eating toast." He munched to prove it. "And drinking tea. Why?"

"Look, I can't explain anything to you at all," Sunny began. "Can you live with that and do me some favours without asking questions?"

"Will you Tell Me All one day?" Mark countered.

"If the day comes when I can, you'll be the first to know."

"All right, what are the favours?"

"How many sleazy tabloids are there in this city?"

"Do you mean the Sundays? I don't know. Half a dozen, maybe. I'm actually reading the maid's copy of the *News,* if you're wondering."

"Far be it from me. Listen, I'm afraid to go out in case they're out there waiting to take more pictures. Can you go and buy me one copy of every paper that's likely to be running this story and bring it around to me?"

"Are you a secret agent?" demanded Mark, in a grotesque imitation of an American accent. "Is this some kind of Commie plot? No, but wait—there are no Commie plots anymore, are there?"

"You watch too many bad movies," Sunny told him.

"And bad movies are too much like real life," countered Mark. "All right, forget I asked. You want the papers.

What are my delivery instructions? Do you have a secret drop in the garden, or what?''

"I do if you can get into the garden. If you come the front way you have to be resolute in not speaking to any reporters who accost you. Can you do that?''

"Do you mean you want me actually to come over the garden wall?'' Mark demanded in awed delight.

Sunny gasped. "Can you?''

"But I told you I lived just around the corner, Sunny. I am three gardens away from you, or is it two?''

"My God, that's wonderful! What about all the neighbours in between? Will they mind?''

"I shall tell them I'm on a secret mission for Queen and country.''

"You—''

"And they'll assume I'm visiting a friend who's not out of the closet yet.''

Sunny laughed.

"It *is* Queen and country, I hope?'' he pressed, mock worriedly. "You aren't working for the bad guys, whoever they are at the moment?''

Sunny said, "Mark. There's no such thing as a Canadian who is working for the bad guys.''

"Of course, of course! How silly of me! For a moment there I'd forgotten. You're all too nice, aren't you?''

"Please don't forget again,'' she chided firmly. "As it happens, however, this is purely selfish and individual. When will I see you?''

"My dear, as soon as I get round to the newsagent you will see me. This is fascinating. Of course I can't resist!''

"Fascinating? It's a nightmare!'' Sunny told him, hanging up. Flinging back the duvet to bury the cats and the newspapers, she discovered a large hairy blue creature with numerous legs nestled in beside her thigh. For a moment she felt her hair stand on end, just like James Bond in the tarantula scene. Then her rational mind informed her that few tarantulas were blue. "Spidey!" she muttered explosively, gingerly picking up the toy by one leather leg and tossing it across the room in disgust. "Damn it, cat, as if I don't have enough problems!"

Lorna Doone leapt wildly out from under the duvet and across the room after the spider. At last she had got it through to this thick human that Sunday morning was *playtime!*

The News of the World had run the shot of her "bleeding wrists" under the headline "'I CAN'T LIVE WITHOUT HIM!' says Jock's rejected lover." They had chosen a picture that somehow looked as if Sunny were deliberately displaying her arms for the camera, and they ran an exclusive interview with her on an inside page. "We've had such passionate nights together," Jock's unnamed rejected girlfriend had told the reporter. "I can't believe it's all over. Jock was the best, the sweetest lover in the world, but fame has spoiled him. Now he wants someone with a title. I can never give him that, but I'll love him till the day I die. And who knows when that will be," she had said with a sob.

"My God!" said Sunny, revolted. "Where do they get this stuff?"

"Listen to this!" commanded Mark, who was reading from another paper. On the front page was a photo-enhanced picture of a woman who had, purportedly, a seventy-seven-inch chest measurement. "'This morning, it seems, there was a terrible FIGHT, during which the macho star reportedly SLUGGED his tiny ex-girlfriend and even tried to *cut her up.* When she resisted his VIOLENT *attack,* she was *thrown* out the door!' I've never seen so many capitals and italics," Mark interjected. "'*She was almost NAKED,* as our pictures show. Fortunately, Jock Prentiss REPENTED after a few minutes and let her back inside. She later left, fully clothed, vowing, "I'll be back!'"''' Mark grinned at her over the top of the paper. "Is that what you said? How brazen of you, my dear!"

Sunny closed her eyes. "How bad is the picture?"

"Well, of course their good taste and journalistic restraint came into play here," Mark informed her, laying down the paper so that she could see the full-length shot of herself, the cat and the broken bottle at her feet, her arms flung up over her face. Her T-shirt had ridden well up, and the exposed part of her body had been decorated with—for it certainly wasn't covered by—the tiny black oblong that is usually reserved for people's eyes in scandal magazines.

Sunny, who never blushed, blushed. "I don't believe it," she said weakly. "Nobody could be so disgusting."

"Well, if it's any comfort, this one is likely to be the worst. It's the latest on the bandwagon, and certainly the scummiest."

"Cold comfort," said Sunny. "Will anybody recognize me from that shot?"

"I suppose that depends on how many people have seen you in a state of undress," Mark said consideringly. "That seems to be an interesting birthmark on your—uh, hip, or is it just a blob on the photo?"

"You've got sharp eyes," moaned Sunny. It was a birthmark, only just not hidden by the black oblong. "Oh, *damn,* what a piece of bad luck!"

"I ask no questions," said Mark. "But how likely is it that the person whom you don't want to know about you will be reading this paper? It really is smut of the lowest kind, you know."

"Right," said Sunny, nodding to herself. "Of course, you're right. Can you tear those pictures and the story out for me?" She set to doing the same for the paper under her hand.

"You want to save this stuff, do you?" Mark blinked at her.

"Yup," said Sunny stolidly. "I want my grandkids to know I had my fifteen minutes of fame, too."

"If it is only fifteen minutes."

"It will be if I can help it," Sunny said firmly. "Do you think your neighbours would mind if I went over the wall to your place so I don't have to use my front door?"

He looked at her. "Probably," he said flatly. "I didn't realize how exposed I'd be up there on the wall until I did it just now. It would make them very uncomfortable unless we explained the why and how." At her look of disappointment, he said, "I haven't got a lot to do these days, you know. I can run errands for you."

Sunny smiled. "That's great, and it'll be a big help if you really mean it."

"Of course."

"But I have got to get out of here twice—once today and once tomorrow, and I really don't want my picture taken for the press. What am I going to do?"

It was a rhetorical question, but Mark looked at her consideringly. "I don't know—you might get away with it. Maybe they'll be more easy-going than I give them credit for. I could come along with you, and that might make it better. And when I explain to them, I'll hint that you really are Jock Prentiss's new girlfriend, yes?"

Sunny sighed in relief. If the press followed her to the meeting with Customs and Excise, she was truly burned. "Tomorrow morning, about nine. Could you make it?"

"Sure."

That only left this afternoon. "Are you going to be home this afternoon?"

"Probably. You do realize . . ." Mark began warningly.

"What?" demanded Sunny.

"If you don't tell me what this is all about someday, my curiosity may kill me."

"Just so long as it doesn't kill me," said Sunny.

"What's that mean?"

"If the press corner you. You won't—"

"See no evil, hear no evil, speak no evil," Mark promised. "Word of an old Etonian."

"Are you really?" asked Sunny, enthralled.

"Oh, you've heard of Eton, have you?"

Sunny grinned in a way that would have warned Mark, if he'd known her better. "Sure I have. That's where Napoleon was finally defeated, wasn't it?"

"*What?*"

"Sure. Wellington said so. 'Waterloo was won on the playing fields of Eton,'" quoted Sunny, going off into peals of laughter. It was another joke that only she could enjoy.

Chapter 12

"What do you want?" Sunny asked. She sounded more ungracious than she had meant to, but she didn't want to see too much of Jock Prentiss. Last night had proved how dangerous he was to her, and she didn't intend to run any more risk of losing her head with him.

Jock stood gazing at her through the window, grinning as if he could read her mind. "We're going to Farid's shop this afternoon, remember? I came by to see what time you wanted to go." He'd tapped on her kitchen window, and since she'd been sitting at the table, she couldn't pretend not to notice him. Now he opened the door behind her and came purposefully in.

"I don't remember you being invited."

"Take it from me, Farid expects me."

For the moment Sunny couldn't decide whether this was the solution to the problem of how to get out of the house or not. "Have you seen this mess?" she asked instead. She was sitting with the pile of clippings in front of her.

"Is that coffee?" Jock asked simultaneously.

"Grab a cup," said Sunny. She enjoyed his company, no question of that. That was what constituted the danger. Last night the spell had been broken, and Jock had brought her home without trying to recapture the mood, but that didn't mean he couldn't do so if he tried. Sunny didn't have a lot of experience with sexual magnetism, but she wasn't underestimating it. To blame her mood entirely on the moon and the summer night was a fast way to go about getting caught unawares again.

With very economical movements, Jock took a mug off the mug tree on the counter, pulled a chair out, sat on it, put the mug down and pulled the clippings around to face him. Feeling oddly domestic, Sunny poured his coffee.

"Cream? Sugar?"

He grunted a negative as he glanced down at the little pile. On the top, as it happened, was the photo in which the little black rectangle failed to protect her modesty. "Ouch," said Jock. "You really got it."

It comforted her to have him express fellow feeling. "They've made up one hell of a lot of trash about us," she said. "Both of us have tried to kill me over your affair with Lady Caro, for a start."

Jock riffled the pile of clippings without bothering to look at them. "Quite a pile," he observed. "Pity royalty wasn't doing anything yesterday. Must have been an empty day." He set his coffee cup down on the pile of clippings, and a little circle of damp appeared on the photo.

"Well, I hope royalty does something today," said Sunny feelingly. She got up and shifted his cup, then moved the pile of clippings to the counter. "Someone's rung the bell a few times, but I haven't answered. When do you suppose they'll get tired of you?"

"Probably when they hear Caro Deane didn't get the part. Why are you saving those, matey?"

"You didn't cast Caro Deane after all?"

Jock raised his eyebrows. "Would you?"

"But you mean—you would have given her the part if it weren't for all the publicity?"

He shrugged. "Probably. She's right for it."

"But that's awful! This might wreck her career!" Sunny was aware of a certain fellow feeling; she sure didn't want this wrecking *her* career.

"Sunny, these people wreck *lives* without turning a hair. One part in a film—an entire career—is nothing to them. But you're right—it was a good chance for her, and it'll bother her like hell to miss it. It's not final yet."

"I think you should cast her, and be damned to them," said Sunny angrily—and impulsively. If his not casting Caro Deane would get the press off his doorstep she ought to be grateful he'd knuckled under. But in fact she hated the idea. "How dare they interfere in people's lives like that!"

"It's a hard world," said Jock.

"*Are* you having an affair with her?" she asked curiously.

Jock grinned. "Did you slit your wrists yesterday for love of me?"

"It's infuriating that they have the right to do this!"

"Oh, come on!" Jock rallied her. "You don't mind having your moment of glory, and nobody minds reading about it."

Sunny narrowed her eyes at him. "How do you know what I mind?" she asked irritably.

"Why are you saving the papers?"

Sunny opened her mouth and closed it again. She could make no answer to that. "All right," she agreed softly. "But just because I save a few clippings doesn't mean I like it."

"You don't hate it, either, do you?"

It wasn't true; she entirely hated it, if it meant that her job would be interfered with. If not for that, Sunny really would scarcely have cared. She certainly wouldn't have bought the papers, let alone clipped them. But it wasn't part of her job to explain anything to Jock Prentiss, and if he wanted to imagine that she was thrilled by the publicity, he would just have to think so. He must have met a lot of star-struck women in his day; if she acted as just one more she would be less likely to arouse his curiosity.

"Well," she said, "this happens to you all the time, doesn't it?" She shrugged and smiled. "But it's the only time I'll see my picture in the papers."

"It bloody doesn't," he said forcefully. He poured himself another cup of coffee and glanced around.

"Oh, really?" said Sunny curiously. "You mean—"

"You got any breakfast on offer? I've about run out of food," Jock demanded abruptly. "And I'm starving."

In the most natural way possible, he just seemed to take over. It was exactly what one of Sunny's brothers might have said in a similar situation. In another minute, she thought, he'll be up rummaging in the fridge.

The front doorbell rang, and Sunny, in her now-famous red T-shirt over a pair of jeans, stood uncertainly and glanced down the hall. "I bet that'll be reporters again," she said.

Jock shrugged. "Don't answer it. You'd better disconnect your bell. You'll be more comfortable."

She slipped quietly down the hall and looked through the peephole. It was the gazelle woman, she saw at once, accompanied by a man with a camera. She moved silently back to the kitchen. "Do you think they're taking it in relays?" she asked. "They seem to come every half hour or so."

Jock was rummaging in the fridge. "You want to disconnect the bell," he said. "Matey, this is great!" he said. "Eggs, bacon—where'd you get all this stuff?"

"Mark went out and got it for me. He's a friend of Emma's who lives a couple of gardens away."

"Right. You think there might be some steaks in your friend's freezer?"

"Have a look," said Sunny, submitting to the inevitable. "Is there anything I can do?"

He missed the sarcasm. "Yeah, toss these in the microwave to thaw," he said, throwing the two solidly frozen steaks he had found onto the counter.

"Australians eat steak for breakfast, just the way all the myths say?" Sunny unwrapped the meat and put it inside the sinister black oven and began pushing buttons.

"Well, it's brunch now, isn't it, matey?" he said with a grin. "It's nearly eleven o'clock."

Farid's shop was in Mayfair, the poshest area of London. It seemed to glow with old gold, from the polished lettering of the name to the faint gold shimmering in the glass of the show windows. It was the sort of place most people wouldn't be easy about entering unless they had money, and that air of exclusivity of course would make it all the more attractive to those who did. Just walking in the door would be an expression of status. A stunningly beautiful antique silk carpet, of a kind Sunny wouldn't have expected to see outside a museum, hung in the window on one side of the door; in the other was a solitary glazed pot with Arabic epigraphy around the bowl. That, too, was museum quality, or nearly.

Sunny was rarely intimidated by such pretension, and she might well have gone into the shop without knowing Farid, and without any intention to buy. As far as she was concerned, an appreciation of beautiful things gave a person at least as much right to look at them as having money did. But her heart quailed a little, for she knew from experience that in such shops the assistants were usually outrageously arrogant, and she was nervous at the thought that perhaps Farid Abul Hassan would have second thoughts about hiring her, even as secretary. Sunny had a friendly and confiding air that made people say her nickname had been well chosen. She would find it difficult to assume an air of consequence.

But inside, the shop had more the air of an expensive Arabian bazaar than a posh West End boutique. Carpets were stacked in odd piles, and antiques placed at random around the shop, with what looked like serene lack of design, but surely could not be. The air was secret and welcoming at the same time, as though you had been given an exclusive invitation to Aladdin's cave.

"Sunny! Jock!" she heard, and from a carved rosewood desk at the back of the room Farid Abul Hassan rose and came forward to welcome them.

"*Salaam aleikum*," said Sunny—Peace be upon you—feeling with pleasure the language on her lips again after a long time. *Kayfeh hallek*, she might have added—How are you?—but that would have been foolish.

"*W'aleikum salaam*,"—and upon you, peace—returned Abul Hassan. "I see you learn my language."

I do, indeed, thought Sunny as he and Jock shook hands and exchanged greetings. How thoroughly, I hope you'll never know.

He walked over to the railing at the side of the room and called down the staircase. "Mohammad, bring tea!" he ordered, then looked at them. "You will drink tea with me?" Scarcely waiting for a nod, he called, "For three!"

They followed him towards the desk at the back, and now Sunny saw the open spread of the *Sunday News*'s pages 16 and 17, and the eight photographs of her Saturday-morning adventure. Farid, settling in his chair and indicating two others for them, looked up and caught her eye. He laughed, a charming, seductive laugh, and his eyes twinkled expressively. "This morning you are famous," he observed with almost naive delight.

"Or infamous," interposed Jock drily. That broke the tenuous bond that was forming between Farid and Sunny, and Farid glanced at Jock and laughed. "You treat women

very badly, my friend! They say it is Arabs who are ignorant of the value of women, but I would not lock Sunny out
of my house in the morning!''

"My door blew shut," said Sunny. "They've doctored the
pictures. I had to wake Jock up and ask him to let me crawl
over his wall.''

"Ah, I see." Farid's eyes, with their spangle of lashes, still
smiled knowingly, and Sunny didn't press the explanation
further. If Abul Hassan thought she was attached to Jock
Prentiss, that might protect her from his own advances. If
it was clear from the outset that the job was just a job, she
might have an easier time of it. A romantic involvement
with a target could be an easy way in for a female undercover operator, but when it came to testifying in court, the
defence would make mincemeat out of your testimony on
the grounds that you were just a rejected woman with more
fury than hell itself. Of course, there might be occasions
when an officer had to be got inside an operation any way
possible, but then you had to be certain that the evidence
could be set before the court without her testimony in the
end. Sunny had never yet been up against the necessity for
such an involvement, and she didn't waste time wondering
whether she could handle one or not. She might never be
faced with the choice, and right now she certainly was not.
Whatever evidence she found, her testimony would almost
certainly be required in any legal proceedings. If Farid Abul
Hassan imagined that her working for him would make her
an easy target sexually, he thought wrong.

So she smiled shyly and flicked a glance at Jock, as
though however much the pictures might lie, there was
something between them. The look was all for Abul Hassan's benefit, and she hoped Jock missed it.

He didn't. In instant response, she felt his hand come to
rest possessively against the back of her neck. "And it was
the beginning of a beautiful friendship," he said jokingly,
but again Sunny sensed the masculine competitiveness in

him, and she saw by Farid's eyes that he read the message loud and clear.

"And I hope," said Farid, perfectly unfazed, "that *we* have the beginning of a beautiful working relationship. Come, let me show you the shop."

All of the main floor space was given over to display, and he led them around his treasures, chatting about those that caught Sunny's eye. There were exquisitely beautiful Indo-Iranian miniatures painted on ivory; pots, bowls and amphorae from the early Islamic period of several countries; beaten brass trays; a silver gun mounted with cabochon emeralds and rubies from Afghanistan; incense burners—all the evidence of the great Islamic civilisation of the Golden Age and after that Sunny had come to know and love during her university years. She had a hard time controlling her instinctive desire to read the inscriptions that many of the artefacts and even carpets carried, but there was no reason to hide her knowledge of the art itself. She wanted a job, and her familiarity with Islamic art, while shallower than her knowledge of the languages of the Middle East, was still sufficient to make her an advantage as a secretary to Abul Hassan. He left her in no doubt that he was impressed and pleased to be getting such a bargain.

The behind-the-scenes area was in the basement, and here was the desk where Sunny would be working. A certain amount of light came through the windows high in the wall that looked out into the areaway, as well as down the stairwell that housed the curving brass staircase that led from the center of the shop down to the secretary's desk. The basement had rooms for storage, as well as a kitchen, bathroom and an additional showroom, and the walls throughout were hung with a king's ransom in carpets.

Sunny was, quite independently of her delight at having got inside Abul Hassan's operation, thrilled. Her years in Rabbit Falls and Fond du Lac were over. At last, at last, she was truly back in the civilised world.

Chapter 13

Sunny didn't waste any time hating Farid Abul Hassan. Emotion of any sort clouded your intellect as well as your instincts, and in any case, he wasn't acting as an individual in this. If Sunny privately felt that she would never do what he did for any reason whatsoever, she was also mature enough to understand that she could not be entirely certain of anything when it came to humanity's—and thus her own—ability to breach the laws of human decency for a "higher" goal.

Farid Abul Hassan was almost certainly the London end of a close-knit network that was supplying Iraq with the materials and tools to manufacture chemical weapons. Weapons that had been used both against Iraq's own Kurdish population and against Iran during the long war, while the West, for the most part, seemed to turn a blind eye.

Only one Canadian cabinet minister had viewed this Western indifference with dismay, and it was at his instigation that the Canadian connection in the supply route had begun to be investigated. Eventually when the trail led to

Britain and the likelihood that U.K. import and export laws, unlike the Canadian ones, were being violated, they had tried to interest Her Majesty's Customs and Excise. The evidence was that the materials for the creation of chemical weapons, as well as other prohibited substances and technology, were being exported from Canada to Britain legally—or so things were made to appear. But the British firms that were doing the importing were suspected of being an elaborate cover for an export operation that eventually saw the goods all the way to Iraq, and proof of that would make the whole operation conspiracy, and therefore illegal all the way along the line, and the Canadian end would be punishable by Canadian courts.

But without conclusive evidence from England that the end use was being falsified, no prosecutions could take place in Canada. It had taken a long time to interest the British, and in the meantime the Iran-Iraq war had ceased and a large part of the Kurdish population was dead, or fled. In such a conspiracy of silence and apathy, Sunny wasn't going to lay the blame at the door of this one man. If genocide was going on, and it assuredly was, once again it was the whole world's fault.

So she had no qualms about drinking tea with Farid Abul Hassan, even though she rather subscribed to the dictum that said you must never share food with an enemy. Farid Abul Hassan was not her enemy in any personal sense. She would sabotage his work, if she could, in an entirely impersonal way. He was only a cog. If it hadn't been him, it would have been someone else. You couldn't hate a *position.*

"This is Constable Sunny Delancey and Staff-Sergeant Jacques Fallon of the Royal Canadian Mounted Police," said the HM Customs and Excise Senior Investigation Officer. In the absence of a Canadian-style national police force, Customs and Excise had wide powers in England, and this officer, though not, strictly speaking, a police officer, would be her commanding officer while she was on this assignment. Sunny had met him briefly on Friday, but everyone else in the room was a fresh face. "Constable Delancey, these officers will comprise your backup team." Sunny wondered if she'd imagined the extra emphasis on the word "constable." "Officers Dinwoody, Pierce, Flood and Rejean." They shook hands with her one by one as he said their names. Three men and one woman, and the woman introduced last, Sunny noted. Ah well, change didn't happen overnight. She ought to be grateful there was a woman on the team at all. She exchanged a friendly grin with Officer Rejean as they shook hands; she was glad to see the twinkle of intelligent amusement and fellow feeling in her eyes.

They were interrupted by someone bringing coffee to the door. That might have broken the ice, the friendly necessity to sort out who got which plastic cup, but in fact it didn't. Sunny mentally girded her loins as she sat in the chair indicated. They resented her. They really resented this invasion of the Canadians into their turf, she realized impatiently. And yet it had been a Canadian operation from the very beginning. What the hell did turf matter, anyway?

Fairchild, the S.I.O., briefly recapped the case in a manner that made it clear none of them was unfamiliar with it. He was a large, blond man with a very quiet voice that he tended to swallow. Sunny had to strain to hear. He finished by saying, "Constable Delancey, as you're all aware, is going to try to get inside Abul Hassan's organisation, which of course we've not yet managed to do." There was a dryness to his tone, but whether it was the dryness of self-deprecation or ironic comment on colonial impatience, she couldn't be sure. She knew that everyone in the room, except perhaps Jacques, understood the tone exactly, and it made her feel isolated. At home a team was a team—but, of course, she'd never worked with anyone outside the force at home. Maybe Bosey would have felt just as threatened if the

Brits had insisted on sending over Officer Rejean to go undercover into the Canadian setup. She made a conscious effort to relax and like them all. It would be fatal to go into this without feeling that the team was behind her.

"Constable Delancey has the very great advantage of being able to speak Arabic," Fairchild was saying, giving the devil its due, unless Sunny was much mistaken. He was sitting with a file open on the low table in front of him, but he didn't seem to need it. "That is the reason she was brought in on this operation at the Canadian end, though I believe you're rather junior, aren't you, Constable?" Again there was the dry note in his voice, as though he perhaps thought the Canadian end of the operation were being run by fools.

Jacques cleared his throat. "Constable Delancey is an officer with six years' experience of police work," he pointed out in a quiet, firm monotone that contrasted strongly with the varied intonations of the English voices. "She is a graduate from undercover training and has worked on several cases since. Her understanding of Middle Eastern languages, religions and cultures is rare amongst police officers and makes her particularly valuable for this operation."

"Quite," said the S.I.O., with a glint of amusement in his eyes. "Well, let's hope your Arabic proves an advantage." Delicate use of the word *hope,* which he probably thought too subtle to be picked up by a Canuck. Sunny merely nodded. "We understand, of course, that there's a further advantage, in that Constable Delancey has a friend living right in Banbury Square. How much of an advantage this will be is unpredictable. We know that several residents of the square are regular attendees of the parties at Number 22, and among them is Constable Delancey's friend. At the moment, I believe, this friend is absent."

He sounded as though that were her fault and not his. She wanted to say, "What a pity you wouldn't let me come sooner," but she repressed the urge, not without difficulty.

She contented herself instead with exchanging a glance with Jacques. He nodded. Since the bull seemed to be presenting its horns, the nod said, she'd better take them. "Emma's away for the summer," she agreed. "But I think I've established a connection in spite of that."

They looked at her in surprise. "We've heard nothing of this," said the Senior Investigation Officer.

"No, sir," she said, "you wouldn't have. I attended a party at Number 22 on Saturday night, and met Abul Hassan through the agency of one of the other residents of Banbury Square."

There was a brief, rather chilly pause while Fairchild, one hand in his pocket, one stroking his ear, gazed down at the file in front of him. "Well," he said, "perhaps you'd better let us know what action you've taken, Constable, before we go any further with this presumably now outdated briefing."

Damn, but the English could freeze you, Sunny thought. There couldn't be another race in the world with such a knack. She wondered why they bothered with conventional weaponry at all—they could just go up to the front lines and freeze the enemy to death.

"Yes, there's been a lot of movement over the weekend," said Jacques, shifting in his chair. "And not without problems. Constable Delancey is going to have to be mighty careful now if she's not to get burned."

That got the fixed attention of everybody in the room. "Perhaps you'd like to take it from there, Sunny," Jacques said.

"Well, to take it in reverse chronological order," Sunny began, as she and Jacques had privately agreed she would, in order to present the best part first, "I've got a temporary job with AlHaqq Antiques starting tomorrow."

A gasp of surprise went around the room amongst the junior officers, but the S.I.O. only calmly consulted his notes. "AlHaqq Antiques," he repeated, as he thumbed through the pages of his file. "That's Abul Hassan's antiques shop, I believe."

"Yes, sir," Sunny said. "Just off New Bond Street. His secretary has left, and I'm going to fill in for a few weeks until he finds a permanent replacement."

They were staring at her now, giving her their full attention, and she took them backwards up the chain of events, avoiding mention only of the journalists, to the party and the meeting with Jock, and the cat and the wind and the locked door. By the end of it they were all looking at her in astonishment.

"Does everybody know who Jock Prentiss is?" Jacques asked then, drawing fire a little to give her a breather.

"That must be the star of *Sydney Streets*," put in Officer Rejean.

"That's right," Jacques said flatly. "And at the moment, apparently, he's involved with an actress who is married to a peer."

Rejean nodded. "Caro Deane," she said. She looked at her S.I.O., who was frowning. "Lord Isham's wife, sir," she supplied. "She's a regular on *Leviathan*."

"This is the man who took you to Abul Hassan's party on Saturday night?" asked the S.I.O., turning his gaze on Sunny.

Sunny only nodded.

"Then there will almost certainly be pictures of you in the yellow papers. Do I understand that you have a sizeable acquaintance in London, Constable Delancey?"

"I went to university here," she said. He was very damn sharp. She hadn't expected to lose control of the conversation so abruptly, but there he was with the whole thing in a nutshell, and next out of his mouth would be the words saying she'd better go home.

In fact, he leaned forward and closed the file in front of him. "Well, that's very unfortunate. You couldn't have known, but very unfortunate nevertheless."

Sunny felt herself panicking. "Wait, wait!" she cried.
"We haven't finished."

He looked at her as only the English can look, and Sunny
was abruptly aware of how rude she had sounded. It just
wasn't done to tell your superior officer you hadn't finished. "Sorry," she said. "But..."

"They took pictures of Sunny on Prentiss's doorstep on
Saturday morning and published them in most of the Sunday tabloids," Jacques put in. "We've brought the clippings. I don't think there's a great cause for despair, but of
course, it's not my decision." He nodded, and she opened
her case and pulled them out. After a split second's hesitation she got up and handed them first to Alex Fairchild.

The S.I.O. went through them in silence, one by one,
scarcely raising an eyebrow. When he had finished he passed
them to the officer on his left and looked at Jacques and
Sunny steadily. "You were educated in England, Constable
Delancey?"

"I took my degree here at the University of London," she
admitted. "School of Middle Eastern Studies."

"How long ago was that?"

"I graduated nearly seven years ago."

The cuttings were making their way around the group in
startled silence, though Sunny could have sworn a couple of
the officers were with difficulty suppressing smiles of hilar-
ity, and if she wasn't imagining it, there was a glint even in
the S.I.O.'s eye. If the English had a saving grace it was their
sense of humour, she reminded herself.

"You're not readily recognizable in any of those photographs," he said. "At least, not to someone who doesn't
know you well." His tone was so dry she almost missed it.
Sunny bit the inside of her lip and began to award him more
points than she'd imagined at the beginning.

"Ah, no, sir," she agreed, wondering how he could do it
without cracking a smile. "I doubt if any of my old friends

would guess it was me even if they saw the whole lot together."

"I presume the photographers are still stationed outside the Prentiss house?"

"They were this morning."

"Have they been taking pictures of you going in and out since then?"

"I haven't been in or out of my own door since the incident Saturday morning," Sunny said. She was beginning to like the man. This is the kind of unflappable guy, she thought, who won the Battle of Britain. Laurence Olivier would have played him in the movie. She had to cough to cover a choke of laughter.

"How did you achieve that?"

Out of the corner of her eye she saw that Officer Rejean was examining the clippings, her mouth twitching irrepressibly. Rejean put up a hand to hide it and cleared her throat several times. Sunny swallowed and forced her gaze away.

"Ah—hmm," she began. "I've twice gone out Jock Prentiss's front door with a wig and heavy sunglasses on, and we weren't followed. This morning I climbed over the back garden walls to get out by way of the house of a friend of my friend Emma York."

"So there won't be any more photos of you running in the papers."

"There may be something in this morning's," she told him, "but, as I said, they'll be of a wig and glasses."

"You have nevertheless been put in some additional jeopardy over this," Fairchild pointed out calmly.

"Yes, sir. But minimal, don't you think?"

Fairchild leaned sideways in his chair and pulled out a pack of cigarettes. Not taking his eyes off Sunny, he put a cigarette between his lips and lit it, then held the lighter and the pack under his rather heavy hand on the arm of the chair. With his other hand he took the cigarette out of his mouth and blew smoke.

"There's no way of knowing the extent of the danger. It will be a matter of chance, and chance is unpredictable. The risk to you personally, as well as to the operation, is greater than we planned for."

"Yes, sir. But I'd really like to go with it."

He was looking at her through the smoke he was creating, and she thought she detected the glint of approval in his eyes. A feeling of mutual liking suddenly, and against the odds, seemed to link them across the room.

It's going to be all right, Sunny told herself, as the tension of the past hour left her in a rush and relief flooded in. I won't lose my chance yet. He's going to let me go ahead.

Senior Investigation Officer Alex Fairchild of Her Majesty's Customs and Excise smiled at her with his eyes only, and she looked back, trying to imitate the eyes-only trick, realizing she had failed when she felt her mouth twitch.

Ah, well, there were some things only the Brits could do. They'd shown that before now. Sunny let the smile have its way.

Chapter 14

One deficiency in her early officer training, perhaps, had been that the walls in the obstacle course hadn't been covered in vines and trellises and roses that were not to be disturbed by the merest leaf, Sunny reflected, as she hoisted herself up on Mark's garden wall and ran nimbly along the brick towards Emma's garden, taking care to avoid the vines and creepers symbiotically attached to the ancient brick along most of the way. It was a question whether the brick held up the vines, or the vines the brick. At Emma's she dropped to a squat and then leapt quickly down. The entire operation hadn't taken more than thirty seconds, but it was still more exposure than she liked. The neighbours seemed to have got used to the twice-daily sight of her gymnastics, but they all also knew the ostensible reason for it, and there was no telling when someone might decide to let the press in on the secret.

So Sunny restricted her use of the route to moments of absolute necessity, which meant going to the antiques shop in the morning and coming home at night. Which, in turn, meant she was effectively a prisoner all the rest of the time. She hadn't seen Jock Prentiss for several days, and the journalists seemed to have given up knocking on Emma's door, but never at any given moment could she count on their not being out there in the square.

It was turning into a very hot summer in London, and the June evening was warm. She was busy pulling her keys out of the pocket of her sundress as she strode up the length of the garden towards the kitchen door, so she didn't see Jock Prentiss until she was almost in his arms. He put up his hands and she stopped abruptly just out of his reach.

"Hi," she said. She hadn't consciously missed him over the past few days, but she couldn't stop the smile she felt inside from appearing on her face. It was a bit like coming into range of a powerful stove when you hadn't realized you were chilled, she thought. Jock, appearing not to notice that she had avoided his touch, stepped forward, put his hands on her bare upper arms and bent to kiss her, in the European fashion, first on one cheek, then the other.

"Hi," he said, and then, as though that little touch had broken some control he might have set on himself, he slowly bent and kissed her mouth.

It certainly broke Sunny's control. A minute ago she had been competently avoiding his touch, but now she lifted her face and opened her lips, feeling his strong arms tighten around her with a sigh of satisfaction, as though she had never considered him a threat to her equilibrium or her work. Her hands slipped up around his neck, and she was pulled even more firmly against the length of his body; she felt how he wanted to wrap her completely in himself, felt her heart soften into need.

At last he lifted his lips and smiled into her eyes. "I wasn't planning on that," he admitted ruefully.

Neither was Sunny, and she groped for the control her rational brain could give her. "Yes, well," she muttered, irritated with her own weakness. Damn it, she was supposed to be a cop. Or at least a cop first and a woman second.

Grinning, Jock rubbed a broad hand against his cheek. "You probably won't believe this, but I'm here on business."

Sunny stepped around him and slipped the key into the lock. Inside, a chorus of howls notified her that the cats considered her arrival overdue. "C'mon in," she said. "Make sure Lorna doesn't get past you."

"That cat still in heat?"

"It comes and goes, I think," Sunny answered absently, as opening the door, she pushed in a foot and shoved the cats back, quickly following the foot in and then bending to hold Lorna as Jock entered. Beetle seemed to lose interest in the outdoors then, either because he was leaderless without Lorna, or because, with Sunny's arrival, he expected a treat.

"Have a seat. I just have to get some Mousers," she added. Jock's eyebrows went up, but he said nothing. "Yes, I know," admitted Sunny with a grin. "But my life isn't worth a nickel if I don't take care of these two first crack out of the cannon. I am a slave. I admit it. But *you* try compromising with a cat! It's just not in the dictionary."

The sound of Jock's chuckle warmed her as she rooted in the cupboard for the cat treats. "Mousers!" she said lightly, shaking the box. Emma was right; the cry would bring them from any part of the house, but as they were right there, it merely caused orgiastic frenzy in them. Lorna and Beetle rubbed against each other and leapt against Sunny's ankles, alternately crying and purring in short throaty bursts. When the first treat came out of the box, Lorna "sat" in the otter position and accepted the treat with great feline graciousness. Beetle watched fixedly but without complaint as she did so, knowing his place was second.

"So, what's the business you want to discuss?" Sunny asked over her shoulder.

Jock, sitting now, leaned an elbow on the table and pulled his ear. "We're casting Caro Deane in the film," he said slowly. "I want to offer you a job, Sunny."

That was interesting. Beetle sat, too, and gobbled the treat as though it might be his last meal. "Really? What as? Gofer on the set?" she asked. She was wearing a white sundress appropriate to the weather, but not very appropriate to a strictly business conversation, he thought. A few tendrils of hair, damp with sweat, were clinging to one brown shoulder. He was aware of a desire that she should turn so that he could see the shape of her breasts again, the warm cleavage exposed by the low top of her dress.

"Ah, no," he said, in some awkwardness. "As my new girlfriend, actually. What do you think?"

She thought she'd heard wrong, that was what she thought. "As your *girlfriend?*"

"Yeah," he said. "I'm really tired of this damn press business, Sunny. I want to get them off my back. I'd pay you well, and it'd all be under the table. What do you think?" he asked again. "You wouldn't have to give up the antiques shop, either, if you didn't want to."

Lorna was sitting up again, but Sunny had lost interest in cat tricks. She quickly dumped some of the little treats on the floor, separated them into two piles, tossed the box onto the counter and turned to Jock.

"You want me to pretend to be your real-life girlfriend?" she asked. "Are you serious?" At her feet, Beetle was already gobbling his little cluster of snacks.

"Yeah, I'm serious." He raised a hand. "Don't turn it down till I tell you about it—it's better than it sounds cold." He wished he hadn't kissed her before making this proposal. Maybe it sounded suspicious. Maybe it *was* suspicious. He didn't seem to know quite what his motives were.

Slowly Sunny crossed the kitchen to the table, pulled out a chair and sank into it, looking at him curiously.

Jock said, "I reckon they're going to go overboard as soon as the news is out that Caro's actually in the cast. What I'd like to do is make it obvious there's another woman in my life and hope they'll lay off a bit. We're not announcing the news till Friday. I'd like to announce at the same time that you've got a part in the picture, too. We'll make the part sound big, but in fact it'll be nothing much. Still, you'd end up in the final cut unless you're absolutely impossible."

Sunny frowned. "I don't get it. What's the difference whether it's me or Caro Deane? They're still taking pictures of you and writing about your private life."

Jock grinned and shook his head. "Nah," he said, drawing the word out. "This is the English, matey. They're not interested in me—it's the peer's wife that's got 'em going. There'd be a day of concentration on the rivalry between you and Caro, and then it'd all peter out."

"Don't you have a girlfriend here who would serve the purpose?" Sunny wondered absently whether he really was having an affair with Caro Deane and was hoping to use this method of hiding it from her husband.

"If I did, I wouldn't be offering you the job, would I?" he countered flatly.

"No, I guess not. Look, I'm sorry—"

He interrupted. "There's good money in it, a lot of publicity—and a film part," he said. "We might even swing a permanent acting union card. It could change your life, Sunny."

It could, indeed. Some wild part of Sunny urged her to fling her organized life to the winds and leap at it, just for the hell of it. But it was a part of her that she had no difficulty in controlling. "Jock, thanks for the offer, it sounds terrific, but…" She paused involuntarily. It would be great cover under the right circumstances, she thought sadly—girlfriend of a star—but these weren't the right circumstances.

"What the hell's wrong with that cat?" Jock asked abruptly, because he needed time to think. Sunny turned her head to see Lorna, still high on her haunches, the little piles of treats at her feet. The cat was staring at her reproachfully.

"Oh, for—! Lorna, you don't have to sit today. Just eat the darn things," Sunny told her.

The cat's gaze remained unblinkingly fixed on her. Sunny began to laugh. "I don't believe it!" she said to Jock. "Do you see this? This cat's been trained to sit for her treats, but she thinks it's *me* who's been trained. And now I'm slipping up on the job. See? I don't get the fun of watching her eat her treats unless I feed them to her one by one." She got up and bent down over the cat, picking up the treats and offering Lorna one, still laughing.

Jock watched silently for a moment. "I think the cat's right, isn't it?" he said.

Still chuckling, Sunny said, "Why, what do you mean?"

"Why are you feeding her those things?"

Sunny froze in the act, while Lorna magnanimously took a third treat from between her fingers and delicately chewed. "My God, Jock, you're right! I've been trained by a cat! Hey, I'm pretty smart, eh? It hardly took me a week!" Sunny's sense of humour was well caught, and she began to laugh in her throaty, contagious way. "Boy, you can't fault me for brains! I bet Lorna's proud of me, aren't you, Lorna? I'm your star pupil!"

It was impossible for Jock not to join in her uninhibited laughter. For some reason he couldn't work out, too, the laughter had a direct link with his loins. He crossed to where Sunny was feeding the cat the last treat and drew her to her feet. "Damn it, woman, what are you packing?" he asked. He drew her against him, though he knew he shouldn't. Women liked subtlety, not these direct full frontal assaults he couldn't seem to help making on her. At least, he thought they did. Ever since he'd been an actor, he hadn't had to put the weights on any woman. They made all the running themselves.

Sunny was out of practice, too. Not many men made full frontal assaults on women they knew to be Mounties. At least, she supposed that was what was affecting her. Usually she had no trouble resisting passes when she needed to, but she was having trouble with Jock, for sure, for sure. Right now she felt as though someone had planted little land mines under her skin all over her body, and Jock was setting them off wherever his hands or his body touched her.

She was saying weakly, "No, Jock," so he bent and kissed her, because he knew that was the way to shut her up. He was dimly aware that this wasn't the way his brain normally worked, but he didn't care. He was right. Once his mouth was on hers, she stopped resisting and wrapped her arms around his neck, so that her body was open to him, inviting. His hands slipped quickly down her back and over the swell of her rump, then stopped there, not pressing her to him, but holding her firm while he pushed against her. The light dress she was wearing hadn't much under it; he knew she could feel how hard he was, because her mouth opened under his with a little grunt, a soft moan. That moan was like meat and drink to him. He wanted to make it louder and longer; he wanted to look into her eyes and know he was giving her pleasure, and he wanted to do that right now.

His hands shifted; one dropped to her thigh and caught the white fabric of her dress, sliding it up to her waist in one rough motion. Underneath, no stockings, only cotton briefs, and as he pressed his strong hand against her rump, the other moved up to cup her neck and the back of her head, and Sunny felt enclosed, protected, captured, and utterly drunk with sensation. In all her life nothing had ever felt as right as what she was feeling now.

It wasn't till the phone had rung four times that she realized it must be her seven o'clock call from Bosey.

Chapter 15

When she pulled her mouth away and her head back, he kissed her throat, and Sunny drew in a breath and tried to mobilize her arms to push him off.

"I have to answer that," she said breathlessly.

"Sure you do," said Jock, not loosening his iron hold on her by a degree. His mouth was moving down from her throat towards the tops of her breasts that the sundress left exposed.

The ringing signals were not spaced as widely in London as they were in Toronto, thus imparting a greater sense of urgency to any ringing phone, which she hadn't yet learned to ignore. The phone had already rung nine times now, and if she didn't answer it, she would have to explain why to Bosey later. She didn't want to have to give him any reason, and she pushed hard against Jock's chest.

"It's a call from home," she said. "Let me go."

Jock came up for air with something like shock and instantly let her go. He couldn't imagine what the hell was the matter with him. He hadn't hung on to a woman who was fighting him off since he was nineteen years old and had got a black eye for his efforts. He had no doubt that Sunny was capable of giving him more than a black eye, and bloody right she'd be, too. He stood shaking his head as he watched her snatch the receiver from the cradle.

"Hello!" she gasped into the mouthpiece, sounding as though she'd run the last quarter mile.

"Sunny?" The voice came faintly, sounding a long way off amidst the heavy crackle and pop of static. "*Crackle, hiss--ma. Can you screek, whuttle?*"

"Emma, is that you?" Sunny shouted. "I can hardly hear you! Can you hear me?"

"*Screek* very bad line. I just called to tell you that *whee-auk, scrack, scrack, fiss, scrack* in a day or two, so be prepared."

"You're coming home? Is that what you said?"

"No, not *scrattle, scrattle, scrattle, SCRATTLE* hope you can hear this. This line's *screeee.*"

"Emma, I didn't hear what you said! What did you say?" Sunny shouted, spacing her words, desperate to be heard, to hear what was so important that Emma should call her from the middle of some Egyptian desert to let her know.

"*Scree* hear a word you're saying. Did you hear me? *Scrack scrack scrattle hiss scrattle...*"

Eventually the line, hissing and crackling, and without the exchange of another word, went dead. Sunny stood staring at the receiver in her hand for a helpless moment before she slapped it back in the cradle.

"Damnation!" she said. "What do you suppose that was all about?"

"No idea." Jock shrugged. "She was trying to tell you something, was she?"

"God, that's the worst line I've ever heard. She must have been trying to call from some village near the dig. I think she was trying to warn me about something, but I just didn't get a clue. Well, in a day or two, that's as much as I got."

"Maybe she forgot to pay her home insurance," Jock suggested.

"No, it wouldn't be anything like that," Sunny said absently. She almost said, "It would be something important to me," then she remembered that Jock wasn't someone she should be thinking out loud to. "Well, maybe," she amended. "I'll have a look around and see if there are any papers or anything."

But she knew that Emma was warning her of something that might interfere with her work, and she was worried. When the phone rang again under her hand she snatched it up. "Emma?" she shrieked.

"Mind the ears, Delancey, mind the ears," said Bosey's slow, level voice imperturbably. "What's happening?"

"Oh, Bo—hi," she said hastily. "Emma's just called me from Egypt to tell me something, but I couldn't hear what it was. I thought you were her."

"Oh, yeah?" Bosey said, on a slightly rising intonation. It was his idiosyncratic way of signalling that he was taking in the data and ready for more.

"That's all I heard, really. 'In a day or two,' that's the only thing I really heard. That and 'be prepared.'"

"Doesn't sound very good."

"No, but I can't think what it would be. What could she possibly find out out there...but never mind that!" she said with ferocious mock gaiety, realizing that Jock was taking all this in. "My neighbour's just visiting me, and you'll never guess who it is!"

Flies rarely got the chance to settle on Bosey. He was nothing if not quick. "Jock Prentiss," he said.

"Jock Prentiss, the actor!" Sunny announced. "How about that?"

"He's there now, is he?"

"Yeah, I was, too!"

"All right, just listen. I'll be quick. You're going to have to call back, anyway. The obvious thing that strikes me is something to do with her ex-husband. He's Egyptian, and he's the target's friend. I want you to start playing very, very safe until we find out for sure what her information was, right, Delancey?''

"Hello? Hello?"

"Yeah, that's right, this line's bad, too. It's cutting us off right now. You'll call as soon as you can."

The line went dead. "Hello!" said Sunny. "Damnation, I must not be living right." She hung up and turned to Jock. "Now, where were we?" she asked.

When Jock smiled she went pink, remembering. "Forget I asked that," she said. "Let's have a cup of coffee."

"I'd rather go back to where we were," he observed mildly. "Any reason why we shouldn't?" He reached for her, one hand taking her upper arm, the other stroking her cheek.

She really had to put an end to this. She couldn't afford to have Jock nibbling away at her concentration and efficiency the way he seemed to do. She'd worked this out in advance, without really believing she would need it. "Look," she said, dropping her head and speaking to the floor. "I'm a married woman, Jock. Pip and I have split up, but I'd still like to get back together with him."

He didn't blink. "I know an easy way to make him jealous." His hand ran from her neck down her arm to her wrist, not lightly, but with a firm masculine touch that made her shiver.

"I don't want to make him jealous. He's bad enough as it is." Poor Pip, what a reputation she was giving him.

"Did you give him cause to be jealous?"

"No, no, but . . ." She trailed off as if helpless to explain, which indeed she was.

"Bad type to get mixed up with," Jock advised sagely, entirely forgetting what his own feelings had been when Abul Hassan had shown an interest in her a few days before. "Man who gets jealous for no reason."

"Yeah, well..." Sunny looked up and grinned. "He'd kind of have reason now, wouldn't he?"

"He hasn't got any right to be jealous if he's let you go and hasn't come back to get you tied up again," Jock pointed out.

"Maybe," she said, "but I have never got over feeling married to him."

He pulled her gently into his hold. "Give me half an hour," he promised softly, "and I'll make you forget you ever knew his name."

She was in no doubt about that. He could probably make her forget she'd ever known her *own* name. There was something about him, both physically and mentally, that just seemed to knock out all her defences. Under his touch, she felt her skin shiver into goose bumps all over her body. She pushed herself away from him, and Jock looked down at her and swore.

"Look at you," he said. She followed his gaze and saw the outline of her hardened nipples pressing against the white cotton of her dress. "It doesn't take either of us a minute, does it?" His hand came up to cup her breast, while his thumb stroked gently. Sunny's breath hissed in between her teeth.

His other hand cupped the back of her neck in a way that was already familiar, and with a twist he undid the button of the halter strap. The two straps dropped forward and slipped down her chest, exposing the thin white cotton of her halter bra. The suddenness of it shocked her into deep sensual response, so that she felt her womb clench and her body melt.

Jock carefully, gently, brushed the straps of her dress down off her breasts. The soft cotton of the bra was very thin; her tanned skin was visible through it, and so was the whiteness of her breasts, the darker colour beginning again at her nipples. She felt his hand at work at her back, pulling at her zipper, and suddenly the dress was at her feet, and she was standing there in nothing but bra and briefs and shoes.

It had happened so suddenly she hadn't been able to muster any defences, but now, slowly, her reason tried to kick into action. "Jock," she protested weakly, feeling as though her rational self were struggling through thick mud.

At the tone of her voice a warning rang in his brain. If he gave her a moment to think she would ask him to stop. Without taking a moment to think himself—he was hardly capable of thought—he sank to his knees in front of her and pressed his mouth between her thighs. He heard her gasp in mingled surprise and desire, and he felt his own body throb almost painfully in response. This was unbelievable. He'd never felt anything like it in his life, not since he was seventeen and it was all new and astounding and everything in life was sex, sex, sex. In those days everything in the world seemed to have a direct connection to his groin. Now it was just Sunny.

The heat of his mouth radiated from her centre to all the ends of her body. It shocked her, and so did her response to it, physical and mental. She could feel her thighs trembling uncontrollably, and she had to fight a desire to open her legs to allow him better access.

"Stop," she said. "Jock. Stop."

She didn't like it. Jock smiled to himself in satisfaction. Man, he was going to love teaching her to like this. To love it. By the time he was finished with her, she would have no shame at all. Gently he stroked her with his tongue, slowly, tantalizingly, to make her want more. He felt her hands touch his hair.

She clenched her hands in his hair and tried to pull him away, but he resisted, and won. "Jock," she said hoarsely. "I want you to stop."

He tilted his head back and looked up into her dark eyes. Her pupils had expanded till there was no colour in her eyes but black. "Sunny," he said, shaking his head, "you don't."

"Yes," she said.

Now he slipped both hands up around her waist and held her firm, looking into her eyes. Damn, she meant it. She was going to be a lot tougher than he'd imagined. "All right," he said then, releasing her. As he got to his feet, he reached down and drew her dress up over her hips. Once on his feet, he expelled his breath mightily and grinned. "We'll do it your way, matey. Or at least we'll try. I'm making no promises. So—what's on the cards now, then? Shall we cook dinner?"

She was a little surprised. She'd had the idea he was only after conquest, and that he would go off with a wounded ego after such a rebuff. "I guess so," she said, trying to disguise from herself her relief that he had not gone off in a huff. "At least—"

"Right," he said, not giving her time to add any riders to that. "And since we can't go out, I guess we're eating in. I got a chicken today. You like chicken?"

Holding her dress to her breasts, Sunny only nodded. She felt highly confused. No personal relationship had ever threatened to interfere with her job before. She wondered what to do; could she keep the two separate? Could she be sure Jock had no involvement, other than social, with Farid Abul Hassan? Ought she to ask Bosey about it—or, worse still—S.I.O. Alex Fairchild?

She had to do something, she reflected, as Jock disappeared out the back door and across the garden to the wall. He was threatening her stability, and that meant he was threatening the case. She couldn't allow that; she had to find some way to handle it. She realized belatedly that it might have been better if Jock *had* taken masculine offence at her sexual rejection of him. Or, failing that, if she had refused his assumption of friendship.

Sunny slowly buttoned the straps of the sundress around her neck, and found herself looking down into her own cleavage as she did so. Suddenly she could feel his mouth on her skin, his hand against her breast, with a clarity of sensual memory that shocked her.

She needed protection, there was no doubt about that. If she was going to be able to resist Jock Prentiss, she had to have help. Where was her guardian angel when she needed him?

When the knock on the door—Jock had disconnected the bell for her—came a moment later, she didn't connect it with her prayer; she merely thought it was some journalist trying his luck at random. She went silently down the hall and looked through the peephole.

Straight into the eyes of Emma's brother, Pip. The man she was supposed to be married to. And pining for.

Chapter 16

"Can you send Ahmad and Mohammad up, please?" Farid Abul Hassan's voice came down the staircase to Sunny's desk with unusual pleasantness. It must mean there was an important client upstairs. The atmosphere in the antiques shop was by no means consistently pleasant, nor did Abul Hassan consider it necessary to treat his staff with respect. Often when he wanted the stock boys he simply shouted their names, so that the place sounded like a carpet shop in some Arabian *souk*.

Sunny didn't mind all that much, though she could see it might become wearing over the long term. However he treated the others, he generally treated her as an equal, perhaps because of the way they had met. For the most part, she found it exciting to be in such an atmosphere, not least because it reminded her of the year she had spent in Egypt as part of her degree.

The two young men were in the little kitchen, smoking, which was against shop rules and probably fire regulations, but although Farid had told her to stop them whenever she caught them at it, Sunny didn't have the necessary tyrant's instinct. So much, she thought, for all those people who think cops are cops because they like to force other people to obey the rules.

Nevertheless, they leapt guiltily when they saw her.

"You guys are wanted upstairs," she told them. "In a hurry, I think."

That last was unnecessary. Whenever Farid wanted someone, it was always in a hurry. The cigarettes were quickly doused, and the two young men, muttering unflattering curses in Arabic, which, of course, they assumed Sunny could not understand, ran lightly upstairs.

Leaving Sunny to the work she'd been doing, which was combing through the shipping records to see if she could find anything questionable. Of course, Farid Abul Hassan had several companies, and it was possible that the antiques business was run entirely on the up-and-up. But their intelligence had said it was the only import-export business he ran in the U.K., and common sense said it was therefore involved in any smuggling operation.

What she was looking for was first, anomaly, and second, a pattern: of shipments, correspondence, imports, phone calls, anything. There was no narrowing things down this early in an investigation. What this meant in practice was that she had to try to be aware of everything that went on in the shop until she picked up some clue about what to examine more closely.

In the typewriter she had a sheet of paper half-typed with instructions to Abul Hassan's shippers, and her ostensible reason for having the big ledger file open on the desk was to check the format and wording of such letters. She was, after all, still in training. What she was in fact doing was paging through the file—which was a record of shipments to the shop's customers—looking for a recurring address, perhaps, or anything else at all worthy of notice.

Ahmad came back down the stairs, still muttering, and disappeared into the back showroom. When he came out again he was carrying the little wheeled gizmo that they used to move very heavy items around the shop. He stopped by her desk. "He don't tell you he want this?" he asked her, knowing what answer to expect.

Sunny shook her head and smiled in fellow feeling. "Sorry, he didn't."

"Up and down, up and down," he said. "He crazy man."

His English was not up to fully expressing his complaint, which it hadn't taken Sunny two days in the shop to understand was valid. Farid Abul Hassan was one of those men who like to feel his power. He did this by making his staff do a lot of unnecessary running around. When he called down, he could easily have asked them to bring up the wheels and so saved Ahmad the unnecessary extra trip. But it was typical of Abul Hassan that he had not bothered.

A minute later they both came down again, slowly and laboriously, for the little set of wheels was almost more of a disadvantage than an advantage on the spiral staircase, and the package they were shifting was very large.

"Why doesn't the mongrel dog's son let us open the parcel upstairs and carry them down separately?" Ahmad was saying softly, while Sunny gazed at him in apparently blank incomprehension. Listening to the stock boys' conversation was good practice for her Arabic, and very necessary, for she had done her "year abroad" in Alexandria, and the Egyptian dialect being very different from that of Iraq, she needed constant input to train her ear for that one moment when understanding might be crucial.

She knew that Ahmad hated Abul Hassan. If his English had been better, she would have sounded him out, because he might have picked up a lot of helpful information, but it was almost impossible to have a conversation with him in English, and until she could be sure neither man was an active part of Abul Hassan's operation, she could not risk giving away the crucial information that she spoke Arabic. Mohammad spoke somewhat better English but was less easy to read.

Both men's accents were very slightly different from Abul Hassan's, which might mark nothing more than the fact that they were from different tribes, or that he was from the city and they the country. Sunny wished she knew. Their skin wasn't pale enough to mark them as Kurds, she thought, for the Kurds, like many Persians in Iran and the Pathans in Afghanistan, were all descended from that mysterious Aryan race that had pushed down from the Caucasus as far as northern India four or five thousand years ago. She wished they were Kurds, for it would have been a tremendous advantage. There couldn't be a Kurd anywhere who wouldn't jump at the chance to help dismantle the Iraqi chemical weapon capability. But until she knew more, she couldn't run any sort of risk of that nature except in a life-and-death situation.

Mohammad didn't reply to Ahmad's complaint, and the little wheeled lift with its heavy burden came bouncing down the last few steps almost out of control. Both men were sweating and cursing by the time it was safe on the ground.

Imports were not of first interest to Sunny, of course, but she was still at the stage of not being able to ignore anything, so she asked, "What is it?" Because she was wearing the persona she had established in her first meeting with Abul Hassan—someone with a deep interest in Middle Eastern art and artefacts—she could get away with an overt expression of purely artistic curiosity. Since it was so close to the truth, it was easy enough to maintain, and it might get him used to dismissing any curiosity on her part as artistic. She hoped.

"Carpets," Mohammad told her.

"New or antique?" she asked. Any Middle Eastern carpet was a delight in this shop, because Abul Hassan of course did not deal in anything except the best, but antique carpets were generally of greater interest, because they would have been done in the villages and possibly by an individual weaver, whereas a modern carpet, though technically hand-woven, might well have come from a city sweatshop, where any number of people might work on it.

Mohammad shrugged. "Probably old."

She jumped up and followed them into the back showroom, where she watched them unpack the carpets and unfold them. They were not very old, no more than thirty to fifty years, she thought, and they weren't very attractive. Although the name of the shop was AlHaqq Antiques, that referred only to things other than carpets. Some of the carpets Abul Hassan sold were new. Carpets were the easiest thing to sell to tourists, he had told her. Most shops needed one bread-and-butter item, and carpets—though of course only the best—were his.

"Do you like them?" Abul Hassan's voice asked behind her. He must have finished with the important client.

"They're not bad," she said slowly. "Are they for upstairs?"

He laughed. "Ah, what a very good eye you have! Yes, you are right! They are not for this shop! They go to the shop in Italy."

"Oh." Well, that cleared up that little mystery. "It doesn't carry the top-quality stuff, I guess?"

He looked peeved. "Yes," he contradicted her, "the top quality, but also not so top quality. Only carpets we sell there. Nothing else. Here we sell to collectors, rich people. There, we sell to everyone."

Well, he wouldn't be the first up-market retailer to have a down-market outlet, though it was interesting to learn that it was as far away as Italy. "What a good idea," Sunny said. She absently pulled the heavy brown paper wrapping out of the way of the stock boys, who were fighting to pull each of the carpets in the pile straight. As she did so, she glanced at the label. It informed her, in Arabic and in Roman script, that the carpets had been shipped from Iraq.

"Brush them down, fold them and wrap them again for shipping," Farid told the men in Arabic, as Sunny turned to go back to her desk, hoping to write down the address before she forgot it. But Farid followed her. "You don't know how to type the documents for shipments to the shop in Italy?"

"I haven't done any so far," she said.

"Okay, I show you," he said.

Sunny sat down, casually closing the shipping ledger file and setting it to one side. "All right," she said, indicating her readiness.

"Why are you reading that file?" Farid asked.

"Oh, just for the format of the shipping letter," she said, indicating the letter still in her typewriter.

"Ah," he said. "Now, these carpets go straight to Italy, and we use an Italian shipper for this. Also, we have special letterhead paper. So first . . ."

It didn't take her long to learn the routine, and when the documentation was typed, the carpets packed and gone, and the shipping letter she had been working on typed, Sunny had nothing more to do.

She had very little work generally; she could understand how he'd managed without a secretary for a few weeks. Even with all the work that had to be caught up, there wasn't a full-time job here. Sunny slipped the last letter into the folder awaiting Farid's signature and then sat with a book about antiques open on her desk. Farid had gone into the back showroom with a client while she was working, and she could not risk reading through the shipping file when he might come out again at any moment.

Besides, reading the art book might well be productive; in a job like this, no information would come amiss. The more she knew about the business, the more likely she would be to find any anomaly in the way it was run.

At the picture of an Isfahan silk prayer rug she paused. In its colouring it was similar to one hanging on the wall in Farid's house; she had looked at it with Jock on the night of the party, and though she had been resolutely keeping her mind away from him all morning, she was suddenly remembering last night.

"Pip!" she had cried in astonishment, tearing the door open and dragging him inside before anyone could get a picture. "What on earth are you doing here?" She slammed the door to and leaned against it.

"I've come to stay for a bit. What about you?"

Pip was the wild sheep of an already pretty unconventional family. His thick, shoulder-length auburn hair as often as not had a henna rinse in it, and bizarre jewellery, all of it occult, was in his earlobes, on his fingers, around his neck. His clothes, when they were not neo-hippy, were all black and tight. He had very intelligent blue eyes and a full mouth; he did whatever he wanted in life, and looked it. Anybody less like an ex-husband could hardly be imagined. You wouldn't dream of him bothering with the ritual called marriage, still less with the one called divorce.

"Oh, damn, damn, damn!" exploded Sunny. "Of all the messes!"

"Why, what's the matter?" asked Pip, narrowing his eyes at her with the intense look that was his hallmark.

He would not have been her first choice of co-conspirator, and Sunny wasted time moaning, "I thought you were in India."

"I'm in London now," he said matter-of-factly. He took a big duffle bag off his shoulder and swung it to the floor. "Are you staying here, too?"

Sunny closed her eyes. Just what she had been afraid of. "Listen," she said, suddenly aware of the passage of precious time. "I've been telling lies about you, and if you stay here you are going to have to back me up. All right?"

"What lies?" he asked. She had the funny feeling she remembered something in his pantheon, whatever it was, about lying being a form of power. She devoutly hoped she wouldn't be violating some power line or something.

"I've told a few people we used to be married and are divorced, and that my name's Sunny York."

One thing about Pip, he didn't waste time on astonishment or questions. "Oh," he said. His head moved a little as he took it in. He paused, his eyes inwardly assessing something—her, or the lie, or his situation—and then said, "All right."

Sunny heaved a sigh of relief. "Do you know what I do for a living, Pip?" she asked, because she wasn't going to tell him if he didn't remember, reminding him only in order to ask him to forget it again.

The look again. "Something very strange," he hazarded. She laughed. "I remember that."

"Yeah, well, please forget whatever you know if you happen to remember. Here I'm a would-be writer, and I'm hoping to come to London to live. Oh—and I didn't go to university with Emma. We met in Canada when your family was living there."

Another silence. "All right," said Pip. "Is there any hot water?"

"What?" Sunny said, startled.

"I've been travelling for days. I'd like a bath."

So her problem and her panic were put into perspective. Sunny laughed. "Yeah, I guess there is."

"Good," said Pip. He started up the stairs, paused and turned. "Sunny."

"Yes?"

"We're supposed to have been married?"

"That's right. It's really important, Pip."

"Yeah, okay. But—we don't sleep together, right? I'm preserving my power at the moment. All right?"

"Yeah, that's all right."

"I mean, I don't even want to pretend we sleep together, you understand? That would be a drain."

"Would it really?" she paused, but Pip never answered such rhetorical questions, and she went on, "Yeah, okay, I'll remember that, Pip."

He turned away again. "Pip, do you want any dinner?" she called after him.

"That would be good," said Pip, nodding. "Thank you." And then he was gone.

It had been quite a meal. Pip didn't eat any chicken, since, he explained to Jock, he didn't eat meat except at very particular times and places. He wore a flowing Indian robe and had left off none of his occult jewellery. He was strikingly attractive in an almost feminine way, and his presence was rather magnetic, and there was no doubt Jock felt it. He certainly didn't seem to feel suspicious about the idea of their having once been married, however weird such a scenario seemed to Sunny. But that he was bristling with masculine jealousy was pretty clear, as also was the fact that Pip refused to engage. Any thrust fell flat in the face of that curious, intense, yet detached gaze.

It was exactly the way Sunny felt in Pip's presence much of the time, but that didn't stop her finding the situation funny.

It fortunately wasn't long before Pip decided to go to bed. "Where are you sleeping, Sunny?" he asked, and she felt Jock freeze.

"In Emma's room," she said.

Pip nodded. "All right." He got up to go.

Jock looked up. Abruptly his power, or magnetism, or whatever it was, seemed as strong as Pip's, and a good deal more threatening. "And where might you be sleeping, matey?" he asked softly.

"In the guest room," Pip said simply. "Sunny and I do not engage in marital relations."

"Good," said Jock. He nodded once. "That's good."

"Good night," said Pip.

When he was gone, all the tension left her in a rush. The worst thing about Pip was that he was unpredictable. No matter what he'd agreed to, she felt, there was no telling what he might say.

"I wish Emma had warned me he'd be here," she'd said to Jock.

"Didn't she? I thought that was why you were here," Jock said.

She remembered giving that impression at Abul Hassan's party. "Yes, well..." was all she said. When you were undercover, too much explanation was more damaging than too little or none, ninety-nine times out of a hundred. She remembered the abortive phone call then. Of course. Emma had got a letter or something from Pip on his way home from India, and had tried to warn Sunny. Well, at least it was better than wondering what the cryptic call had been trying to warn her of.

"So, you think you're in love with him?" Jock asked.

"Well, I'm not hoping to get back together with him for the sake of the kids," she said drily. "Of course I'm in love with him."

Jock was shaking his head to contradict her. "Why?" she demanded irritably, masking her fear that it was far too incongruous a match to fool him.

"You aren't in love with him, matey. You're curious, maybe, hypnotized, but you don't love him. Who broke it up?"

Oh, Lord, she hadn't got that far. "Well, I..." She hesitated. Never having been married, it was difficult imagining how someone would respond to such a question. "I guess *I* did, really." She shrugged.

"Why?"

"I don't know." She decided to fall back on irritation as a way out. "Why are you asking?"

"I think that's pretty obvious, isn't it? You tell me you love him and don't want to get involved with me. But you don't love him. You left him once, and I can see the reason why."

She was curious in spite of herself. "Why, then?"

Jock shook his head. "Because you're only fascinated, as I said. But that's no basis for marriage. You'd be a fool to get involved with him again. Have him as your guru, not your husband. Why don't you come and sleep in my house tonight?"

Sunny only shook her head and laughed, and he had left soon after, without having tried to do more than lightly kiss her good night. Clearly he couldn't make a move on her with Pip right there in the house.

Sunny had felt a little deflated once he'd gone. It was a while before she realized that what she was feeling was disappointment.

¶

Chapter 17

For the next few days she used the excuse of Pip's presence to avoid Jock Prentiss. Not that she any longer admitted the possibility that he might be involved with Abul Hassan's conspiracy, for the more she knew of Jock, the more she was convinced that he could have no part in anything so appalling as chemical genocide. And there was nothing whatsoever pointing in Jock's direction.

If he was innocent in his friendship with Abul Hassan, she was free to get involved with him, if that was what she wanted. But she was living a lie, and however much she might have liked to, she couldn't tell him the truth. It was better to keep him at arm's length. In any case, Sunny told herself, he was a famous actor and could only be interested in her for a fling, and did she need that? No.

Over the next few days, when Jock called, she made excuses and tried to concentrate entirely on work.

As in any trading enterprise, at AlHaqq Antiques there were shipments in and shipments out. In a factory, of course, what was shipped in was transformed into something else before it was shipped out, but in the antiques business, there were no raw materials. As well as importing, Farid bought from and sold to both traders and private citizens, and except for the odd bit of carpet mending and cleaning, or silver polishing, or framing, no transformation of the product took place.

This theoretically made it easy to follow what happened to any particular artefact. Every item had to be numbered for stock-taking purposes; that number was assigned to an item the moment it entered the shop and remained with it till it was sold and shipped.

For some reason it wasn't that simple. It was, in fact, confusing. Numbers sometimes seemed to be assigned to nonexistent articles, while some items seemed to be assigned a number only when they got sold, and Sunny hadn't been in the shop three days before learning that fraud went on *vis-à-vis* customs duties. Like any carpet dealer in Ankara, it seemed, Farid commonly matched goods going abroad with documents that understated the price a foreign customer had paid for them, so that they could be taken through Customs at home without paying the heavy duty due; he even, Sunny felt sure, made false declarations to Customs on items he was importing for trade.

In fact, Sunny began to fear that what was really going on in the shop was nothing more than import-export tax fraud, and she said so one day when she was reporting, as usual, at a Customs and Excise "safe house."

She had been describing the various ways he avoided customs duty for both himself and his foreign clients. "And then there's the Italian business, which I can't figure out at all," she told Fairchild. Sometimes the whole team sat in on these briefings, but often, as today, it was just her and the Senior Investigation Officer.

Fairchild lit a cigarette. "Yes?"

"Another lot of those carpets came in from Iraq today and went straight out to Italy."

"Ah," said Fairchild, in some satisfaction. Much of police work meant finding a pattern, and while twice couldn't be counted a pattern, exactly, it pointed to an area worth watching. "Tell me about it."

"The carpets come in from Baghdad. I managed to get the address this time," Sunny began. "They're unwrapped, examined and maybe brushed, and then wrapped up again and sent out to the shop in Italy. I don't think there can be much doubt the carpets aren't really of a standard for the shop here, from the little I know of carpets. Some of them are badly worn, some made out of wool dyed with modern chemical dyes, which nobody in Mayfair would be caught dead with, some just not attractive enough."

Fairchild blew out smoke. "Does Abul Hassan know that before the parcel is opened?"

Sunny shook her head. "I can't tell. He only makes a cursory examination, but then, the quality is readily apparent—at least, it seems so to me. If he told me one of the badly worn ones was five hundred years old and worth fifty thousand pounds I wouldn't know the difference, of course. The whole antiques business is ripe for fraud, anyway, isn't it?"

"All right, carry on."

"I typed up the shipping documentation on a sheet of the same letterhead I told you about last time, which he supplied me with again from a stock in his desk. Today I made a mistake and asked him for a second sheet, and he made an excuse to see the ruined sheet and then threw it in his own waste-paper basket." The letterhead was of a firm with an address in Southampton, which Fairchild's team last time had investigated and discovered to be an accommodation address. "When that's done, he phones the Italian shipping agent, and they come and pick the package up."

"How does it travel?"

"By sea, as far as I can establish. The customs declaration I type for the shippers puts the value at only a few hundred pounds each, and I don't think that's wildly low, but, as I say, I don't know enough about carpets."

"What's his purpose in bringing these carpets through England?" Fairchild asked suddenly.

"Pardon?"

"Why are they shipped through England, with all the attendant necessity for clearing customs here, if they're on their way to Italy? He'd be better off shipping everything straight to Italy and passing on only the best to England. Wouldn't he?"

"Maybe there's no one in the Italian shop capable of judging the carpets," she said.

"That's the obvious answer, of course." Fairchild never pulled any punches if he thought Sunny was being stupid. "Let's look at some others. Is it possible that these carpets don't leave England, and that it's an operation designed to save on customs duties here? Those carpets may look worn to you, but to some people they may be museum pieces, as you said."

"I'll keep my eye open for any of the ones I've seen coming back into the shop for sale," Sunny said, forestalling him. She didn't mind having it pointed out to her when she was stupid, but it was a matter of honour with her to reestablish some claim to intelligence as soon as possible.

"I think this is something worth watching," Fairchild said. "Let's get the Italians working at that end, trying to trace those shipments coming in."

That was when she broached the idea that had been growing in her mind for some time. "Do you think he can be using the antiques shop for any of the chemical smuggling if he's indulging in so much fraudulent activity there?"

"Why not?" asked Fairchild in his quiet voice.

She looked at him. "Surely he realizes what would happen if Customs got suspicious and went in there and started going over his books? They'd flush out all the anomalies, wouldn't they? Not just the false declarations, but anything else.''

"You may be overestimating us." He smiled at her, nearly indetectably, but she was beginning to suss him out. "Someone looking for simple evasion of customs duty would be more likely to stop whenever he found it, don't you think? Abul Hassan may be running the fraud as a deliberate gambit—in order to have something small to sacrifice to protect what is more important." Sunny noted his particular use of the word *gambit* with secret admiration. Fairchild never used language sloppily.

"Yes," she said.

"In any case, it never does to assume that the members of other cultures reason according to our own rules, does it? I should have thought there was a very good chance that this kind of activity was so much a part of the Middle Eastern mentality that it would astound Abul Hassan to know that here we care very much about it.''

"Yes, I guess so," said Sunny.

"But you would know more about that than I do."

It didn't feel that way just at the moment. Sunny grinned self-deprecatingly. "Maybe," she said dubiously, meaning, "Don't get the idea I think an Arabic and Hebrew degree has made me an expert on human nature."

"There is also a possibility that he simply can't resist screwing the authorities out of their due, whatever else he's doing," Fairchild continued. "I sometimes think crooks have been caught oftener through the little passing dishonesty they couldn't resist than for the big one they were spending their energy on."

"Let's hope Abul Hassan doesn't get caught for his petty sins," Sunny said, appalled, because of course that was true. Whatever his reasons for the import tax evasion, if Sunny had been working for another branch of HM Customs and Excise, what she had found would have been instant paydirt. She and Alex Fairchild, therefore, agreed to keep the information to themselves. They didn't want the regular Customs people spoiling their operation with an untimely investigation into fraud.

Sunny was getting more and more committed to this job the more she was in a position to actually do something. It was one thing to hate what Iraq was doing with chemical weapons; it was quite another to think you yourself might actually stop it. Before, such a possibility had been rather nebulous, depending on many external factors. But now that she was inside the organisation, it might only depend on whether she managed to suss out the system. And now she was becoming a zealot. Through her action, thousands of Kurdish lives might be saved, and perhaps those of other populations and peoples in the future.

The terror of chemical weaponry was that it could be used exactly as it was being used: for genocide. A machine-gun raid, or even a bombing, could somehow be escaped by one or two inhabitants of a village. A child hiding in a ditch, or a family in a basement, might just miss death and be left to carry on the traditions and the gene pool in however vestigial a form.

But no one escaped a direct chemical attack. A village so attacked was a village destroyed for all time, and a people systematically subjected to such attacks was one of the lights of creation forever darkened, one of the instruments in the great symphony forever silenced: a blow to all humankind. If each man's death diminishes me, as the poet believed, how much more must each people's death diminish the earth.

Sunny could hardly have put such thoughts into words, but they were within her, and they were what drove her, made her determined to find whatever there was to find in Farid Abul Hassan's organisation.

When she left the shop just before six on the Friday evening that week, Officer Rejean, dressed as a London meter maid, was giving a car opposite a parking ticket. Sunny's eyes passed over her without recognition, while Rejean adjusted her hat. Sunny walked around the corner and into the underground station, crossing over to the bank of pay phones. She lifted the receiver of the last phone in the row and put in a ten-pence piece, shifting her body so that she could hold down the button without its being seen. She didn't dial. When the phone rang she released the button, and collected her ten pence, which had fallen through.

"Delancey," she said. Her heart was thudding; a call from the backup team could be anything from the news that she'd been burned and the target was gunning for her to the simple information that Fairchild wanted to see her urgently.

"It's Pierce, Delancey. Thought you'd better know the mob are really hopping over there in Banbury."

"Right," she said. This was no more than she'd been expecting. According to Jock, the news that Caro was cast in the film would have been released today. "Just the usual, or something special?"

"Just the usual, as far as we can see." That meant that they were at Jock's front door and in the square, but she wasn't in much danger of running into them anywhere else. It meant it was a reasonable risk to go home.

"Okay, thanks for the warning." Sunny made her good-byes and hung up. The automatic turnstiles were down again, so she joined the long line, flicked her weekly pass at the solitary guard at the barrier and went down the escalator to catch her train. The guard had hardly glanced at her pass. With enough aplomb a person could travel anywhere on the London Transport system carrying only an outdated Zone One pass, Sunny reckoned as she squeezed into a train already full to bursting. But that was nothing new.

There was no one but the maid home at Mark Snell's house, but in any case, these days Sunny only said hello as she passed through to the garden. She noticed nothing untoward as she made her usual quick journey past her neighbours' back gardens, aside from a dog who took exception, presumably, to her passing out of the reach of his teeth. Still, Sunny gained the protection of Emma's garden with a feeling of relief. She pulled out her key and ran lightly up the garden to the back door. She would be glad to get inside.

The door didn't open when she pulled it. She must have left it unlocked when she left this morning, then locked it just now when she thought she was unlocking it. Sunny put the key in and turned it again.

A horrible chill started in at the base of her spine when the door still didn't open. The bolts. It could only mean that Pip had bolted the big bolts on the inside of the door. "Oh, God, oh, no," Sunny prayed, turning the key yet again.

She was locked out. It simply hadn't occurred to her to explain to Pip that she used the back door, and in any case, he was usually sleeping when she left in the morning. How typical of her! This was Blunder Woman, all right! She pounded on the door, but she could hear the cats inside yowling, and they wouldn't do that if anyone were in the house. Lorna, in particular, was savvy enough to go and plague Pip for a treat rather than wait by the door for Sunny's return.

Sunny turned and glanced up at the windows of the houses facing onto the gardens all around. The evening sun was catching those on the upper floors, making them flash with dazzling gold light. Suddenly the scene seemed hostile. Any one of the windows might hold a photographer who'd talked or bribed his way past a servant or a resident who wanted to be part of the excitement.

Pip was unpredictable. There was no telling when or if he intended to return. But she had to get out of sight, and she had two choices: go back to Mark's house and throw herself on the mercy of the maid, or go over the wall and see if Jock were home.

She hardly knew the Snell maid and couldn't afford to trust her. On the other hand, she had made up her mind to avoid Jock Prentiss.

So much for brilliant intuitions and answers to prayers. Pip had been in the house less than a week and already he'd proved a liability. And today of all days, when she absolutely did not dare risk an attempt via the front door!

It would be entirely in character if Pip were on a plane bound for Goa or Tibet at this moment, Sunny thought irritably as she hoisted herself up and over Jock's garden wall. She hoped he was.

Chapter 18

Jock greeted her with surprise. "Hello, what's up?" he said, holding the door wide. Sunny pushed quickly past him, feeling very paranoid. The scent of cigarette smoke was faint but nevertheless telling in the room.

"Have you got company?" she asked, her heart sinking. If it was Caro Deane and she was interrupting something, what the hell would she do?

"Production meeting," Jock said briefly. "Never mind that, what's the matter?"

She wondered how he knew something was the matter. "Pip's gone and bolted the back door so I can't get in," she explained. "I've got the front door key on my chain, but is the square full of press?"

"Yeah, it is." He rubbed his chin. "Do you want me to break a window and get you in, or would you rather come in and stay till Pip gets back?"

"Well, if you're in a meeting..." she said hesitantly.

"Never mind that, you'll like them. Come on in and meet my team." He didn't seem to know she'd been deliberately avoiding him.

There were half a dozen men and women lounging around his sitting room, the air full of smoke and the floor littered with coffee cups and papers. On a small table was a stack of what looked like scripts; against the wall behind a small sofa another table held a big metal coffee-pot and all the necessaries. When Jock introduced her and mentioned names all round the room, there was a mixture of Aussie and English accents as they casually greeted her.

"Grab a seat," Jock commanded her, nodding at the empty two-seater sofa. "I'll get you a coffee." When he'd filled a cup and added cream and sugar, he handed it to Sunny over the back of the sofa and then came around and sat beside her. Immediately the room fell into focus. The people were not sitting randomly around the room, but in a pattern relative to the sofa. With Jock absent from the sofa this pattern had been invisible, but when he sat he became the focal point of the room. Sunny thought she could almost see the power lines snaking around the room from his position.

"Right," he said. "Where have we got to? Lisa, you were talking."

Lisa was a thin, rather striking redhead, angular but graceful, in her late thirties. She was holding a clipboard on her lap, a cigarette and a pen in one hand. "Right, we were just moving on to fifteen, right?" Her accent was strongly Australian. "Now, we've pretty well done the deal for the exteriors for this with the Earl of...what the hell—" she glanced at her clipboard "—Stavely, at Stavely House. For those who haven't seen the photos, it's bloody magnificent, exactly what we're looking for." A small cheer went up among those assembled. "We're not sure yet if he'll let us have it for interiors. Harry's got to get out there and have a look anyway, and, Jock, I think you should go with him, because if we want it, the faster we sew it up the better, with this guy. He's a little unpredictable, and we want to get his signature on a contract before he goes buggering off on his travels, which he may do at any time."

"Right," said Jock. "Shall we do that tomorrow?"

"All right by me," said the man named Harry.

Lisa sighed relief. "That would be great, fellas. Okay, so..."

A man quietly cleared his throat. "Ah, Jock," he began. He was brushing his nose apologetically; he was English.

"Dev," said Jock.

"Stavely's got the reputation for being difficult. He's a bit of an eccentric. I didn't realize that Stavely House was a possibility here, or I'd have warned Lisa. He might turn out to be more obstructionist than you're counting on."

Jock nodded. "Yeah, thanks, Dev. Lisa, you'd better have the contracts drawn up both ways, and I'll try to get his signature tomorrow. If we don't get it immediately, we'll go with the next one—Lanyons, is it?"

Dev coughed. "Even if you were to get his signature, I wouldn't want to count on his not causing a problem."

"If he signs a contract, he'll stick to it," Jock said, and Sunny heard a note in his voice that meant it wouldn't be a very wise man who tried to cross him.

Lisa's quick smile showed her approval. "It really is a peach of a place, Jock," she said. "I've been all over it, and some of those interiors are fabulous."

"Right," said Jock. "Sixteen and seventeen we'll discuss later. That takes us to eighteen, does it?"

Sunny was fascinated; she generally was when confronted by something that was entirely new to her. She sat in silence, drinking her coffee, watching whoever spoke, trying to make sense of the specialised language when she did not understand a term. She was surprised, when Jock looked at his watch and said, "Right, it's getting late, let's call it a day," to discover that she had been sitting in the room for two hours and the sun had nearly set.

Everybody seemed to get up and leave at once, saying goodbye to Sunny and moving through to the hall in Jock's wake. He stood chatting with them at the door, and when he opened it and flash bulbs started going off, he merely laughed. "Don't give any interviews, now," he warned his team, and then, with a few more comments, they were gone, and the closing door shut out the babble.

Then Jock was standing in the sitting-room doorway, looking at her, and suddenly she could feel each beat of her heart. "So," said Jock. "What's been happening?"

It occurred to her, too late, that one of his production team might have gone in Emma's front door and unlocked the back door for her without causing too much suspicion among the journalists outside. "Damn," she said aloud.

Jock looked enquiring, but there was no use crying over it. She shook her head. "It's what I said. Pip seems to have bolted the back door before going out today. It must be the most responsible thing he's ever done in his life, and I don't know why he picked today to do it! And I just can't face walking up to the front door through that mob. Do you mind if I wait here till he gets back?"

Jock grinned. "You can park here till the cows come home, for my money. And if you'd like to reconsider my offer, we can go out and brave that lot together and go to a restaurant for a meal. What do you say?"

Sunny was shaking her head before he'd finished. "I can't," she said. "I'm sorry, I can't. Anyway, Pip may be home already. Could I use your phone?"

But there was no answer, and Mark wasn't home, either. She was reluctant to break in except as a last resort. Sunny tried to put her brain to working out a solution, but if there was one, it seemed she couldn't concentrate hard enough to find it. After a few minutes she followed Jock to the kitchen.

"Every time I see you, you're cooking," she observed. There was a sharp smell of garlic in the air. "I think you should have been a chef instead of an actor."

"Actors make more money," he said. "You want salad?"

"Sure. Does that mean you're only in acting for the money?"

He glanced up. "Sunny, matey," he said, "any grown man who stands around in front of a camera pretending he's something he's not for any reason other than money is either lying or out of his mind."

"Golly," Sunny observed admiringly. "Do you say that kind of thing in your press interviews?"

"Usually," he said. "You want to help or just look decorative?"

"Help," she said.

He waved a hand. "Salad fixings in the sink," he said. He was rubbing something into four thick chops on the cutting board. After a moment he reached out to turn on the gas under a pan, and the smell of melting butter was added to the smell of garlic. Sunny's appetite, always healthy, was instantly stirred.

"Boy, am I hungry!" she exclaimed. "I wonder if I'm eating more in England than I do at home?"

"If you are, you look as though you work it off pretty hard."

"I do at home. I guess I'd better join a gym if I'm going to stay here. I'll be getting flabby in another week or so."

"Must be plenty around."

"The problem is those jerks on your doorstep. I feel like a prisoner here."

He glanced up from the stove, where he was gently shaking the frying pan to mix the garlic and spices into the melted butter. "You worry about them too much," he said. "If you just came and went, ignoring them every time, they'd soon lose interest in you. In fact, they've probably ess you counted doing the cups at the station. "I'd better try phoning Pip again," she said then, "before he goes to be—" She stopped, because she had glanced at her watch and it read after midnight, which couldn't be right. "What time is it?" she demanded in amazement, shaking her wrist as though the watch might be broken.

Jock looked at his own watch. "About twenty past twelve."

"Where did the time go?" she wailed. They must have been sitting over the meal for two solid hours, and she'd hardly noticed. This whole evening had gone by without her noticing. She ran to the phone in the sitting room, although a few seconds couldn't make any difference. "If Pip's not home, it'll be too late to call Mark now!" she berated herself as she counted the ringing tones. When she'd counted ten she knew Pip wasn't there, but she held on for another ten just in case he was asleep or in the bathroom. Or perhaps because she was afraid of what would happen when she hung up.

She did so at last, not looking at Jock. "What am I going to do?" she asked worriedly. "We can't break a window now. Someone would call the police for sure."

At Jock's prolonged silence, she at last looked up. He was smiling faintly at her, one eyebrow raised, and sensation rushed up and down her spine so that she visibly shivered. He was standing where she had left him, just inside the doorway. Now he crossed slowly towards her, and she felt the buildup of a tension so strong it was nearly tangible. Her body felt a powerful need to touch him, but her brain told her she must not, and she stood immobile, watching his approach as though she'd been hypnotized, knowing she should move away, but unable to give her body that simple command.

already forgotten you. You were good for one day'
that's all."

She couldn't explain, so she remained silent. "Any
she said, after a bit, "I can go to a gym on my way
from the antique shop. I don't have to make a special
ney."

Jock didn't make any of the conventional arrangem
for seduction, such as candlelight or soft music. He set
table in the kitchen, though the dining room was more
timate. And his conversation over dinner was easy a
friendly, talking about his day and asking about hers.

That this was more intimate than a blatantly seducti
conversation would have been didn't quite impinge on Sur-
ny's consciousness, but she nevertheless felt she was under
siege throughout the meal, without having anything tangible to protest against. In spite of their being in the rather
large kitchen, a feeling of intimacy imperceptibly entered the
room and surrounded them, cutting the lighted table off
from the darkness outside that symbolized the rest of the
world. Intimacy was something that Sunny had not often
experienced, and she was surprised at its effect on her,
without quite knowing what it was. What she felt, mostly
unconsciously, was that she was not allowed to trust Jock,
and that that was a great pity, since he was entirely trust-
worthy. And since she disliked censoring her conversation
she kept away from too much discussion of herself or Far
Abul Hassan and the shop, and talked instead about h
family. Jock told her about the plot of his film, and ab
the actors and his production team, and she found it
fascinating, because it was a world she knew nothing ab
and he had the power to bring it to life for her. It wa
first really personal conversation they'd had.

When the meal was over they did the dishes togeth
it was the first time Sunny could remember ever v
dishes with a man other than her father and broth

Chapter 19

At the last moment she was released from immobility and rather spasmodically stepped away from him. Her foot got entangled somehow with the telephone cord, and the phone jumped from the table with the little *ping!* that was characteristic of British telephones. Whirling to catch it, Sunny knocked against the lamp. Immediately, she abandoned the phone and tried to save the lamp, which, gently eluding her, fell off the table, flickered brightly and went out. They were plunged into shadowy darkness, the light from the hall not reaching more than a few feet into the room. There was a short silence, broken only by the sound of the dial tone.

In the darkness she felt Jock's arms go around her, and his voice said in her ear, "Well, that takes care of the phone and the lights." They began to laugh together, soft, intimate laughter that said everything, that confessed everything—her fear, his determination, mutual desire.

Then of its own accord her face lifted to his, and they were kissing with little hungry thrusts of their mouths, until her arm slowly encircled his neck and his arms tightened around her body, and then they moved from desire to passion, and as she gave herself up to its embrace, Sunny knew there could be no going back now. It was no longer a question of volition. She had never experienced passion before, but its mark is unmistakable, even to the uninitiated: not merely an advance on desire, but an emotion of an entirely distinct kind. The sensual angels were attending in number, but the dark angel of passion is another order of being altogether. He carries everything before him, and Sunny instinctively recognised his power and submitted.

Jock was having a little trouble. He, too, though he had great experience with ordinary sexual desire, had had little or none with real passion, and it was a loss of control that frightened him. This wasn't the simple loss of reason that he had experienced sexually as a teenager, but a deep and confusing disturbance of his inner self, a loss of will, a submission to something that seemed to be beyond himself. He wrapped her to him not because he wanted to be inside her, but because she *was* him, because somewhere in the regions beyond time he had lost her and now she was found.

He lifted her up in his arms almost without volition, and Sunny lost all her orientation in space. When she felt soft pressure against her back, she hardly knew it was the sofa, or whether she was upright or prone.

She knew the pressure over her was Jock, and dimly she knew that he half unbuttoned, half pulled open her shirt, was drawing down the strap of her bra to release her breast; she felt air and then his lips against her breast and moaned her response to the touch. She pulled at his shirt, releasing it from his trousers, and slipped her hands up into the heat against his back, and when he lifted himself and put his arm up and ripped the shirt over his head, flinging it on the floor, she pressed against his warm flesh with a sigh of satisfaction.

Now he slid an arm under her and lifted her body so that she was arched up against him, and kissed her throat and neck and told her nearly incoherently that she was beautiful. When she moaned and sighed his name, he took hold of her face in one strong hand and lowered his mouth for her kiss.

It was too new, too startling, too much for both of them. They could neither wait, nor tease, nor toy, for those are the attributes of desire, but passion, when it has sway, knows only one way: its goal is union. Jock dragged her skirt up between their bodies and roughly, urgently, pulled her briefs down; then he lifted his hips while she opened the buttons of his jeans to release his urgent flesh, and then, wild, he thrust into her, and he heard her cry of gratitude not with his ears but with his whole being.

He cried out himself then, or perhaps he had never stopped; he could not be sure. He had no finesse; he could only push into her, trying to get deeper and deeper into her being, searching for that place in her that he had been banished from sometime beyond time. He called her names that had never passed his lips before, words like Beloved, and Perfection, and knew that he loved her. In some remote place in his being he loved her with a love so perfect it was divine.

She called his name, then pushed up against him and clung and cried out incoherently, and when he felt her body's convulsive quivering around him, he gave himself up to necessity with a hoarse shout and felt life itself flood through him with a pleasure he could scarcely comprehend.

It was impossible to say how long they lay there, half-unconscious—not asleep, but in some other region beyond themselves—before gradually consciousness returned. Jock raised himself on one elbow, and she saw his smile faintly in the shadows and smiled herself. He stroked her temple and her hair, then her cheek, then her lips, and slowly bent and kissed her.

"Unbelievable," he said softly, knowing the word must fall flat on her ears, because it was so far from expressing what he wanted to say. He opened his mouth to try again and then shook his head and gave up. He was suddenly aware of her skirt crushed between them, of his jeans still around his thighs. The phone was sending out a screeching signal that he only now heard. "What *was* that?" he asked.

Sunny laughed lightly, a lazy chuckle of pleasure and satisfaction that stirred him beyond all reason. "You've got me there," she said. She had never felt so close to anyone in her life, except perhaps her parents when she was a very young child.

"Let's go up to bed," said Jock, and she struggled to straighten her clothes and, still drowsy with contentment, followed him upstairs.

Later, he asked quietly, "Sunny, are you on the pill?"

"No," she said.

"God, we took a risk. Will you get pregnant?"

Snug in his embrace, she calculated, "Probably not."

"We won't do that again," he promised, although he was dimly aware that he might be pleased if she were pregnant. "It was a stupid risk. I don't know what the hell got into me."

Or if he did, he didn't feel like admitting it to himself just at the moment. Life was complicated enough without him imagining he'd fallen in love with a mystery woman.

In the morning there was the sound of pounding on the front door. Jock awoke to discover Sunny tucked in against his body, wrapped in his arms and legs as though unconsciously he'd been afraid she might get away. He slowly let go and sat up, the duvet falling away from her as he did so.

She rolled over on her back and smiled up at him. "I wonder who that is," she said.

"If it's another naked sheila with a cat I'll let you deal with her," he promised. She watched as he slipped out of bed naked and reached for his navy bathrobe. He had a stocky, beautiful, masculine body, and he was very sure in his movements. Sunny smiled with pleasure as she watched him, so that he bent over and kissed her. "Don't get out of bed," he ordered her. "I'll be right back."

But she did get out of bed, slipping into the polo shirt Jock had worn last night, and went to the head of the staircase and listened. When you were undercover you never knew what might come out of left field at you, and it was best to be ready for it.

". . . feel about the news?" a man's voice was saying.

"I haven't heard any news, matey. It's too early to put the radio on," Jock said drily. "What do you want?"

"You weren't aware that Caro Deane has left her husband, then?"

"No, I haven't, and I don't care one way or the other."

"She left her husband's house last night and moved in with Brian Richfield," the reporter went on. "How do you feel about that?"

Jock laughed. "If it's true, matey, I feel like cheering. I wish her all the best. I told you bastards you were barking up the wrong tree. Now, go sit on Richfield's doorstep for a change and leave me alone."

She heard the door close and the chain being replaced, and stood waiting at the top of the stairs, grinning broadly as he turned and climbed the stairs to her.

"That's it?" she asked incredulously. "They don't care about you anymore?"

"They probably won't remember my name by tomorrow." He swooped on her, caught her in his arms and half dragged, half carried her back into the bedroom. "And they're sure not going to interrupt my life any more this morning. Is this my shirt?"

"Mmm." Sunny nodded.

"You look pretty cute in it, matey. Almost as cute as you did the other morning. There was something I really wanted

to do that morning. I think I'll just do it now, if you don't
mind.''

Sunny was still asking, "What—" when he sat her down
on the edge of the bed and knelt between her knees. He
pressed one hand against the small of her back and with the
other pushed her to lie down.

Before her head had reached the tumbled duvet, she felt
the heat of his mouth between her thighs.

Chapter 20

Lorna Doone bit her on the ankle as she stepped into the kitchen, and then smiled at her with a slow blink, pretending it had been a love bite. Sunny shook her head.

"It's not me you should be biting," she informed the cat. "You have a go at Pip when he gets home, if he ever does."

Beetle was sitting beside his food dish, his eyes stretched wide with anxiety. Beetle had been rescued by Emma from a life as a starving stray, and he lived in constant fear that whatever meal he had just eaten was his last. Last night's missed dinner had confirmed his worst expectations, and he had suffered far worse than Lorna. *He* would not have dared to bite Sunny—at least, not before she had fed him breakfast.

"Anyway, you could have caught a mouse or something," Sunny told them unrepentantly as she put food and milk into their bowls. "That's what cats are supposed to do."

Lorna gave her a long look, and then her eyes moved uninterestedly away. As far as Lorna was concerned, cats were supposed to eat, sleep and be magnanimous when pleased, and she was scrupulous about her duties. She wasn't about to take any nonsense from Sunny, who manifestly was deficient in her own end of the contract.

Jock had risked taking her keys and going in the front door when she asked him, unlocking the kitchen door for her, though she could tell he thought this avoidance of the press was extreme. A note on the kitchen table informed her that her "loving ex-husband, Pip," had gone out of town for the week-end and had locked up before doing so.

"No kidding," Sunny muttered aloud, and then laughed. So far she had no doubts about what she'd done. There was nothing in the undercover manual that said you had to forego a private life when you were on a case. Officers involved in complex drug cases often seemed to do so, of course, partly because of the odd hours, partly because of the high lifestyle appropriate to anyone dealing drugs in a big way. It might be necessary in such circumstances to become totally involved with your undercover identity twenty-four hours a day.

But it was also psychologically very difficult to return to the ordinary life of a salaried police officer after any length of time spent in such a life. It was actually, Sunny believed, healthier and sounder to maintain an ongoing link of some sort with your real self while working undercover. It might have been wiser—she thought it would have been—not to have got involved with Jock. But she had tried and failed to keep her distance, and now that she had failed, she felt submerged in an unfamiliar contentment, the contentment that said love would conquer all, and that involvement in life was never a mistake.

And this was the weekend, and she was free to be herself—though of course that didn't mean telling Jock anything that might blow her cover—and Jock had asked her to drive down to Stavely House with him, and she was going to go. And, in fact, though she didn't care to think of Jock in this way, it even added credence to the cover she had set up with Abul Hassan.

So she bathed and dressed with a clear conscience, if a slightly less than clear head. She was in a glow of happiness, and she didn't look too closely at what that meant.

Harry accepted her presence in the car without surprise, climbing into the back seat of the rather battered old Mercedes without comment, except on the fact that it was rather too good a day for viewing a location, because everything looked good in the sun, and then if you had to shoot on a rainy day, there would be problems you hadn't anticipated.

To which Jock only replied, ''We're going to be there at least three weeks, Harry. We're bound to have some sunny days for the exterior shoots,'' in a tone of voice from which Sunny gleaned the information that Harry enjoyed his pessimism.

''How come no chauffeur today?'' she asked Jock as he negotiated the long drive through central London. London being without any central bypass road whatever, this was often the longest part of any trip to the countryside.

''I don't like chauffeurs much. I used the company car a couple of times when the press was really heavy, because you can get in and out fast, and they can't corner you when you're trying to park. But I prefer driving myself.''

It was a beautiful day, and Stavely House was a fascinating stately home, parts of it dating back to the time of Henry VIII, a beautiful hodgepodge of all the architectural styles and periods since then. Lisa, the red-haired production manager, met them there and, having taken them all around the rooms and locations she thought were particularly suitable and got Jock's approval of her find, led them at last to the Earl's study. There the other three sat mostly in silence while Jock and Stavely negotiated for terms.

It was an education, watching Jock at work. He was hard, but seemed fair, and it was clear he would put up with little dithering. Sunny caught herself thinking again that it would be a sorry person indeed who crossed Jock Prentiss.

It didn't surprise her in the least when the contract for both interior and exterior shooting rights was signed, but it had been an impressive piece of manoeuvring.

"Well, I didn't think I'd ever see a mere colonial take on a Brit and outface him like that," she told Jock with a grin as they headed for the cars. "I wish you could—" She broke off and pointed. "Look, isn't that a hawk up there?" Her heart was beating so wildly she almost expected to faint. She had almost said, I wish you could take on Alex Fairchild for me. Because the Earl of Stavely had in fact reminded her a little of her superior officer. What a blunder that would have been!

Jock looked at her. "It's a raven."

"Oh, is that all? I guess it's closer than I thought, it seemed bigger. I didn't know ravens' wings fanned out like that. There's a Canadian artist on the West Coast who paints peregrine falcons and stuff, and in flight their wings look like that at the tips."

They had reached the cars by this time, and Jock set himself briefly to arranging that Lisa should take Harry back to town. Sunny leaned against the car and turned her face up to the sun, closing her eyes. Now she knew why some of her fellow officers said they avoided any private life when involved under cover! The human urge to confide in those close to you must be pretty universal, and particularly so, perhaps, for women. For the first time she wondered if those people who said women did not make the best undercover officers might be right. It certainly seemed like her feminine, intuitive nature that wanted to trust Jock, and her logical side was horrified now by what she had nearly said.

If she kept up a relationship with Jock Prentiss, she would have to be constantly on her guard. To Sunny, who had hardly ever been anything *but* on her guard all her life, the thought was suddenly and confusingly appalling. On a dimly felt level she was like someone who is shown the sight of the promised land at last—through barred gates.

They drove, in silence for much of the time, through the perfect June day in the English countryside. "Isn't England beautiful!" Sunny exclaimed. She had had wide experience of Canada's scenery, and she loved it, but Canada's wilderness was young and fresh and vigorous, and England's old and time-worn beauty was of a totally different order: rolling fields as far as the eye could see, broken by hedgerows that now, in early summer, were full of blossom and buzzing insects; church spires of great age dominating thriving villages that still clung to their skirts as though in memory of the life-blood they had once drawn from such buildings; streams and rivers of marvellous peace.

"Hampshire certainly is."

After a while, seeing her enjoyment, Jock turned into the quiet roads, and thence into the country lanes. Both sides of the road were protected by overhanging trees that formed a rich leafy arch above their heads, rooted in great hedgerows rich with the colour of summer flowers. Sunny couldn't have named any of them, but she found the clusters of pink and white and yellow and blue deeply satisfying against the constant background of England's extraordinary greenness.

As they approached a pretty village, a sign by the side of the road read Cream Teas In Church Hall Today. Sunny let out a crow of delighted laughter, and when they shortly reached the second sign reading Cream Teas Here with a hand-painted black arrow, Jock slowed and turned in.

The church hall was a rather unimaginative postwar building, built not too far from a supremely imaginative church obviously many hundred years older. They collected cups of good strong tea and a plate of homemade cream-filled buns and cakes from a counter where a little sign informed them that Money Raised Today Will Be Used Towards the Refurbishment of the Church Bells; and they walked out the back to a few tables placed against a fence dividing church property from a farmer's meadow. Off to the left there was a stile. Jock headed for it and, balancing the tray on the top, climbed over. Sunny, the full skirt of her white sundress billowing in the breeze, agilely followed him, and then, to the apparent amusement and approval of the locals sitting at the tables, they strolled out into the meadow and sat down to enjoy their tea.

The sun was hot, and the tall grass was very dry, but underneath, the earth was still rich and moist. When they stretched out, the grass was high enough to block their view of everything but the bell tower, and they could have been almost anywhere. A fat bumblebee buzzed slowly in the vicinity of the plate of cream buns and eventually came in for a landing on a little blob of jam and Cornish clotted cream. They watched it lazily, drinking and eating in drowsy contentment.

"I wonder what it's like to live in a country where wherever you go you know that people have been walking there for hundreds and hundreds of years," Sunny mused.

"Different," Jock agreed. Like her, he came from a country where there were places you could walk and almost believe you were the first human being to set foot there.

"I bet this has been a farmer's meadow for a thousand years," Sunny said, lying back and squinting up at the sun and feeling that somehow, when she wasn't watching, life had got perfect.

Jock, watching her, grunted softly. After a moment he looked away. A few minutes later he said, "Let's go have a look at that church, Sunny."

"Sure," she said, and they got up and brushed off the crumbs and picked up the tray again. "Are you a fan of old churches?"

He said, "I might like to use it in the film. It's got something, hasn't it?"

Something in the way it clung to the small hill on which it was built, and the ancient fallen tombstones all around it, gave it a feeling of power, as well as great age and richness. Sunny nodded. "You think they'd be willing—" she began.

He said, "There's a bell refurbishment fund, isn't there? They'll get a lot more money renting it to me for a week than they would in two years of cream teas."'

They spent half an hour climbing about amongst the graves and a little grove at the back of the church, then wandering up and down the aisles inside, before Sunny happened upon the little wooden door that opened onto a narrow flight of worn steps that led up to a tiny chapel.

Jock drew his breath in between his teeth. "Perfect," he whispered. "Bloody marvellous."

The atmosphere here was deeply impressive, and Sunny, who had grown up with little religion of any kind, was fighting an almost irresistible urge to cross herself. At last she decided that submitting was the easier part of valour and she hastily performed the ritual, without having any idea if she was doing it the right way round or not. "Boy!" she whispered, the same impulse that enforced the ritual on her presumably making her reluctant to use her more usual profanities. "This place has some atmosphere!"

Jock was shaking his head, though not in any negative way. "This'll go right down onto film, if we do it right," he said quietly. "You notice we don't want to talk loudly in here? I'll use a small unit—just one camera if Harry can manage, and the actors. It'll be perfect. Let's go see if we can raise the vicar."

He was really excited, she realized, the way an artist might be excited over an idea. She said, "I thought you were only in this business for the money."

He followed her down the stone steps, worn in a deep groove by centuries of human feet. "Man, a close-up of those steps as he walks up, that'll say it all," he said, and grinned at her. "Acting—that's the business I'm in for the money. Producing and directing—that I love. You must feel the same in your writing, that feeling you're telling a story to thrill people or entertain them."

"Yes," she agreed briefly.

"To me, film's not all that different from being an artist, but art on canvas is out-of-date nowadays. You can't reach people through art the way Rembrandt, say, did. He was an artist of his time, but that medium isn't really the most appropriate medium to our time, see?"

"Yes," Sunny said again.

"Even what you do," Jock said as they crossed the nave and pushed open the massive, centuries-old door and stepped out into the light of day, "isn't . . . can't reach people the way it used to in the days before film. It can't affect them as powerfully as film does—even though it must once have affected people just as powerfully."

She had the feeling that a real writer would have argued with him. She knew she should have repeated the answer to that argument that had been made by a famous Canadian writer—that in reading fiction people used their imagination and conjured up the images that were most potent for them individually, and that was every bit as powerful as film, which could have only the potency of someone else's view, however striking the imagery was.

But she did not want to say it. It was a lie, not in itself, but because she was not a writer. And she did not want to lie to Jock when he was telling her the deepest kind of truth about himself.

Chapter 21

The filing system of AlHaqq Antiques was a shelved cabinet full of large ledger files, like books, with their description on the spine, and looked like a small library. It was quite unlike any Canadian system Sunny had ever known, and at first she thought it inefficient, but in fact it was not. It was merely less efficient for her own purposes. There was, unfortunately, far less chance of misfiling a paper when you had to take the book off the shelf, punch holes in the paper and fit it over the ring binders, than when you had only to pull open a drawer and slide a paper into a file, as she did in her desk at home. This meant that she could not be caught searching in an inappropriate file and use as her excuse some misfiled document. Except for those files broken down alphabetically inside, a misfiled paper would be right on top of any file it had been put in.

It meant that she couldn't often risk a fishing expedition in the files. Someone might walk in on her at any time, and Farid had very sharp eyes for any discrepancy. Fortunately he was often out of the shop, for he visited his other businesses regularly. At such times his place was taken by a woman he had introduced to Sunny as his mother. The woman had no English, and rarely spoke, even in Arabic, and Sunny was convinced she was not his mother. She and Sunny contented themselves with smiling whenever they met.

Sunny saved most of her exploration of the files for the times when Farid was absent from the shop, hoping that the woman's lack of English would prevent her discovering that Sunny was searching files she had no business in. She didn't worry about the stock boys, who weren't likely to know which files were in the secretary's purview and which were not.

She went through all the obvious files first, the overseas shipping orders, the customer sales records, the receivables, the payables, the banking, the VAT file. She found nothing that looked suspicious, nothing that fell into a pattern. Some customers were repeat customers, of course, but not at regular intervals, and few were abroad.

She took the names of all repeat buyers, all of whom were in either England itself or the States, and their bona fides were quickly checked out by Fairchild or Bosey. They all were what they should be: ordinary customers.

More and more, without ignoring other possibilities, she began to focus on the carpets that came from Baghdad and were regularly shipped to Milan. On the surface, her suspicions were a little ridiculous. She was looking for exports to, not imports from, Baghdad, and of what importance could carpets going to Italy be? But amidst all the petty fraud and the overpricing and even, she began to suspect, false valuations on the part of "experts" that Farid engaged in, this was the one anomaly that struck a note with her. Her cop's nose told her there was something in it, and though her fear was that she would discover it was just another, more elaborate fraud, she had Fairchild's instinct also on her side.

She could find no file that kept tabs on the carpets that were being shipped to Milan. That in itself was very curious. She had earlier got the address of the shop, and Fairchild had had it checked out through Interpol. According to the Italian police it was indeed a carpet shop. They had stopped a couple of parcels of imported goods at Italian customs, but nothing suspicious was found. They were prepared to stop and search the next shipment from England, whenever Sunny notified them of its being sent.

There should have been a file on the shop. In that file should have been copies of the documentation she typed for the shipping agents. At Farid's instruction, she had made plain paper carbon copies each time she typed a letter on the strange letterhead. But she was never asked to file such copies, which would have been normal procedure. After delivering the copy with the original upstairs to Farid's desk, she never saw it again. And where were the billing records? As far as Sunny could see, no payment ever changed hands over those carpets, and no bill ever came from the Baghdad company.

When the third shipment occurred, Sunny was particularly vigilant. That was when she noticed that the stock numbers assigned to the carpets did not fit into the sequence of numbers used for the other carpets in the shop. Carpets were generally assigned four digits and a letter, paintings and other works of art five digits. Ceramics got three digits-hyphen-two digits, and metal objects letter-three digits-letter. The carpets going to Milan were assigned five digits and a letter. There was no file anywhere in the system that kept track of anything with five digits and a letter. As far as AlHaqq Antiques was concerned, the carpets received from Baghdad and sent to Milan did not, and never had, existed.

Which was fitting, because according to Italian customs, the shipment never arrived in Milan.

* * *

"Feel like that party at Andrea's tonight?" Jock asked Sunny over the breakfast table one morning late in June.

"Remind me who Andrea is," she said, wrinkling her brow. Andrea was probably someone she had met on the set or at a party recently, but for the moment Sunny couldn't place the name.

Jock had disappeared from the pages of London's tabloid press, and the journalists from Banbury Square, between one minute and the next. Even Brian Richfield's reign hadn't lasted longer than a week. The gutter press, after all, thrives on speculation, rarely on fact. There was endless meat in the possibility that Lady Isham might be cheating on her husband, scarcely any in the demonstrable fact that she had left him for a readily identifiable man.

So Sunny had begun to use the front door again, though she never felt comfortable doing it, and she had slipped into the habit of being with Jock as though it were the most ordinary thing in the world, as though she had never done anything else.

It sometimes seemed to her that one night and one day had changed her life. She felt as though she were becoming rounder, fuller, richer. The old rules by which she had sustained herself seemed questionable, even though she was never quite sure what those old rules were.

Of course, she told herself, it was a pity she had to be feeling this—whatever it was—around Jock, who had never suggested that what they had together was anything more than a casual love affair, and who never would. She knew enough about the world, she told herself firmly, to understand that rich and famous actors didn't carry on with ordinary, nondescript policewomen for very long, however good a figure the policewoman had, and however exciting their sex life together was.

And it was exciting. If there was one time in which the inner barriers she so carefully maintained were in danger of being torn down and burnt up for firewood, when they were assailed simultaneously from without and within, it was when Jock was making love to her. Up to now, poor Sunny had really believed that sex was, in her not very original phrase, "vastly overrated," and whenever her hormones had sabotaged her ivory tower, she had found the whole thing pretty...what? She had never quite found the word for that combination of disappointment and emptiness sex had made her feel.

But Jock, having thrown her off her balance when she was in a situation where she was already without most of the social support system she was used to, had changed all that. When Jock made love to her, he did not let her hide from him, or not much. He was deeply possessive when they made love, so that she felt as though on some inner level they had bonded somehow, and the act of making love was only the physical expression of some profound nonphysical fact; it was as if he understood that fact within himself, and sex was his way of informing her of it. It was animal not in its passions, but in its sweet obedience to the will of nature. For the first time in her life, Sunny began to consider the lilies in the field with something like envy—not because they toiled not, not because they did not spin, but because they did not set themselves against...divine will. They just gave in to necessity. For Sunny the individualist, who had always felt alone, this was something like heresy. It made her nervous. She did her best not to think about what she was doing, and worked her damnedest to hold on in the teeth of the wind.

On a purely practical level, too, her life became unrecognizable. Jock bought her a car, and now she often drove to wherever he was filming at the end of her working day to pick him up. If they went home they cooked dinner together, but often they went out, generally somewhere different each time, because Jock was adventurous about food and liked to try new places and new foods at least as often as he cooked. They generally went home early, where Jock often had a production meeting and where a screening room had been set up for the viewing of each day's rushes. At that point Sunny would go home to Emma's and call Bosey or Alex Fairchild, or both, and do her own work. Then, usually, she went back to Jock's for the night.

She had established that habit early, saying that it was because having Pip and Jock in the house together made her uncomfortable. Her real reason was, of course, the work she was doing, and the phone calls. She had to do everything she could to prevent Jock coming in on her unexpectedly and discovering her at work.

She was slowly collecting a file of documents relevant to the antiques shop, and each night she spread them out on the table and tried to make sense of them. She spent hours on the telephone, the London and Southampton directories in front of her, trying to track down the "Italian shippers" who handled the carpets. She called Milan, trying to find out anything she could about the shop there, sweet-talking whatever police officer she got on the line into going out to the shop in his spare time to check around. She went over all the possibilities with Bosey, Fairchild and, more recently, Constable Rejean, who, like herself, was getting committed.

If Jock had walked in on such activity it would have been very difficult to explain away.

Sometimes she felt her life was split in two, that she was becoming two different people, or even three. In Jock's world she was a star's girlfriend, of whom not much was expected intellectually once they checked out her body, and whose bright mental functioning was often a surprise, and—to men, anyway—not always welcome. In Bosey's and Fairchild's world, she was a junior officer of whom they expected hard work and whose mental functioning was taken for granted. Her femininity was never an issue, scarcely even noticed. And at the shop she was "the best secretary" Farid Abul Hassan had ever had, even though her typing wasn't the fastest. She was always a step ahead of him, she caught on quickly, she worked hard, and her presence seemed to keep the staff in a good humour much of the time. He made no bones about the fact that he liked her, but he was afraid of Jock Prentiss. If Sunny ever indicated willingness, she felt he would move very quickly, but he never once made a move positively identifiable as a pass.

She was deeply involved in life, on all levels, in a way that she had perhaps never been before, and she found it exciting. But more and more she hated the lying.

She had never had to lie in her private life before because of an undercover operation and she had never realized it would bother her.

Of course, that helped her in her efforts to keep Jock psychologically at arm's length, because that was the only way to handle the problem of her living lie. And although at times she felt she didn't want to be at arm's length from him, she knew it would be better for her in the end. It was simple: if she didn't keep Jock at arm's length she would get hurt. The requirements of the job, in fact, were going to save her a certain amount of heartache later.

So it was ridiculous to feel cheated, especially when she hardly knew of what. It was stupid to think, as she sometimes did, that if she just let go emotionally with Jock everything would be fine. It would not be fine, and if she let go emotionally, she would only have more pieces to pick up later.

"I said," he said now, patiently calling her back from wherever she had wandered to, "Andrea is the one playing my sidekick. Do you want to go?"

"Oh, right!" Sunny said stupidly. How could she have forgotten Andrea's name?

Other than the restaurants, she rarely went to public places with him. If he suggested they drop in at a theatrical party, she saw no reason not to go, but if he mentioned a nightspot that catered to the film world, she generally found a reason for refusing. Such places attracted the paparazzi as a matter of course, and there was a distant but real possibility that some photographer who had caught her on Jock's doorstep might recognize her, and a much greater possibility that someone would consider Jock Prentiss's unknown girlfriend worth a photo.

"All right, why not?" she said, but if it had turned out to be the name of a club instead of an actress, she would have pleaded tiredness.

"Then I guess you'd rather I picked you up back here?" Jock said.

"All right," she said again. "I'll take the tube this morning. Save me finding a parking space."

"I wish you'd quit that job and get down to some writing," Jock said. "You don't have to be so bloody independent, do you?"

Of course it looked like madness, working full-time for Farid when Jock would have supported her so that she could spend her time writing the novel she was so keen to write. And since there was no rational explanation she could give, Sunny had to fall back on a sort of female unreasonableness, which translated, in Jock's ears, into a lack of trust of him.

"I just think it's a good idea to keep my independence," she said feebly, when what she really wanted to be able to do was tell him how excited she was by this job, how committed to nailing Farid, how close she sometimes thought she was to the centre of the thing. When she would have liked nothing better than to outline the whole case to him and hear his ideas on it, because Jock was imaginative and his ideas might be very different from her own, and that could hardly have failed to be productive.

"Didn't anybody ever tell you you can take independence too far?" Jock said, shaking his head, feeling what a fool she was to turn down such a leg up in her career as he was offering her, yet knowing he couldn't force her.

"I know what I'm doing," Sunny said, which was perfectly true on one level. But to Jock it merely sounded cold.

And some undercover officers did this kind of thing for years, she told herself later, on the way to work—and turned in men who trusted them and who had considered them friends. She didn't really mind lying to Farid Abul Hassan all that much, or letting him trust her when she intended to betray him, because what he was doing was deeply horrific—because he had set himself outside the family of man and therefore outside the normal rules of honour that bound human interaction.

But she minded like hell lying to Jock, and that added another impetus to her work: she couldn't wait to crack the case so that she could tell him some, at least, of the truth.

Chapter 22

As luck would have it, there was a fire scare somewhere in the underground that morning, and ever since the King's Cross fire all such alarms caused massive response and maximum delay in the system. After taking one train and two buses, Sunny arrived at the shop forty-five minutes late to find uproar. The Italian shipping agent had called to say that yesterday's carpet shipment for Milan—the fourth since Sunny's advent—had been picked up without the customs declaration. It could not go out in this morning's container unless the paper was found immediately.

Farid had gone looking for it in the shipping ledger file, though why he imagined it would be there she couldn't think. Sunny felt hot and sweaty from her prolonged bout with London Transport, and she used the irritation to cover her excitement. This had to be a break, the kind cops lusted after on every difficult case. "Why are you looking for it in there, anyway?" she demanded rudely of Farid, who was sitting at his desk in the back of the shop vainly paging through the fat ledger file. "Those declarations never get filed there."

It wasn't till he looked up slowly at her that she realized she had made a very bad mistake. "Which declarations never get filed here?" he asked softly. He thought she hadn't noticed. Good God, she thought faintly, I never realized before that his weakness is that he underestimates people.

Instinct told her not to try to back off. She looked at him. "Farid," she said, "I have never yet filed anything handled by Traviata Shipping in that file. Now," she carried on as though that fact were not of the least importance except as it reflected on her efficiency, "I gave you a folder of letters to sign just after lunch yesterday. Where's that?"

The direct attack had the desired effect. A little guiltily, Farid set the file on his knees and began pawing through the chronic disorder on his desk. After a moment he located the plastic folder with several typed letters in it, still, Sunny saw at a glance, to be signed. But the letter to the shippers, which had certainly been among them, was there no longer.

"You've taken it out and signed it, I suppose, and then put it somewhere. Are they sure it's not in the parcel?"

"Yes, they are sure," said Farid coldly.

"Then it must be up here somewhere. I'd have noticed if it had come back downstairs by mistake," Sunny said, dropping her satchel to the floor. That almost made her laugh aloud. She'd have noticed, all right. "Now, where might you have put it? What were you doing yesterday when that shipment was brought back upstairs?"

Whatever Arab men thought of women, they revered their mothers, and Farid began to react to the mother's-taking-care-of-it tone in her voice. "I was sitting here," he said. He pawed futilely through a few papers.

"What do you normally do with the papers—how do you attach them to the parcel?" she asked. She wished she could ask him all the other questions in her head as easily.

"I put it in the envelope and use this tape to attach it to the paper of the parcel," he explained.

"And you just forgot to do that altogether?"

"No—they said the envelope was empty. So it must be I forgot to put the paper in the envelope."

Enoch, Moses and Abraham, what a break. Sunny had a hard time not bursting into song. "All right, let's go over it. I bring you the paper, you sign it, yes?"

"Yes," he said. She realized suddenly that he was afraid. That was what made him weak, made him look to her for direction—Farid needed a saviour. The case was sitting in her hands.

"Did you sign it yesterday? Do you remember doing that?"

"Yes, I think—I am sure I signed it."

"And what do you normally do after you've signed it?" God, she sounded like the perfect secretary; this didn't sound like an interrogation at all. Miss Efficiency, that was her.

He hesitated. "I put it in the envelope."

But the hesitation told her the truth. She said matter-of-factly, "But you have to make a note of the stock numbers, Farid. Do you do that before or after you sign the customs declaration?"

"Oh, yes!" he said, pretending he hadn't been hiding that part of the ritual. "Well, at the same time, really."

"Ah, well then, I suppose you've looked in your Milan file—it wasn't there?"

The phone rang on his desk then, and Sunny turned to answer it. "AlHaqq Antiques," she carolled. "Good morning."

Farid was shoving his hand in between two of the stacked carpets behind his desk, but Sunny pretended not to see, concentrating on the phone.

"Abul Hassan, please," said a thickly accented voice, and she knew it was the "Italian" shipping agent as clearly as if she'd been told.

"One moment, please," she said, and turning, signalled silently to him.

He was holding a black book, large, square, about an inch thick. A white tag on the spine read, "Ann Barr." He reached for the phone, as if he, too, knew who it was.

"Yes?" he asked.

She heard the crackle of a short burst of speech from where she stood beside him, but without being able to decipher it. Farid said two words in Arabic, and then, with a glance at her, switched to English. "Yes, just one moment," he said. With his other hand he laid the book down on the desk and opened it, then flicked over a page or two to the last written-on page.

Sunny watched eagerly, but not seeming to take much interest in the book itself. When the last page lifted to reveal the protruding white edge of a sheet of loose paper, she pounced on it as though that were her only interest. "Here it is!" she hissed gleefully.

She didn't look at the book again as he closed it. She had seen all she needed to see in that one glance. The pages of the book were covered with lists of stock numbers, all of them consisting of five digits and a letter. And in the back of the book was a plastic folder containing copies of customs forms. Sunny felt like cheering.

Her great fear had been that no record was being kept, that he simply destroyed the copies of the papers she made for him. But whatever was going on with the Milan shipments, Farid was keeping his tail well covered with evidence that he'd done his part.

"Do you want me to courier it over there?" she asked, when he had hung up the phone.

Farid hesitated only briefly. "Yes, yes, that is best. My car is in the garage. It will take too long to get it, and their delivery truck is out."

"Sure," said Sunny cheerfully. "I'll do that now." Without waiting for his reply, she crossed the shop and went downstairs, kicked off her sneakers and changed them for the low heels she pulled out of her satchel. All absolutely standard procedure for the morning, but her heart was thudding.

She quickly fixed hair and face in the bathroom, as usual, and ran cold water on her hands and pressed them to her temples. Her heart calmed. She must not be nervous with what she did next. She must be absolutely business as usual.

She made the pretence of looking up the courier number in the previous secretary's little red book of numbers, but the number she found there was not the number she dialled.

"Fairchild," said his voice, and she breathed to calm herself.

"This is AlHaqq Antiques," she said. "I have an urgent delivery item. Can you have a bike here immediately?"

"Sure," he said. "Where's it going?"

"The address will be on the envelope. This is really very urgent. It has to be there within half an hour. Do you have a bike available now?"

"Sure," he said. "That's AlHaqq Antiques at the regular address?"

"Yes. It's very urgent," she repeated again, stupidly, a little surprised at how easily he understood and played ball, though doubtless she shouldn't have been.

"Right you are," said Fairchild imperturbably, and hung up. There had been nothing in his voice to hint that the possibility of there being a break in the case excited him, but Sunny knew better than to expect it from him. The Second World War, after all, hadn't been won by people who got excited over every little thing.

Then she drew out one of the courier company's delivery forms and ticked the Prepaid box. She took ten pounds out of petty cash and went upstairs.

"I need the address of the shipping agent for the delivery form," she told Farid.

"Bring it here," he said from his desk, waving his fingers to summon her. She crossed to him and handed him the delivery form and the money. "I couldn't find our billing number," she said. "So I told them we'd pay cash." Farid was certainly smart enough to notice later if the billing for this never appeared on the courier company's statement.

"All right," he said. He waved her away. "You can go down to work now. I will give it."

"It's nine pounds sixty," she said, going. "He owes you forty pence change."

"One moment," he called, and her heart gave a little kick as she returned to his desk. She looked enquiring, but it was only that Farid had signed all the letters in the folder that she had typed yesterday. "These letters should not have waited overnight," he pointed out softly. However much he shouted at the stock boys and sales staff, he never shouted at Sunny.

"Yes, I know, Farid, I'm sorry," Sunny said contritely. If she had not had her job to protect, she would have pointed out that it was counterproductive on his part to take the folder, read the letters without signing them and then slide it into the chaos of his desk, all of which was Farid's nearly invariable practice. It caused Sunny unnecessary work, since she generally had to climb the stairs, ask for the folder, find it on his desk, put it in front of him again and return to her desk, two or three times until the thing was done. Yesterday it had simply gone out of her mind.

"All right," said Abul Hassan as she took the folder from his hand. "Deal with them now."

Sunny turned and strode away. He let her nearly reach the stairs before he called her back again.

"Yes?" she asked, turning.

Farid held out the shipping ledger file. "You can take this now," he said.

There it was again—that unconscious reminder of his power.

That he was doing it to her now was clearly a reestablishment of his authority after his loss of face earlier. He had let her take control, and now he was taking it back. Sunny understood all this and crossed the shop with good grace, letting it appear in her eyes that she knew he was doing this deliberately and found such pettiness humorous.

As she approached the desk she reached out for the file, but he didn't immediately hand it over. Instead he held up a slip of paper. "This paper was in the shipping file," he told her, his eyes briefly on the paper as he glanced at each side of it. She didn't need to look closely to see that it was covered with her own handwriting and doodles. "Among the February shipping orders." That charming accent, in which every consonant was given its full value, seemed suddenly harsh to her ears. Sunny braced herself as his eyes left the little slip of paper and moved up to find hers. His gaze this time was dark and intense and very searching: the real Abul Hassan.

"How did it get there?" he asked politely.

Chapter 23

"I've no idea," said Sunny lightly. "Why, what is it?"

Abul Hassan shrugged. "Nothing, I think. Just a scrap of paper." He passed it over to her, and Sunny glanced at it.

"Sorry," she said, shrugging, too.

"Is that your writing on the paper?"

It was. Nothing significant, just a doodle and a few notes that she thought she remembered making when she was learning the use of the typewriter, which had a small word-processing capability. Nothing incriminating in that, but how to explain its presence in amongst the February orders? She wondered suddenly if Farid had already compared the paper with examples of her handwriting elsewhere—papers on her desk, perhaps. Or perhaps he just knew her writing by now. It would be too risky to deny it was hers.

"Yes," she said casually, "it's my writing, all right. But I can't say how it got in the file. Is it important?" She managed to inject a note of lightly stirring curiosity into the question.

"It seemed to be marking your place," he said.

"Oh, well, maybe it was," she agreed easily. "I'm still copying the shipping letter from a letter in the file every time I type one. It could just have got caught one day and I never noticed."

He nodded then and handed her the shipping ledger, letting her go. But she could not be sure her explanation had satisfied him.

Downstairs the stock boys were standing near her desk, talking in whispers. "Mohammad! Ahmad!" Abul Hassan called over the railing, for no other reason, Sunny suspected, than that he didn't like to think they had no work to do. She didn't like the feeling that he had followed her across the shop and watched her down the stairs. "Come up, please!"

"Ya Allah!" muttered Mohammad as he passed her. "We'll be caught now for the next half hour," she heard him say in Arabic. Ahmad, above him, lost his footing somehow, and fell with a loud shout, slithering down the spiral to the ground at her feet.

Mohammad made a grab to save him and then leapt down behind. "What's happening?" Abul Hassan cried from above. "What happened?"

"Ahmad's fallen," Sunny called briefly, feeling immediately guilty. They hadn't had much experience of her chaos-causing propensities in the shop, but she recognised the signs herself. "Are you all right?" she asked, bending over Ahmad.

"I'm okay," he said. With Mohammad's help he got to his feet and sat for a moment on a pile of carpets. Then he stood up. "Air," he said. "I like to go out."

With Mohammad's help he climbed the stairs. "I need some air," she heard him say to Farid in Arabic. "I'm all right, but I want a cigarette."

"All right," Abul Hassan agreed. "But not you, Mohammad!" he called, as the two men went to the door together. "There is a carpet here that is not folded properly."

Mohammad reluctantly turned back from the chance of a cigarette. "Smoke two," he said to Ahmad.

But Sunny wasn't listening any longer. She was standing staring at her desktop. Five minutes ago, on her way up to Farid, she had left the customer's copy segment of the courier form right in the middle of the desk. Now it was in her otherwise empty out tray.

Only the stock boys had been in the basement. What was their interest in the form? And how could they read it, anyway? They scarcely *spoke* English.

"Nice work," said Fairchild. "We got the address."

"*Geronimo!*" shouted Sunny excitedly. "What is it?"

"Well, it looks like any small shipping agent's premises. The name over the door is not Traviata Shipping, but it seems otherwise perfectly straightforward."

Which was not to say that it was. "Are we going to get a search warrant?"

Fairchild drew in a deep breath, and she knew instantly there was going to be a problem. "Sunny," he said, "we don't really have any grounds for doing so."

It was an old story; she hadn't been a cop for six years without discovering that it was just when you were on to something that someone would pull some bureaucratic crap on you that tied one hand behind your back.

"Aw, damn it!" she exploded.

"Well, they're right, up to a point," said Fairchild, and she realized with surprise that she had got to the stage of talking to Fairchild in shorthand. A whole conversation had just passed between them in two quick sentences. And she had once thought him uncommunicative.

"Yeah, all right," she said. "But you know I'm right."

Fairchild chuckled down the wire at her as if he had just made the same discovery and it had caught him by surprise. "Yes, I know you're right," he admitted. "But we need some grounds."

"I don't know what the hell we're going to get that we haven't already got," she said, knowing he knew what she was going to say before she said it but saying it anyway. "Can we at least get some surveillance on the place?"

"Surveillance costs money," Fairchild explained. "We've already got *you* under surveillance. But I'm working on it."

"Take the surveillance off me," she offered, but Fairchild only laughed.

When she hung up it was already seven o'clock. Sunny tried to put the whole thing out of her mind, and, climbing into a warm bath, concentrated on her transformation into Sunny York, star's girlfriend, with nothing on her mind except having a good time at Andrea's party.

"How do I look?" she asked, twirling for Jock's approval two hours later. For a woman who used to pride herself on being able to dress for anything in under twenty minutes, start to finish, Sunny was certainly making a lot of fuss about her appearance these days. Part of it, perhaps, was the desire to create a believable cover as Jock Prentiss's latest flame, but Jock was a maverick himself, and people really would have accepted Sunny however she presented herself. And she knew that, so she had to face the fact that there was a part of her that wanted to compete with the women she was meeting on their own ground. She was less eager to face the fact that part of her, too, just wanted to feel beautiful in Jock's eyes. It was a new feeling for her, but somehow she was giving in to it. Sometimes she felt as though she had been fighting the current all her life, and now, with Jock, she was almost ready to let life carry her.

He was a generous man, and he bought her anything that happened to catch his eye, or hers. Sunny had learnt to be reticent about admiring anything at all in a shop window, but her gasp of admiration when she saw this dress had been irrepressible, and she had not protested when he shepherded her in through the door of the very famous, very expensive shop.

It was an extremely fashionable, tight, short, clinging dress in sea-green silk that left one arm and shoulder and most of her back bare, and curved delicately and, it seemed, precariously, low over her breasts. Any sort of bra under it would have been impossible, a fact that would be instantly apparent to any male eye. Her other arm was snugly encased in silk down to the wrist, where the fine tapering point had a little loop that fitted over her middle finger. Attached along the length of the arm and across the sweepingly cut back down to the hem was a lightly billowed half cape of the same fabric.

It might perhaps have been designed with a modern, anorexic figure in mind, but between Sunny and the dress some chemical transformation occurred, so that neither was quite what it had been before. She looked like Venus caught in a high wind, a piece of silk momentarily plastered against her body, which, with any luck, the next gust would blow away. Although current fashion would have dictated black stockings and shoes, by instinct tonight she wore flesh-coloured stockings and tan shoes, enhancing the illusion of near-nakedness without quite realizing that that was the effect she was creating.

She had moussed her layered hair back off her face in a rather wind-swept style, and the illusion was pretty well complete.

It felled Jock with one blow. Being a man, he didn't consciously take in much of the detail. He saw great legs and that incredible body in a dress that was half off and should come all off; he knew that there wouldn't be a straight male within a half-mile radius who wouldn't want to assist it in the coming off; he dimly realized that he would kill any man who tried; and it all translated into a burst of pride and a pressure in his groin that was all too familiar these days around Sunny.

What he said in answer to her question, therefore, was, "We didn't make love last night."

Sunny began to laugh. This naturally made her breasts tremble. Jock's animal brain watched, fascinated, for this to cause the silk to slide away, and when it didn't, he decided to help it along. He took a couple of quick steps, wrapped his arm around her, registered the fragile slenderness of her waist against the strength of his arm with a surge of passion, and bent and kissed her neck. He began drawing a line of kisses from her ear all the way down her neck and across her bare shoulder to her arm. He lifted her arm into range and continued down to her inner elbow, and thence to her wrist and her tender palm.

Sunny had never seen such naked admiration and desire in any man's eyes before, or perhaps the sight had never thrilled her before. Why Jock's admiration should thrill her so particularly she didn't allow herself to ask, nor why his touch should be so stirring, but by the time his mouth was against her palm she was trembling, almost shivering.

He felt it and thought his groin would burst. It was a passion that was almost frightening, worse than the first time, or better, he wasn't sure which. He placed her arm around his neck and ran his hand from her shoulder down over her full hips to the hem of her dress, hard, pressing her against him, and then bent to her mouth and gently kissed her. He was torn between a desire to rip her clothes roughly out of his way and take her in the most direct way possible, and a desire to treat her like porcelain. The kiss that started out gentle increased in pressure and passion.

Sunny, opening her mouth under his, felt her heart stir painfully with need, felt her body yearning for a union much greater than the mere physical, and suddenly she was afraid. She must not allow herself to feel so much for Jock. She must not risk the work she was doing, as she would if the impulse to confide in him became much stronger, and she must not risk being hurt, as she inevitably would be if she let herself feel too much for him. In short, she must not allow herself to make love to him in this powerful, passionate mood.

She began to resist him then, so that what fell on his ears next was her saying, "Jock, not now, please. Jock."

He couldn't believe it. He was sure that if he made love to her now the world would come to an end. "What the hell are you talking about?" he muttered, tightening his hold as she struggled in it. He had for a moment the clear and certain feeling that if he hugged her tightly enough she would become part of him, would become absorbed into him, and then he would never need to search for anything again. "Don't stop me," he begged her hoarsely, for he felt on the verge of deep and amazing discovery. "Sunny, for God's sake!"

But she was in full panic now. The tone of need in his voice set off a skyrocket of passion in her, and it terrified her. She was on the edge of a chasm of completely giving in, and trust did not come easy to her. What she was afraid of was her vulnerability. What she translated it into was a fear of compulsively confiding in him things she was duty-bound to confide in no one. She reacted automatically as she had been taught to react to close personal threat when unarmed.

Jock heard the shout and felt the stinging pain simultaneously, and his brain cleared of passion and need and their place was taken by a flooding disappointment, as though he had been reminded of a lifetime's missed chances. Obediently he stood back from her and looked at her beauty, and he could have wept for that lost discovery he had nearly made.

"Sorry," he said flatly. "Right, then! Ready to go? Do you need a coat?"

She looked up at him, and her heart trembled with regret for her own lack of courage.

Chapter 24

The party was more a wild romp. There were nearly a hundred people already there when Jock and Sunny arrived, in half a dozen rooms throughout the house. It was far larger than Sunny had anticipated, and therefore more dangerous. Andrea Bellamy had one flat of three in a large Victorian house, and the party was a joint one between her and the inhabitants of the other two flats. It had been billed as a "Summer Solstice" party, and many people had taken this as an invitation to dress in what they imagined to be pagan fashion. The woman who owned the basement flat was, according to Andrea's hastily whispered information, "an aging hippie," so there were any number of people wandering around in long flowing dresses and robes, with circlets of flowers in their hair, male and female. One middle-aged, bushy-bearded bear of a man had, in addition, long ropes of old-fashioned love beads around his neck, so that he looked like a cross between Prospero and a sixties guru.

The latter apparently was the comparison he preferred, because he kept muttering "peace" at people and waving his arms benevolently. He bumped into Jock and Sunny in the kitchen, where Jock was opening a bottle of wine for Sunny. His eyes widened as he saw Sunny. "Piece!" he said loudly in admiration.

Jock merely glanced over his shoulder. "All mine, matey," he said casually, and turned back to his work with the corkscrew. The guru raised his eyebrows at Sunny. "Ah, what a love-child you would have made," he told her sadly. He had a Canadian accent. Feeling distinctly treasonous, Sunny merely smiled at him, not opening her mouth to reveal her own accent. "That's the story of my life—twenty years out of sync with life. Far out. Far freaking out." He wandered off.

"That guy's book was up for the Booker Prize a few years ago," someone in glitzy punk informed the kitchen. "Can you believe it? He looks like a bag lady at Stonehenge."

Most of the black-dressed punk people were invitees of the top-floor flat, and large numbers of them were, Sunny's experienced eye told her, on drugs. One thing that made partying with Jock uncomfortable was the amount of drugs that seemed to be a part of the film crowd's life. Drugs made Sunny nervous. She had made her share of arrests of people on hard drugs, and she frankly thought anyone who willingly got involved with drugs was a lunatic. A drunk who was disorderly had usually lost motor control and was, therefore, easier to handle, even if he was violent. Someone on drugs, especially a mixture, could be cunning and, if he got violent, might have the primitive strength of ten men, so that he was virtually uncontrollable.

So Sunny was nervous around drugs and as a result was not enjoying herself very much. When they had been at the party an hour, she no longer wanted to contain her discomfort. She just wanted to get out. She had a strong feeling of foreboding that she couldn't shake. Deep in conversation with his assistant director, she suddenly missed Jock, who had been carried off by a work-hungry actress some time ago. She murmured her apologies rather abruptly and moved off, searching for Jock.

The house was big and crowded, and he wasn't tall enough to stand above the crowd, but she found him quickly, as though she had radar. He was in conversation with several other men and women, among them the hungry actress.

"Matey," he was saying, sliding his arm around her as she slipped into the circle beside him, "there are—or were, till recently—tribes in Africa who've learnt how to eat meat without killing anything. They just walk up to a cow, slice back a flap of skin, cut off a steak, slap the skin back in place, cover it with mud so it'll heal, and there you go. What you might call conservation farming."

There were noises of distaste and discomfort, and some laughter, from the group.

"It would be interesting to speculate," said a rather dry male voice from Jock's other side, a voice whose owner Sunny could not see, "whether or not such meat would be considered kosher."

The comment caught Sunny smack in the centre of her crazy sense of humour. She let out a wild hoot and collapsed into laughter and, not having registered her presence in the circle, everybody turned to her in surprise. Jock began to join in first, but it was inevitable that the others would follow, and they did so, till very quickly the group was in uproarious laughter. Others in the room began to turn curiously towards them.

The laughter subsided, and the dry voice on the other side of Jock said, "I recognize that laugh. It can only belong to one person." Before she could make a move, he stood forward and grinned at her. "I knew it!" he said triumphantly. "Sunny Delancey! What are you doing back in England?"

There are two kinds of people in the world: those whose brains, under sudden stress or threat, turn to mincemeat, and those whose brains clear and become capable of almost superhuman functioning. Sunny—in this instance, at least—fell into the latter category. Part of her seemed suddenly to draw back from the situation, giving her the ability to analyse it and decide what to do. Her first priority, she saw, was to get her old studying buddy Iqbal away from everyone else. At the same time, she was smiling delightedly and saying, "Iqbal! What are you doing here in the cesspits? You're supposed to be enshrined in academia!" She hugged him, grinning, then took his arm and began to draw him away from the little crowd around Jock. "Come over here and talk to me!"

He tried to talk, but she kept up a rattle of commentary. "Excuse us, everybody, but we've got a lot of things to talk about that would only bore you," she said quickly, and then, "So what are you doing these days, Iqbal? Are you married? What are you working at? Boy, it seems years since we struggled through"—she caught herself on the verge of saying "Arabic verbal noun construction" and said instead, "our homework together!"

They were away now, safe from the ears of anyone who knew her. "Yes, I'm married, very happily, one boy and another child on the way," he said.

The immediate danger was over, but she knew there was still a problem to deal with: how to make sure Iqbal didn't mention to anyone what he certainly knew—that his old friend Sunny was a cop. "And what are you working on, these days?"

"Still writing," he said. "If you can believe it, I'm here tonight because I'm working as advisor on a feature film about Muslims in Britain. I'm lecturing now, and I'm on a government race advisory council. I'm the token ethnic Brit, if there is such a thing. And what about you? Is life with the Mounties all you wanted it to be?"

She would have to trust him; there was no other way, Sunny decided abruptly. She couldn't let him loose like a time bomb, not knowing when or if he would say something that would burn her. She had him over by a wall now, and she glanced to right and left. They were between two rowdy groups, quite isolated. She leaned a little closer.

"Iqbal," she said, "listen, I've got to trust you. Can I trust you?"

He blinked nervously. "I think so," he said. "I guess it depends on what you want."

She said, "It is absolutely essential that nobody here finds out that I'm a cop—in fact, nobody anywhere. Iqbal, it's tremendously important. Please, will you promise not to mention it?"

It was a small enough favour, but he looked at her blankly, steadily, as though he were appalled by what she'd asked, and said nothing. She opened her mouth and said softly, "Iqbal?" but something in her already knew.

Jock's grip was tight around her waist, and she felt him bend and kiss her throat, and went cold over her whole body. "Of course he won't mention it, will you, matey?" he was saying. "Can't let this bunch know you're spying on them, can we? Somebody might get nasty with you."

Jock's front door closed behind them with an ominous sound, which only went to prove, Sunny thought distantly, that human perception could be thoroughly distorted by emotion. There was light filtering down the hall from the kitchen, but now he flicked on the overhead.

"All right, let me look at you. Let me get a good look," he said, and Sunny stood there, taking it, knowing there would be more and that she would have to take that, too. She couldn't explain, nor could she leave Jock in this mood, whatever her own personal feelings were. She had to make some attempt at damage control. She was making a superhuman effort to keep her own feelings at bay, to remain cool, not to think of what it would mean to her to lose him, as now she surely must.

"Damn, you're beautiful," he said roughly. "I shouldn't have let you stop me tonight. I should have made love to you one last time before I knew, shouldn't I?"

She closed her eyes, because she was wishing it, too, wishing they'd had that one last time to say goodbye.

He saw it in her face. "Shouldn't I?" he repeated roughly, wanting her to admit it.

"Yes," said Sunny. She opened her eyes at him. "But it's too late now, so let's get this over with."

He knew it was too late, but somehow hearing her say it made him angry. He stepped towards her, not knowing what was wrong with him, feeling as though something was carving him up inside so badly that he didn't know how he could still walk. "Maybe not," he said, putting his hands on her arms, his sensory detectors registering the contrast of warm bare flesh under one hand and cool smooth silk under the other and sending the message direct to his loins. "I could always pretend for half an hour or so, and you—hell, you've been pretending all along, haven't you?"

"No," she said.

He pulled her into his hold. He wasn't sure what question she was answering, anyway. He caught her full lower lip between his teeth and sucked lightly, something that always stirred her—unless she'd been faking that, too. He supposed she had, but he did it anyway, because he liked it, and because he would never do it to her again.

Sunny closed her eyes and lifted a hand up to his shoulder. It was stupid, and probably dangerous, but she wanted him, and she knew she would never get another chance. Men like Jock didn't take betrayal lightly, and she was in the position of not being able to explain anything. She might never be able to explain, and even if she could, one day down the road, would he be interested by then?

She knew he would not. All the way home in the car, sitting beside a silent Jock, she had told herself that whatever might have been between them would never be, now. It was finished, as probably her job was finished. That was just the way it was. But now he would make love to her one last time to remember, if she let him, and with his kiss on her mouth, how could she say no?

"That's my girl," he said, his approval only faintly tinged with bitterness, and she felt his arms under her knees, and then he was carrying her up the stairs, though she knew she was far too heavy, and then she felt the bed under her back, and Jock over her.

He was fierce, but not brutal. He pressed and held her tightly, but only to excite her, only to possess her, never to punish. All her senses were heightened, and his firm touch filled her with passion, and when he watched her face and listened to her cries she knew he could not be certain whether it was a real or pretended response, and there was nothing she could say to him.

But he was being driven. He did everything he knew she liked, and everything he'd been saving up to try on her—all the process of discovery that he had imagined would last months or years telescoped into one night, into one tiny hour. He felt as though he were living his whole life with her in one hour, when he hadn't even realized he intended to live his whole life with her. So the learning and the loss happened all at once, like discovering you love someone on their deathbed.

"Afterwards, you'll tell me," he said softly, hardly knowing what he was saying, "but not now. Now you'll just tell me if you like this—ah, you do like this," he said in satisfaction as she gasped and then moaned. "I imagined you liking this, my sweet, my darling. I thought you would make just that sound, but it's even better than I imagined."

Suddenly he pressed her back on the pillows, and he was between her legs, his mouth on her eyes, her forehead, her face, her cheek, her lips, in a frenzy of kisses. "Lord," he said, "Lord, I can't wait, when you look at me like that I'm—"

Whatever he would have said was drowned by the cry she made as he entered her, hard and strong and already nearly out of control. He drove into her over and over, because he was beyond subtlety now; he only wanted what he wanted, and what he wanted was her cries in his ears, her pleasure, his pleasure, everything.

She had reached her peak; she was making the high whimpering noises that he had learnt meant she was there, that he could let go, or maybe they didn't mean that at all, but only that she was faking it. He didn't know. She was a woman, what could you ever know for sure?

"You do that so well," he said admiringly, knowing that her cries were sending him over the edge, real or not—such was her power over him. "Oh, my sweet, you do that so well. Do they train you for this? I bet you were top of your class, my darling, and to think I thought it was all for me." And then he couldn't speak anymore; he could only wrap his hands under her hips and hold her up to his thrusting body as he took his pleasure from her, crying out as he did so, and still, in spite of everything, wishing that this act might somehow make her part of him forever.

Chapter 25

Later she lay in her own bed, sobbing. She wasn't used to crying; she had rarely cried in her life, even over her father. Now it was like a storm, so maybe she was crying all her tears at once. It certainly felt like it; it felt as though it would kill her. Sunny could hardly believe she had so many tears in her.

Lorna Doone and Beetle kept watch at the bedside, showing their concern in various feline ways like sitting beside her head in silence or, when their attention span had run its brief course, pouncing on the corner of the duvet, which trembled as she wept, or leaping onto her quivering stomach.

So sometimes she laughed through her sobs, and that lightened the misery, but it didn't prevent her getting the worst headache she'd ever had in her life.

She had explained nothing; there was nothing she could explain. To tell Jock that neither he or his colleagues in the film world were her target would have been to tell him that her target was Farid Abul Hassan. Jock wasn't stupid; he would have sorted that out at once. And she simply could not jeopardize the operation now, not when what had happened only today might be the break they needed. Not when a casual word from Jock, unthinking or deliberate, could burn her and the operation to the ground between one second and the next.

"All right," he'd begun.

But before he could go on, she'd said quietly, "Before you say it, I may as well tell you that I am not going to tell you anything."

"Maybe," he said. "But I'm going to ask. There's nothing you'd want to be investigating me for, unless Aussie internal revenue have taken to hiring Canadian Mounties, which I doubt. So—you were using me? You're using me to get to someone else?"

She wished she could deny it. But she *had* used him—whatever had happened later, at the beginning she had used him to get to someone else. That was the horrible truth. "I can't answer that," she said stonily.

"But I can see it's true," he said. "I remember how eager you were to meet actors and writers, and you've met quite a few of those, haven't you? What is it, drugs? That's the big preoccupation these days, isn't it? Hell of a lot of drugs in the film world, I guess. An easy way to target suppliers. Always somebody trying to buy."

"I can't answer anything you're going to ask," Sunny said again.

"I just bet you can't," he said drily. "That was some operation, a half-naked sheila with a cat in heat coming to my door. I should have realized it was too classy for the press to invent."

She said, "That wasn't calculated. That just happened."

"Uh-huh." He was of two minds about whether to believe that. "And now we know why you were so concerned about the press, don't we? You thought someone would recognize you and blow the whistle."

It couldn't hurt to tell him that. It was obvious. Sunny smiled tentatively. "You thought I was saving the clippings because I liked it," she reminded him.

But he was not to be reached so easily. "I thought a lot of things that I was dead wrong about, didn't I?" he said.

"I don't suppose you'll believe anything I *can* tell you."

"Try me," said Jock.

She said, "It was no part of any plan to meet you. It just happened that way."

"And you took full advantage of it?"

She didn't reply.

"Farid, too, I notice. Think he's bringing drugs in with those carpets he imports, do you, matey? I doubt it, you know—Farid provides whatever will bring the people he likes to his parties, that's all. He just likes to have certain people around him, and he knows the ways to get them."

That was almost certainly true, and an excellent cover for his operation it was, but still she didn't reply.

He said suddenly, as if it were torn from him, "Damn you, I wish I *had* stripped you naked and thrown you out to the wolves that morning! It was about what you deserved."

She had lain there beside him, feeling his anger flow over her, stabbing her like little knives, because she had to. She had to know what he was going to do. Would he burn her, announcing to anyone he'd introduced her to that she was on the drug squad and he washed his hands of her? Or might she convince him to keep quiet, just for a few days, just till she had time to finish her work?

If not, the thing was as good as lost, anyway. She said, "Will you believe what I tell you?"

"I don't know," said Jock. "Try me."

"I can't tell you much," she said evenly. "But as far as I know, no one who is a particular friend of yours is under investigation. Can you believe that?"

He didn't answer directly. "How about anyone I introduced you to?" he asked drily, as though she'd underestimated his sense of what was right.

She couldn't stand the way he was looking at her, as though he didn't know her at all, as though they'd never shared anything whose memory he would treasure. Sunny pushed the thought out of her field of consciousness. She said, "Does your protection extend to everyone you know, no matter what they might be doing?"

"Matey, I don't like being used," he said flatly. "If I'm going to betray someone I know by introducing him to an undercover cop, I'd like to know about it beforehand, you get me? I'm good for my word, and I'd like to keep it that way."

There was no answer to that except the entire truth, and even that might not satisfy him. Sunny swung her feet over the edge of the bed and stood up. Looking down at him, she said, "What are you going to do about this?"

"What might I do?"

"You might tell everyone you've introduced me to that by mistake you've introduced them to an undercover officer." She began to pull her clothes on, briefs and pantihose and the beautiful green dress. "If that's what you're going to do, I'd like to know in advance."

"Why?" he said. "Why should I tell you that? To give you a chance to make some quick arrests first?"

She breathed deeply and struggled with the dress's fastening, and he casually reached up and did it for her. The automatic intimacy of it knocked them both out of their defensive positions for a painful, shocking moment of seeing how far down the road of togetherness they had, almost without knowing it, travelled, and how far apart they had moved tonight.

"Jock," she said flatly. "This isn't a movie. This is life, and it's important. It would help if you could take my word for it that it's more important than what you think I've done to you. If you are going to burn me to the people you know, someone is likely to kill me, and maybe other people, too. If that's what you're going to do, please tell me now."

His eyes widened, and she could tell she'd shocked him. He cursed once, his voice a whisper. "You're telling me the truth, aren't you? I've got that kind of power now—if by some bloody stupid slip of the tongue I let somebody, and I've no idea who it is, know about you, I could be responsible for your death. Is that the situation?"

It was, though she hadn't quite looked at it that way before. "That's about it," she said. "What are you going to do?"

"Damn you!" he said passionately. "You give me that kind of power, and then you ask me what I'm going to do with it? What the hell do you think I'm going to do with it?" He thought there couldn't be anything in the world so painful as discovering you loved someone like this—at the exact moment you realized that the person you loved didn't exist. His heart was coming apart at the seams. He realized now that he would have killed anyone who tried to harm a hair of her head, and she was standing there calmly, coldly asking him whether he intended to let someone kill her— worse, to deliberately cause someone to kill her.

"I don't know," she was saying steadily, and he cursed again.

"Well, you should know! If you had any kind of honesty, but I guess you haven't, you should know! Of course I'm not going to 'burn' you—is that what you call it, just like in the movies? I'm never going to say your name again, if I can help it! Does that satisfy you?"

"It will if you say I have your word on it," she said.

He laughed once. "Right," he said, shaking his head. "That's the worst of you bloody spies, isn't it? Your own word's not worth stink, but you like to count on the honour of the people you're taking along for the ride."

She had to take it, even if her heart broke in two. She said steadily, "Will you give me your word?"

He discovered suddenly that he was nearly crying. "Yes," he said. "Yeah, if you need it on such a matter, I give you my word. Now, will you get the hell out?"

She couldn't understand why she couldn't stop crying. She had always known it had to be over sometime. It was one of those relationships whose end is inherent in its beginning. He was an actor, after all. He was used to picking up and discarding women, and she'd been preparing herself for the inevitable from the beginning.

Last night, before the party... there had been something in the air then, something between them that might have meant...something, if only she hadn't been afraid. If she'd let that happen, if they'd had that moment of feeling truly connected, maybe after the party she could have said, "I love you," and he would have trusted her without explanations.

But it had frightened her, the look in his eyes, the passion in his touch, the sweeping need she had felt in herself to give in, to trust him. And the fear that she might gamble—and lose.

Sunny abruptly sat up and punched a pillow, startling Lorna and Beetle into flight. "Damn it!" she said aloud. She was being ridiculous. Who was she trying to kid? She might have given in to loving Jock last night, but no way would that have been binding on him! Jock was rich and famous and inhabited a world where his name got linked with the wives of peers, and just because that didn't matter to Sunny didn't mean it didn't matter to him or the rest of the world. She was a nobody, a Canadian cop, that was all, and she'd damn well better start doing her job and stop feeling sorry for herself!

In the heat of this mood she got up and stomped down to the kitchen. Lorna and Beetle, who had nobly given up all idea of this evening's Mousers when they'd seen how upset Sunny was, now felt it would not be undignified to make the small lapse in routine known. As she filled the kettle, first Lorna and then Beetle carefully "sat" at her feet. When she didn't notice, Lorna mewed delicately and questioningly.

Sunny glanced at the cats and away, and then did a double take. "Oh, for goodness' sake!" she exploded, beginning to laugh. "It's two in the bloody morning! Don't you cats ever forget anything?"

Laughing even harder, she opened the cupboard and brought out the Mousers. It's a relief to laugh, she thought, as she crouched down and fed the delicate Miss Lorna a treat. It clears your brain of all the self-pity. She was laughing so hard her hand was shaking.

"Sunny! What's the matter?"

She turned quickly, her hand pulling away from Beetle's mouth. Following it, Beetle promptly fell over. "Pip!" she gulped. "Where did you come from?"

"I just came in. I was trying not to wake you, and then I heard you crying. What's wrong?"

"I'm not crying, I'm laughing," Sunny said, almost believing it herself. She wiped her cheeks, where tears had started to flow again.

"I can see that," Pip said drily. "Is there anything I can do? I mean, I'd like to share the joke."

That made her laugh again, which made her cry again. "What's the *matter* with me?" she exploded. "I feel like a basket case! Remind me never to let my emotions run away with me ever again!"

Pip just stood there, laughing softly. "I don't think life's that easy, Sunny," he said.

Chapter 26

Bosey thought it was getting too dangerous and that she should come off the case, but Alex Fairchild seemed to think Sunny was made of sterner stuff. If she wanted to carry on, he was perfectly prepared to let her do so.

Sunny wanted to carry on, so she argued with Bosey, and threw Fairchild's name into the balance, and said that neither Iqbal nor Jock would betray her and she was prepared to stake her life on that.

"That's exactly what you're doing," Bosey pointed out. "I hope you're right."

"Look," she said, "Fairchild's working on getting a search warrant. If he gets it, it'll be a big help if I'm there to finger the date of the next Milan shipment. Let me stay on a little."

Bosey said only, "If you've got Fairchild's okay, it's not for me to say. He's running the operation over there. But I would like to point two things out to you. First, your cover is precarious at best, and second, you have no evidence *of any nature* that links that shipping agent with any shipments to Iraq. You may be putting yourself in jeopardy for a bit of petty fraud, Delancey.''

''No,'' she said. ''Bosey, you have to take my word for it. No.''

She was grateful to Alex Fairchild for his calm assumption that it was natural for police officers to take risks with their lives, for his lack of fuss, for his matter-of-fact acceptance of her willingness to risk herself on the word of her friends that they would not betray her and, most of all, for his faith in her instincts. He thought she was right. He was doing what he could to enable them to get inside the shipping agency office, one way or the other.

But she was afraid that Bosey's fears might eventually get through to Fairchild and convince him to pull her off the case, and even she knew she couldn't stay there forever. Information had a way of seeping out, once it had gone beyond a limited number of brains. The mere existence of the knowledge that she was an undercover officer in two additional brains, Jock's and Iqbal's, might easily tip the balance. Now it might come out from any direction. It was volatile.

But what could she do to hurry the thing along? She could keep on looking for proof, convinced as she was that all the proof they needed would be there in the shipping office next time there was a shipment of carpets to Milan, and she could wait for that next shipment. And she could carry on looking in other directions in case she was wrong. That was about all. But there were few other places now to look.

The sudden descent into relative inactivity nearly drove her crazy.

Of course, there was also the fact that her evenings were free, completely free, for the first time in weeks. She certainly never saw all the new acquaintances she had made, through Jock, over the last weeks. And of course she couldn't call up any old friends from university days, and

Pip was away more often than he was home. And you can only work out at a gym so many hours a week.

She had any number of explanations for the restlessness she felt. None of them got near admitting to herself that she missed Jock with a hollow loneliness that was complete and brutal.

Perhaps because she couldn't admit it to herself, she made the foolish mistake of accepting an invitation to Lisa's party. Lisa, Jock's location manager, was one of a few film people Sunny had met whom she really liked. With the others she had often had the feeling, perhaps because she was playing a role herself, that they were hiding behind some facade, that the person she met wasn't the real human being.

But with Lisa she had felt comfortable from the beginning. Lisa was strong and abrupt and open, and there was no nonsense about her. Sunny liked her. So when, answering her phone one night, she heard a rough, "God, woman, I haven't seen you for ages, what's happening?" her first response was to laugh.

"Isn't it obvious?" she asked drily.

Lisa said, "Well, you've broken up with Jock, but so what? I can't stand the idea that someone's only 'Jock's girlfriend'—do you know what I mean?—and when he stops seeing her, suddenly she doesn't exist. You're not Jock's girlfriend, you're Sunny, right?"

She felt her eyes burn with unexpected tears. "Roight," she agreed, in horrible imitation of the Aussie accent.

Lisa laughed. "Right. Well, then, there's a party tomorrow night. I want you to come. Will you?"

"Will Jock be there?"

Lisa sighed. "He's been invited, but I don't know if he'll turn up. It's a preshoot feed-the-workers party. We've got a tricky early dawn shoot with a midnight call, so no one's going to bed. But probably Jock'll have too much work to come. But what does it matter whether he comes or not? I'm inviting *you*. Will *you* come?''

"All right, thanks," said Sunny, not sure what the hell possessed her. But she would go crazy if she stayed cooped up with the cats much longer. She was almost beginning to imagine that they answered back.

She would have given three years of her life for another look in the book labelled "Ann Barr," but it remained resolutely out of sight. On the day after Lisa's call, when she went up with some letters for Farid to sign, she saw a corner of it just visible between two carpets in the stack behind his desk and forced her eyes to pass over it without a flicker. She spent all day in tense expectation of the news that another shipment had come from Iraq, but no shipment arrived. Late in the afternoon it suddenly occurred to her that the fuss that had happened last time might have been enough to cause Farid to alter his arrangements for the handling of such shipments, and then she really did hit rock bottom. What if he changed his shipping agent, too? What if the whole investigation fell apart because they'd moved too damned slowly?

She had looked up the names "Ann Barr" and "Barr Ann" in the London residential and business directories and the Southampton directory. Surprisingly there wasn't even one listed. She called every "A. Barr" she found, using the name "AlHaqq Antiques" or "Farid Abul Hassan" whenever she had the faintest suspicion, but got no result. She had even called Milan and got one of the police officers there whom she had talked to before to look up the name in the Milan directory.

He had done so, but had protested that it wasn't an Italian name. "Anna," he pointed out to her. "This is the Italian form of Ann. I will look up Anna Barr, too."

"Thank you," Sunny had said, not attempting to dissuade him. Such little bits of nonsense were often the trig-

ger to something useful. But there was no "Ann Barr" and
no "Anna Barr"—not even an "Anna Barra"—in Milan's
directory.

On a desperate impulse, which she certainly should not
have obeyed, she went upstairs next time Farid had a phone
call and waited till he hung up. "Yes?" he said politely as he
did so. His call had been in English, to the advertising
manager of a magazine he bought space in; he wasn't worried about her eavesdropping.

"There was a long-distance call while you were talking,"
she said. "We got cut off. I thought you'd like to know."

"Where was it from?" he asked.

Sunny shook her head. "I don't know, the line was very
bad, and they didn't say the city. I'm not even sure the call
was for us. But I thought I caught the name Ann or Anna—
Tar, maybe. It was a really bad line, and it just went dead.
But they were shouting. It sounded urgent."

Farid shrugged and shook his head. "It was a wrong
number," he said. "If not, they will ring again." And he
looked as though he really believed it, but nevertheless,
Sunny went downstairs and watched her phone for any sign
of it lighting up with an external call from Farid's desk.

It didn't do so. Farid made no attempt to call Ann Barr,
whoever she was, all the rest of the afternoon. It could only
mean two things: either it was impossible that Ann Barr
should be trying to call, in which case Sunny's mention of a
similar name had almost certainly aroused his suspicions, or
there was no such person, or shop, as Ann Barr.

But then why was it written on the spine of the Milan
shipping record?

She pretended to herself that she didn't care whether Jock
came to Lisa's party or not, but it didn't stop her dressing
for him. Not that she put on anything very attention-getting,
like the green dress, but she dressed as stylishly as perhaps
she'd ever done, in black trousers and vest and short boots,

another of the outfits Jock had bought for her, slicking her hair back from her forehead in a wet look that was held in place with gel.

She looked as though she belonged to his world; there was no doubt about the transformation she had undergone in the past weeks. She might not look like a star, but she had certainly never looked less like a police officer in her life. It occurred to her suddenly that perhaps she should have given him back everything he had bought her. The keys of the car, of course, she had shoved through his mail slot the day after Andrea Bellamy's party. The car was still parked where she had left it in the square a few doors down; as far as she could tell, Jock hadn't touched it. But until tonight she'd had no cause to dress in any of the clothes he had bought her; she hadn't thought of them.

But probably she should return them all. Women always did, as far as she knew, though it seemed a pretty stupid custom to Sunny. What would Jock do with them?

As she came down the stairs the cats attacked her, yowling. They sensed that she was going out, and they wanted to be sure they got fed before she did so.

"All right, all right," Sunny said, walking to the kitchen. She looked in the fridge for the half can she had left there this morning, but it was gone. "Damn it," she said, "it *can't* be my memory! That's the third time this week that's happened! Are you guys getting fed by Pip, too? Where do you put it all?"

Beetle hadn't gained any weight, as far as she could see; naturally the greedy one would be Lorna, who was certainly looking fatter than when Sunny had arrived. "Emma will come home and won't recognize you," she warned the cat. "And we'll have to change your name to Tugboat Annie or something."

Oddly enough, she found conversation with the cats comforting. She didn't like the idea much, but that was the way it was, and Sunny was big on facing life as it was. She

wondered for the first time if Emma had got Lorna Doone
because she was lonely after the breakup with Rafiq. She
realized that she had never really discussed it with Emma,
or certainly not her feelings about it. For the first time she
saw it as a tragedy, what before had been just words to her:
a broken marriage. If Emma had felt anything like what she
was feeling, how had she survived?

Lorna finished the food in her own bowl and then
growled until poor Beetle slunk away from his. Sunny
watched the proceedings with interest, but without taking up
his defence. It was his business if he wanted to give Lorna
Doone supremacy. Besides, if she started anything the least
bit emotional now, she would ruin her eye makeup.

People were glad to see her, but by no means as glad as
they had been when she was Jock Prentiss's girlfriend.
Sunny amused herself by wondering if that was because
Jock's mantle had given her an aura of importance, or
whether they had been currying favour with her as a possible pipeline to Jock. This thought gave her a bitter pleasure, though she was not often cynical except when her
spirits were low. By this means she established the fact that
her spirits were now low.

As if she didn't already know. Sunny, standing over the
food table, snickered to herself. Lord, she was reaching se-
nility early: first talking to cats, and now laughing to herself in a corner.

"What's the joke?" asked a voice beside her. She put a
salmon cracker in her mouth and glanced up, chewing. A
man named Simon, one of the heavies in the film, was
loading a little plate with sandwiches.

"It was an in joke, I'm afraid," Sunny said, when she had
swallowed.

It made him laugh. "You want to be careful with in
jokes," he warned her. "The in group gets smaller and

smaller. Come on over here and share my sandwiches. I'm feeling lonely."

"Me, too," she said, although up to a minute ago she'd been talking with Lisa and two other women she liked. The problem was, she couldn't settle to anything.

"You and Jock not an item anymore, I see" was what Simon said to that, slipping an arm protectively close to her back as he shepherded her back to his corner. "Does that leave the field open for the rest of us?"

She wasn't sure what to answer to that. She turned up to him with a half smile, but he was looking past her with eyes suddenly gone wary. Sunny turned. Jock was standing in the doorway, looking in their direction, and Simon melted away. "Hi," said Jock, nodding to Sunny, and she managed to smile and nod, and then he turned to talk to someone beside him, and the moment passed.

The two women she'd been chatting with earlier came up and surrounded her protectively with a smoke bomb of chatter and laughter and waving arms, and she laughed with them, though she had no idea at what. After a few moments Lisa came over to add to the confusion, and she really did make Sunny laugh.

They looked after her for the next few minutes, making sure she was recovered. Oddly enough, it seemed clear to the women that Jock had ditched Sunny, and yet none of the men who had shown an interest in picking up the pieces during the first hour of the party, Simon included, showed any inclination to make a move on her with Jock in the room.

She was talking to Harry, a safely married man in his late forties who had joined the group, when Jock at last approached, his face by this time unreadable. She felt the current, like an electromagnetic field, drawing her to him, and stepped back in the vain hope of moving out of range without actually being forced to run away. Then she pulled herself tight.

"Hello, Sunny, how are you?" he said, and she managed to nod and mutter something. "I've just got to have a word with Lisa—and you, Harry," he said. "Tried to get you earlier, Lisa, but your phone's off."

Lisa jumped, her hand going automatically to the cellular phone hanging from her belt. "Hell, is it?" She pulled it out and looked at it. "Damn, it is! Sorry, Jock!" She pushed a button that set a red light glowing. "What's up, then? Is there a problem?"

"Lisa, I've just been out to the location. There's a bloody great lorry parked just in front of the warehouse doors. Is that ours?"

"Yeah, it is, Jock," Lisa said. "We parked it there to make sure no one else would get that space. I didn't want to have to knock on every door in the neighbourhood at two in the morning to try to find the owner of some car," she explained humorously over her shoulder to Sunny. "People don't like that much."

Sunny laughed. "You'd think they'd be thrilled."

Jock waited patiently for this by-play to run its course. When it did, he said, "And who would have thought you'd have to put a guard on a sixteen-wheeler parked on the level?" and Lisa's head snapped up and she stared at him.

"Oh, no!" she protested. "What is it? What's gone wrong, Jock?"

The flicker of a smile touched his expression, making Sunny suddenly aware that he hadn't really smiled since he came in. He raised a hand and scratched his ear. "Matey, all sixteen tires are flat," he said. He began to chuckle. "Sorry to break up the party, but that's going to take a while to fix."

Lisa let out one explosive curse, but wasted no more time than that. Turning her head, she called, "George! Poppy!" very loudly, and from two different parts of the room a man and a woman, sensing catastrophe, set down their glasses and started towards her at speed. "What's the time?" she muttered, checking her watch. "Blow, it's after eleven! George, Poppy, they've let the air out of the tires on that lorry out at the warehouse. Poppy, you get on the phone and find somebody who'll come out and blow them up, and George, you get out to the warehouse immediately. I've got guards on the film trucks, but I never thought to ask them to keep an eye on the lorry!"

Sunny stepped back to watch, intrigued and a little bemused by the way Lisa went into action.

"What's the address of the warehouse?" Poppy called suddenly from the corner where she had gone to make her calls.

The name Ann Barr popped into Sunny's head, seemingly unconnectedly. Perhaps because everyone was suddenly busy with their work, and that was Sunny's work. Ann Barr...

"The warehouse! What's the street address?" Poppy called again.

The warehouse...Ann Barr...*anbar*... Sunny froze where she stood, almost unable to believe what her brain was telling her. Ann Barr...*anbar*... was an archaic Arabian word for warehouse. If she hadn't made the connection before, it was because on the spine of the stock book it was written in Roman script.

"Warehouse," Sunny muttered softly to herself. A warehouse is where you store things. It's not a shipping agency at all.... It's where Abul Hassan is storing those damned chemicals before he ships them! It has to be.

So we don't need to wait for the next Italian shipment, she thought. If I'm right, it'll all be there right now.

Chapter 27

"The address you want'll be down there, miss, and then first on the left," said the cab-driver worriedly. "You sure you'll be all right?"

Standing in the dark, unfamiliar street now, Sunny shivered. "Yes, thanks," she said, paying him. At the last moment she had the feeling she should ask him to wait for her there, but her words were drowned out by the sound of him shifting into gear, and she let him go.

Probably she had been gripped by some temporary madness, back there at Lisa's place; she shouldn't be doing this, and certainly not without at least having informed someone on her team.

But it was only a recce. She didn't intend to try to get into the shipping office, or at least, only if the chance offered. What she wanted was to check the premises, because she was afraid that Farid Abul Hassan had got spooked in the past few days and might move out of the premises before Fairchild made his move. If possible, she would look in a window. That was all she intended. She wanted to find some evidence that her sudden inspiration tonight was a reasonable hypothesis, so that tomorrow she could convince Alex Fairchild that they should take some action.

It was a warmish night, but she was cold with nerves. Sunny moved quietly, almost invisibly, down the street to where it debouched into a road running almost at right angles to it and turned towards the street that led off to the left a hundred yards away.

London was not built on a grid system, as Sunny's made-in-Canada brain always unconsciously assumed it was. When she got to that street, it wasn't the one she wanted. She retraced her steps and at last found the little cobbled laneway—hardly more than a hole in the wall—that led into an industrial courtyard.

At the end of the lane she paused, gazing into the courtyard. It was cobbled, lighted only by the moon, and looked as if it belonged to another century. She saw the arms of a pub and several tradesmen's signs hanging over the yard, and except for their faint swinging in the wind, there was not a movement anywhere.

She herself must be nearly invisible in the gloom. She had asked to borrow a sweater from Lisa, who, busy on the phone, had simply waved her into the bedroom and told her to help herself to whatever she needed. Sunny had found a black shirt and black scarf and, tucking them under her arm, had quietly left the party. Jock had left a few minutes before, and the rest were in motion, preparing to leave; her departure had been unremarked.

She wished the place had been on an ordinary street, so that she could have the comfort of a free escape route. If this laneway were blocked, she would be a prisoner. Sunny stood there for several minutes, watching, until, by good luck, a band of clouds moved in and shadowed the bright moon.

Nothing moved, and at last she crept forward, keeping to the shadowy side of the courtyard and flat in against the wall. The doorway of the shipping agent, she thought, must be the one directly opposite the lane entrance. As she crept towards it, the moon began to slide out from behind its cloud cover. She slipped into the relative safety of a doorway and breathed again. She glanced up to where the moonlight caught the sign painted on the wall of the doorway just above her head. Tonbridge Plastic Mouldings, it read, and Sunny caught her breath on a gasp. It was the name of one of the plants on the list of suspected Iraqi-owned factories. She was sure of it. Not one of those that Abul Hassan owned outright, but one they suspected was importing the chemicals with false end-user's certificates. And it lay at right angles to the shipping agency offices. Inside, the spaces might easily communicate.

Well, there was proof enough here, and danger enough. She didn't need to go any further tonight. If this wasn't enough to spark a search by Her Majesty's Customs officials, the colonials might as well pack up and go home. Why the officer whom Alex Fairchild had sent to investigate the address hadn't noticed this fact, she didn't understand, but then, she herself had been eating and sleeping all those names for much longer than the British team. Besides, the plant address for Tonbridge Plastic Mouldings was in Tonbridge; this address was certainly not on the list.

She wished the moon would get back behind the cloud. The shadows now were darker and sharper, it was true, but the chance of the moon reflecting from her face or hands or even her leather boots, was much greater. Sunny slunk back in the shadow of the doorway, looking up and praying for the cloud to cover that bright eye.

She did hear the faintest squeak behind her, and did whirl instantly, but her reaction was too late. The squeak came not from the door opening, but from it swinging to again. Her assailant had a grip on her before she could even get an arm up, and her mouth was covered almost before she had taken in the air to scream.

Not that a scream would have been any help in this area, Sunny thought, but she would have liked to try. She tried to kick, she tried to break the painful hold she was in, but there were two of them now, and whatever was pressing into the back of her neck was causing her to lose consciousness very effectively. She fought wildly to stave off the blackness, but there was really nothing to be done.

She awoke in darkness, feeling she hadn't been out for very long. She was on her back, and only dimly conscious.

"She won't be out for long," said a voice above her head. She must be on the floor. "What are we going to do with her?" Sunny kept her eyes closed as light from a flashlight ran over her body.

"...her, first of all," said a second voice. "It will be better if she doesn't recognise us." She could understand most of what was being said, though her brain felt groggy and ill-equipped to cope with a foreign language. Sunny tried to concentrate.

"All right, have you got an..."

"Use her scarf."

"Right." She felt hands at her throat and breathed to relax against the tension building in her body. Her scarf was pulled from under her neck and pressed against her eyes. He was competent, whoever he was. He made a good job of the blindfold.

"That's good enough. Now let's get the job done. We can't waste any more time with her. We'll have to take her with us when we go."

"Is there anything to tie her hands with?"

"Over on the table. Make it quick." There were steps that receded and then approached again, and she was rolled over and her hands firmly taped together behind her back.

"Now let's get going."

She heard them creep silently off, but they didn't go far. Whatever job they were doing was in the same room. Sunny lay quietly for a moment, till their concentration should move from her and onto the work they were doing. Then, slowly, she turned her head and body till she could press the blindfold at the side of her head against whatever she was lying on, and slowly dragged her head down, trying to dislodge it.

She was lying on something that provided a lot of friction; it was a moment before she realized that it was a carpet. In spite of everything, her heart beat in excitement: a carpet in a warehouse? And she could tell she was on a pile of them. Surely they could only be here to be shipped?

It took her a dozen attempts before the blindfold rode up far enough to free one eye. She could see nothing except faint shadows in the blackness. The two men were behind her in the room; she would have to risk moving without knowing whether they were looking her way or not. Sunny slowly rolled over on her bound arms to her other side and lay motionless as the flash suddenly played over her.

"She's waking up."

"Yeah, we'll be through in a minute. Bring the light back, I nearly dropped the . . ."

Now that her left eye was uppermost, she could see what they were doing. She lay watching in astonishment for a moment, trying to make sense of what she saw. Against the concrete wall of the warehouse, on metal shelving that covered the walls of the room, were several rows of painted metal cylinders. Two figures wearing gas masks, eerily outlined by the light of the powerful lamp they carried, were creeping along the row. At each one they paused, and one man fitted a complicated-looking gadget over a sealed intake valve and opened it. The other, carrying a large tank on his back, lifted the hose attached to the tank and fitted its nozzle over the cylinder-intake valve.

Now the first one brought the light close over what must be a measuring device on the hose, and the one carrying the tank pressed a lever and held it for several seconds; then the opening procedure was reversed and the cylinder sealed again.

The gas masks muffled their voices, the light threw huge shadows over everything, and the whole scene seemed too horrific to be real. Sunny found that she was shaking.

Well, she'd walked into the lion's den, for sure. She almost certainly would not get out alive. The only reason they hadn't killed her already was undoubtedly that they intended to interrogate her, with perhaps a little additional factor being that the disposal of her body would be easier if they killed her somewhere else. Sunny didn't waste time on thinking about it. The thing to do was act, and she couldn't do anything if she was crippled with fear, as more than one instructor had drummed into her.

Of course, she would try to get out alive, but she had to bear in mind that if she didn't succeed, her business was to cause as much fuss in dying as possible, so that someone would notice and some kind of word would get to Alex Fairchild.

The best distraction, of course, would be a fire. But if her suspicions were right, and they almost certainly were, the cylinders that they were tinkering with over there contained chemicals of one sort or another. She knew nearly nothing about chemical reactions to fire, but some nerve gases required high temperatures for their formation. She knew that much. She simply could not risk the possibility of wiping out even a small part of London with nerve gas in her attempt to send up a signal flare.

In fact, in her ignorance, she could not do anything that endangered those cylinders in any way. That limited the scope of her activities very considerably. And if she simply attacked the men physically and the chemicals killed the three of them, it would be Farid who would learn about it, not Fairchild, and her death in such a way would be useless.

They had two more cylinders to go, she reckoned. If she wasted time trying to free her hands, she would be lost. What she had to do was get out, if possible, and raise the alarm before they could catch her. Quickly Sunny pushed the heel of one foot against the toe of the other and dislodged first one boot and then the other. The boots were not noisy, but she must be absolutely silent now.

The most dangerous time must be when the lid was off and the nozzle being fitted; that was when they would be most concentrated, and with a little luck the process was too dangerous to be interrupted even if they saw her move.

She rolled over again, her eye stretching wide in the darkness, looking for the door. There it was, deep in shadow, but there was no mistaking the way the steel shelving that lined the walls stopped right there. Sunny listened for the clink that told her that the lid of the cylinder was being carefully lifted, then rose soundlessly to her feet and began to run. If there was anything on the floor she was a goner, but she couldn't waste time picking her way.

There was a shout behind her as she reached the door and turned sideways to pull the handle with her bound hands. It was locked, or rather bolted, she could tell by the way the lock gave but the door held. Her eyes stretched wide, trying to see where the bolt might be, and at the same time she pulled as hard as her muscles could stand at the door. She would either break the bolt or establish where it was.

Below the lock, thank God. She couldn't possibly have reached above it. She crouched, her back to the door, feeling down the seam for the bolt, but she was too late. They had set down their equipment and were running towards her. She wouldn't—there!

Her hands found the bolt and struggled with it, snapping it back just as they reached her. Sunny stood and let fly a kick that caught the first man in the groin, but he was too well trained to crumple. He gasped and shook his head, but he nevertheless reached out and caught her.

It was absolutely useless for a bound woman to try to take on two strong men, and Sunny needed to conserve her strength. She screamed then, a short hoarse scream that was immediately stifled by the second man, still encumbered with the tank, but strong enough, nonetheless. They dragged her back to her bed on what she could see now was a small pile of carpets and forced her down.

"If you scream any more I'll knock you out," said the man with the tank, in English. Sunny didn't respond, and he didn't let go of her mouth.

The second man got up and went over to collect the lamp from where they had dropped it when she ran, pulling off the ugly gas mask as he did so. When he returned, training the light onto the ground at his feet, there was just sufficient glow for her to see his face. It was Ahmad, one of the stock boys at AlHaqq Antiques.

Sunny's brain performed the trick it sometimes did when she needed it most, pulling her back from the scene, and allowing her to distance herself from both her fear and her surprise. Ahmad flashed the light in her eyes. "If you scream, I'll hit you with this," he said, in English. "Are you going to scream?"

She had one card to play, and it had maybe a five percent chance of taking the trick, her detached brain informed her. Sunny shook her head impatiently, and as soon as her captor released her mouth, she said softly, in Arabic, "Well, Ahmad, you! And this, I suppose, is Mohammad! Why was I not informed that you would be here tonight?"

Chapter 28

There was a silence in the gloom. Following up her advantage, Sunny said, "And will you please take that light out of my eyes? You're blinding me."

Ahmad turned the light to the ground as if automatically. She could see that the two men were gazing at each other in surprise and confusion. "Well?" she demanded.

"It was not our job to tell you," Mohammad said softly, from his station behind her head. "Why are *you* here tonight?"

Well, that was certainly the question she hadn't wanted them to ask. "If no one has told you, I certainly won't," she said. What a ridiculous game of bluff it seemed, or it would have been, if the stakes hadn't been so high. Sunny felt as though she were fencing with someone behind a blanket. If only she could guess what they were doing. What on earth would you do with the chemical raw materials for nerve gas prior to shipping them that would entail adding something to the cylinder?

She said roughly, "Have you left the lid off one of the cylinders? You'd better go and finish the job before we're all poisoned!" There was a little hesitation, and then Mohammad got to his feet. "You, too, Ahmad!" she said. "Let's get this finished. And get this tape off my hands before you go!"

Ahmad slowly shook his head. "I don't think so," he said, and her heart sank at the knowing look in his eye. As Mohammad released her and rose, Ahmad had carefully shifted his position so that any attempt to move or scream on her part could be quickly forestalled. They were too intelligent, too efficient. Sunny began to abandon hope of escape and started thinking of ways of leaving some kind of trail for Fairchild, something that would lead him to look at the warehouse.

Mohammad went off with the light, leaving them in deep shadow. She heard the clank of metal on metal, and the hiss of escaping liquid. "Who are you—CIA?" Ahmad asked conversationally, and Sunny's skin went clammy all over. Her armpits seemed suddenly cold, and part of her brain engaged in curious appreciation of the possible reasons for such a sensation.

"Don't be a fool!" she said flatly. "Take me to Farid and let's get this sorted out before you do something you're sorry for."

Ahmad only laughed, and then they were silent until Mohammad returned with the light, stripping off his mask again. He set it down on the floor and squatted in front of her, gazing at her with a worried frown. They didn't quite know what to do with her, she could see that. "Take me to Farid!" she said, trusting to fate to offer her a means of escape, of signalling, anything that would prevent them from killing her out of hand.

Mohammad lifted his arms in a shrug and looked at Ahmad. Obviously they wanted to consult, and they could not do so in Arabic now, knowing she understood, nor could they leave her without first gagging her and tying her more securely, and they had no wherewithal to do that. Sunny understood their dilemma as if they had spoken it aloud.

"Az, ma lasohd?" Mohammad asked. *What shall we do?*

"Amarti lekha. Haia tsarich l'hiot..." Ahmad began. *I told you so. It should have...*

Something was wrong. Her brain was taking in the language and interpreting for her, and at the same time she had the wildest feeling of incongruity. What on earth was it?

"Well, so, you are spying on Abul Hassan?" Mohammad said calmly in English, waving Ahmad to silence. "I am afraid that you will have—"

He broke off because Sunny was staring at him in amazement. Her brain had finally figured it out. *Ma lasohd?* "What to do?" That wasn't Arabic! That was the favourite expression of submission to fate on Kibbutz Yad HaShofet, where she had spent two incredible summers. Sunny's mouth slowly fell open.

"Hebrew!" she gasped. "You speak Hebrew! You guys aren't Iraqis, you're Israelis! You must be from Mossad! My God, what a relief!"

"Why are the RCMP interesting themselves in these chemicals?" Ahmad, whose real name was Zvi, asked a few minutes later.

"They probably came from Canada originally, that's why. We're trying to prove fraudulent end-use declaration so we can stop the shipments out of Canada."

"Why do you care?" he pursued. "As long as the exports out of Canada are legal?"

She looked at him. "Don't you know what these chemicals are?"

"Of course I know."

"They're the raw materials for the manufacture of chemical weapons in Iraq," she said anyway.

"We know," Zvi said again. "Why is Canada concerned about it?"

She said, "They've been using chemical weapons against the Kurds and the Iranians. They're trying to wipe out the whole Iraqi Kurdish population."

"That's not all he's trying to wipe out. But there's been no international interest in stopping him up till now."

"Well, we're interested. Especially after the supergun. For all anyone knows, the supergun was supposed to shoot chemical weapons. Someone's got to stop it, because they won't stop at using it on the Kurds, will they?"

Mohammad, whose name was Gadi, laughed. "Are *you* telling *us?*"

She looked at him for a moment, then shook her head in appreciation of the point he was making. "Right," she said. "I guess Israel would be next on the list, wouldn't it?"

"These weapons were developed by Hitler's scientists during the war," Gadi pointed out. "Nerve gas, I mean. Of course, lethal agents like mustard gas were used already in the First World War, but those Hitler developed, Sarin and Soman and others, are much more efficient and deadly. Large parts of the record were destroyed, but it is certain that they were tested on human beings in Germany during the war." He didn't add to that, leaving the rest to her imagination.

"I know," Sunny said.

"The Kurds now, like the Jews then, have sent delegations to every Western government asking that this genocide be stopped. And like the Jews, they have received no response whatsoever."

There wasn't anything to be said to that.

"But Israel cannot afford such blindness." Again he didn't add the obvious. "When the Kurds came to us, we understood the logical extension of their catastrophe."

"Do you know how the pipeline works, exactly?" Sunny asked.

"Oh, yes. Very exactly. You don't?"

Sunny decided to risk calling a suspicion a certainty for the sake of having it confirmed. "I know that the stuff goes out under cover with those carpet shipments to the shop in Italy, but we haven't been able to trace them even to Italy, never mind beyond. Italian Customs have pulled a couple of searches, but there's been nothing so far."

They looked at each other, seeming to consult, and then tacitly decided to tell her. "That's because they are never shipped to Italy."

"Really!"

"There is an Iraqi agent—or, at least, a bribed employee—at the shipping firm. His job is to take the shipment destined for Italy, with all the relevant papers, and place it by mistake in the container going to Iraq."

Sunny stared at them, then smiled and shook her head. "Brilliant!" she said. "It's absolutely, brilliantly simple. That explains why all the papers are on the false letterhead. If a customs agent *did* happen to search that particular container, he'd find a shipment for Italy, but that wouldn't raise his suspicions. And if he searched that particular shipment, he'd find the stuff, but it would be entirely untraceable."

"You're absolutely right. I knew you were too intelligent to be wasting your time as Farid's secretary. What's the address on the false letterhead? We've never managed to get a look at it," said Gadi.

Fairchild was going to kill her, anyway; she'd broken enough rules tonight to get her fired five times over. And if the Israelis were doing something to stop this horror, she was in no mind to impede them. So she told them the address on the special letterhead. "But it's only an accommodation address," she said. "As far as we could discover, it's an arm's length rental from an ordinary accommodation address facility."

Nobody wrote anything down, but she could tell they'd both committed the address to memory.

"So what were you doing tonight—testing the stuff, or what?" she asked.

"I think we've had a fair trade-off of information, don't you? I don't think we're going to trade any more secrets till we know for sure who we're dealing with," said Gadi. She had to admit he was right. She had almost no information to give, and what they had traded so far was small potatoes. But what the two men were doing to the shipment was vital information, and probably fatal to them if she weren't who she said she was. "We're wasting a lot of time, let's get out of here."

They all suddenly became aware of the passage of time and got to their feet. The two men didn't offer to free her hands. "I'm still your prisoner?" she said, struggling to slip her feet into her boots one by one as Zvi bent to hold them for her, knowing that if the bonds had been on *their* wrists, they would certainly still have been her prisoners.

"We can't take your word," Gadi said apologetically, shepherding her towards the door. "We have to know who you are before we let you go. Hold her, Zvi," he said.

She stood quietly in the dark beside Zvi while Gadi took the light and moved systematically over the room, making sure they had left no evidence of their presence behind. At the pile of carpets, the light paused where the shadow was doubly black.

"What's that?" he asked, walking forward to pick something up.

It was Lisa's black scarf, almost invisible in the gloom. Picking it up, Gadi crossed to where they stood by the door, ran the light once more round the room, then doused it. Quietly he turned the handle and opened the door a crack, then opened it wide and silently went through, careful not to let the tank on his back clank against anything. He stood in the moon shadow of the doorway for a long minute and then stepped around to the right, keeping against the wall, and waved them to follow.

Sunny came next, no more eager than they were to make any noise. She followed Gadi around the edge of the doorway and stood waiting as Zvi closed and locked the door behind them. Moving in admirable silence, he crossed the little recess of the doorway and joined them.

"All right," Gadi whispered, and then the sound of a step against the cobblestones across the courtyard electrified them all.

"FREEZE!" shouted a voice from the darkness. "All right, *freeze*, you bastards. We've got you surrounded!"

Jock Prentiss stepped out of the shadows on the other side of the courtyard, and the moon glinted off the big .45 he had levelled on them. "Sunny, you get going. There's a car out on the street," he commanded. "You other two, don't move a muscle. Don't even breathe."

Detective Matt Patten was coming to the rescue, just like in the movies.

Chapter 29

Sunny recovered quickly and, ducking under the range of Jock's gun where it was levelled on the two men, she ran quickly across the courtyard towards the lane. From her vantage point there, she called quietly, "Don't shoot, Jock, for God's sake! We don't want to make any noise. We've got to get out of here." Then she turned towards the two men. "Sorry, fellas," she called cheerfully. "Catch you later!"

Jock thought she was out of her mind. She was a prisoner, but he wasn't to make any noise rescuing her? But he was in no position to argue; it was a damn sight better than if she'd asked him to shoot them. "Keep me covered!" he ordered his imaginary cohort in a doorway behind and beyond the two men; then, his gun still levelled on them, he slowly began to back across the cobblestoned yard in Sunny's wake.

As Matt Patten, he realized suddenly, he would have made a run for it, waving his gun all over the place, but he suddenly understood how woefully inadequate such a technique was in the face of real danger. If they pulled guns and started shooting while he was running, he would have a hell of a time aiming. Not that it would do him any good, with only blanks in the gun.

Once in the protection of the covered laneway, he turned and ran flat out after Sunny, whose long moon shadow stretched towards him from the mouth of the lane. Man, she was lithe, he thought admiringly. Her arms were tied behind her back, but she was running straight, no problem with her balance. "Right!" he called, and her shadow abruptly disappeared as she turned sharply to obey him.

A moment later he was on the street. She was running ahead of him, more slowly now, looking for his battered Mercedes along both sides of the road. He caught her up as she reached it, pulled open the driver door and half lifted, half shoved her in and over. Somehow the keys were in his hand, and the engine started without a hitch, and in another second they were away. As they roared past the lane entrance, he saw the two men running hell for leather up the road to a white van.

Sunny was laughing. She couldn't help it. Every time she opened her mouth to speak, she collapsed into laughter. After a moment, Jock gave in and found it a terrific release for the tension he'd been under for the past half hour.

"That was wonderful!" she said when she could speak. "That was just like the movies! I've never seen anything so exciting!"

Jock was a little chastened. "Isn't that the way they do it?" he asked.

Sunny laughed again. "I think Bosey would rather die than shout 'Freeze, you bastards!' at anyone, and I don't suppose Fairch—my superior officer on the English side even has the words in his vocabulary. But they're very impressive! Where did you get the gun?"

He threw her a look and grinned. "Off the movie set, where do you think?"

She blinked. "You mean it's not even a real gun?"

"It's real enough, I reckon. I don't know. But it's only loaded with blanks, so it's a bloody good thing you *didn't* want me to shoot those two."

Sunny sobered suddenly. "You came after me without even a gun?"

He said, "You ever tried to find a working gun in England in a hurry? They don't grow on trees, you know."

"And what about the people who had us covered in there? What did they have?"

"There was only me. I thought it would be a good idea if whoever had you thought there were more."

She said, "But you might have been killed."

"So might you, matey, and that's what I was concerned about."

She turned and looked at him, motionless, her arms still fixed behind her back, all laughter stilled at last as it sank in. "Jock," she whispered protestingly.

He reached out one strong arm and pulled her in against him as, with the other, he firmly guided the car through the rain-damp, silent streets. He realized now that he'd never been so scared in his life as when Sunny had come out of that doorway with her hands tied. "Yeah, I know, matey," he said. "But what can you do, eh? What can you do?"

As the big Mercedes roared through the night and the empty city, a cat on a corner turned its head curiously to watch it pass.

"How did you find me?" she asked later.

He said, "After the party, I went out to my car and waited for you to come out. I wanted to talk to you. But when you came out, you stood there putting on a black scarf and shirt, and that seemed pretty strange on a warm night. When you caught the taxi, I followed you."

She gasped. "I didn't even think to look for a tail! Bosey would kill me if he knew!" She repressed the thought that Bosey might well kill her, anyway, for her actions tonight.

"I was at a distance when you got out, and by the time I'd parked, you'd disappeared. But you suddenly came back the other way and turned into the alley almost in front of me. By the time I thought it was safe to follow you through, you'd disappeared again."

She said, "The thing's kind of wide-open now. Probably I'll be able to tell you some of it soon."

He caught her hand and held it, not answering.

"I heard you scream, but I didn't know where it had come from. I was just about to start kicking doors in when you all came out. Who were they, anyway, and what was all that rig they were carrying?"

Sunny laughed. "They were Israelis," she told him, because she was probably burned now, and so were they. "And they were trying to make the world safe for the minorities."

"You're a police officer, Delancey, not some kind of freelance," Bosey said. "What the hell do you think you were doing?"

She knew he was right. She said apologetically, "I was having some personal problems. My judgement slipped. I'm sorry."

"You're damned lucky personally that it was the Israelis you bumped into, but I have to say there are people who aren't pleased about it."

"At least they're on our side," she offered feebly.

"We don't necessarily always cooperate with people who are on our side," Bosey said. He was good and mad, she could tell. He'd probably had some explaining to do about why he'd thought Sunny was experienced enough for an international job.

"I was temporarily insane," she said.

"I'm glad you admit it," said Bosey. "I'll talk to you later. You have some holiday coming, is that right?"

"Yes, sir, I've got four or five weeks due."

"You're taking it now, you understand me? As of this moment you're on holiday, and if you still have a job at the end of it, I'll let you know. With luck, in five weeks things will have cooled down a bit."

She figured he was wise. "What should I do now?"

"Nothing. You should do absolutely nothing now, do you understand me, Delancey?"

"Yes, sir," she said.

Alex Fairchild said, "I thought you'd like to know we had a meeting with your Israeli friends today. They asked after you."

"Did they tell you what they were doing in there? What was that stuff they were putting into those tanks?"

"They didn't like us knowing, but we had most of it figured out. Apparently their scientists have discovered an agent of some kind that renders the reaction that turns those chemicals into a nerve gas inactive, without giving any signals that it's doing so. The stuff still looks and responds the same as the toxic gas, but it's nearly harmless."

"Yeah?" said Sunny delightedly. "But that's terrific! That means that all the stuff being stockpiled over in Iraq—"

"Well, not all of it. But they say they're getting to a large part of this particular chemical. Of course, Iraq is manufacturing more than just this one. They're pretty upset with you, of course. They're assuming that the information will leak to Iraq now."

"Oh, God," she said. "Will it?"

Fairchild shrugged. "Hard to say. But all it means is that they'll find out that some part of their chemical stockpile is inactive. They'll have a hard time testing it, won't they? It might even be a good idea if they know we know they're shooting blanks, if it ever comes to that."

He didn't seem to object to her ad hoc approach to police work. Sunny said lightly, "So will you give me a job if I get fired?"

"If it happened, I would certainly expect you to come and talk to me," Fairchild said calmly.

"You're on," said Sunny.

"Lorna Doone, what on earth is the matter with you?" Sunny said shrilly. "What are you doing? Jock! Jock! Come and look at the cat! There's something wrong with her!"

Jock strode out to the kitchen, the Sunday paper in his hand. "What's the matter?" he asked.

"Look at Lorna Doone! She's never acted like this before! What's the matter with her? I think she's eaten something poisoned. I think she's dying!"

Lorna Doone had nested in the dirty laundry basket. She was making strange mewing sounds, twitching and straining, getting up and lying down again, and every now and then calling to Sunny for help over her shoulder.

Jock took one look and laughed. "She's not dying, Sunny, she's having kittens! Where were you brought up, anyway?"

"Kittens! But that's—but I took such *care!* How could it have happened?"

He grinned at her. "Only one way that happens. If you're not sure, I could show you." He put his arm around her and kissed her lightly.

But she was distracted. "Oh, golly, Emma'll kill me! Are you sure?"

"I'm sure," he said, with an odd tone in his voice, and she turned and looked into the basket, where Lorna's first kitten lay against her flank, a tiny glistening ball.

"Oh, gosh, is that it?" said Sunny in amazement. "Oh, boy, are we supposed to do anything?"

Lorna cried up at her from her position on her side, but whether it was an announcement or a cry for help, Sunny couldn't tell.

"Animals usually manage," said Jock. "But cats like human company sometimes. Seems like that's what she wants."

So Sunny watched the little miracle of birth four times over the next hour, watching Lorna unerringly transform four little unrecognisable glistening balls into four tiny kittens.

"Siamese!" she exclaimed. "Two of them are Siamese! I've never even *seen* a Siamese in this neighbourhood! Jock, am I allowed to pick one up?"

At her insistence Jock was keeping her company while she kept Lorna company. "If she'll let you, it won't hurt them."

"It's so soft! Isn't it amazing! Look, Jock, this one's got folded ears, just like its mother! We've probably got a new breed here!" she laughed. "Siamese fold! Isn't it cute! I can't wait to tell Emma!"

"Siamese!" said Emma. The wire crackled, but she was in Cairo, and the line was by no means bad. "That must have been Maggie's cat, that day he got out. But I was so sure Lorna hadn't seen him."

"Wait a minute," said Sunny. "Do you mean this cat has been pregnant all the time I've been here?"

"Well, of course. I thought you knew. A cat's gestation period is seven weeks, Sunny."

"I've been driven crazy trying to keep that cat away from males for you and all the time it was already pregnant?" she demanded indignantly.

Emma laughed. "Was it a terrible bore? I'm awfully sorry, Sunny."

"You're going to be a lot sorrier than you think," Sunny predicted direly. "You remember the most virile man in the world?"

"What—oh, you mean Jock Prentiss? Have you met him? Isn't he a dish?"

"Yes, yes and yes. And it was all Lorna Doone's fault, so you can blame her. I'm afraid he's been took, as they say."

"*Jock* has? By you? Sunny, that's wonderful! How did it happen?"

"I told you, the cat. I'll explain it all when you get home. I'm glad to hear you're not seriously heartbroken, Emma," she said drily. "A very short time ago it was 'hands off,' if I recall."

"Yes, and I like the way you obeyed me. So what—it's serious, then?"

Sunny laughed a little. "No, of course it's not serious, if by that you mean permanent. I mean, look at him, and look at me."

"I'm looking," said Emma. "So what?"

"Well, I just bear in mind that it's going to be over someday, that's all."

"Has he said so?"

"Men don't say so, do they?" In fact, Jock had asked her to move in next door. Sunny had refused. "But I know. So you can have a chance at him later, if you're still interested."

"Well, don't give up too easily. And I'm not still interested. I have no time for Jock. That's really why I called. Raf is here, and we're going to try again. Isn't that wonderful?"

Sunny would not have understood two months ago, but now she did. Before, she had accepted Emma's reading of the breakup at face value. Now she understood that it had never been that easy. "Emma!" she said. "Yes, wonderful! Terrific! I'm so happy for you!" Because even over this line she could hear the note in her friend's voice that said it was what she wanted.

"We're coming back up to London in a couple of weeks, only for a week or two. But it would be nice if we could have the house to ourselves. Would that be all right? Maybe you could move next door with Jock. That would be nice, too, wouldn't it?"

"Yes, sure," said Sunny faintly. What *would* she do? Manifestly she shouldn't go home yet. "Well, it's all right for me, I guess. Have fun dislodging Pip."

"Oh, Sunny! Did he arrive? I got that letter and was horrified he'd mess up your work. Was it all right?"

"It's a long story," said Sunny.

"I'll hear it all when I come. Say hi to Jock Prentiss for me! Bye!"

"Ow!" Sunny cried. "Ow, ow! They've got nails like little needles. Ow!" Jock laughed unsympathetically. They were lying eight in the bed this Sunday morning: Jock and Sunny, Lorna, four kittens, and Beetle, who was as proud and possessive as if he were himself the father. The kittens, small and fluffy, were playing all over Sunny, attacking her hair, her scratching fingers, even her eyelashes. *"Ouch!"* she said again. Lorna Doone watched placidly, her purring a constant background of sound in the room.

"Do you want to keep a couple of them?" Jock asked.

"Where would I keep them?" she asked. "I won't be able to take them back home with me."

His heart started to thud. He said, "You could keep 'em next door, I guess, couldn't you? With me?"

Sunny's fingers abruptly stopped making the little scratching motions that were exciting the nearest kitten. "What do you mean?" she asked levelly.

He said gruffly, "Sunny, I love you. Why won't you move in with me?"

A hand clamped her heart so that it stopped beating. "Jock," she whispered. "Jock..." She tried again. "Jock, if I don't retain some independence now, what'll I do when you leave me? It's not fair to ask me this."

He leaned over her. Suddenly he was almost angry. "What do you mean, 'when I leave you'?" he demanded. "Who said anything about leaving?"

She could not reply.

He said, "I love you, do you understand that? I want to marry you." He hadn't meant to say that yet; he'd meant to save it till he thought he had a better chance. "I didn't want to ask you till you'd had more time, but you like being with me, don't you? Just stick around and I swear to you you'll get used to the idea." A little urgently, he kissed her. "Will you?" he asked when he lifted his mouth.

"Jock," she whispered.

He said, "I know you've got a job, but you like it here, don't you? I'm not asking you to come to Oz, but we could live here. You said you thought you could get a job with that bunch here if you wanted. Why don't you take it, and I'll stay here making movies? That'd be all right, wouldn't it?"

She opened her mouth, but she couldn't say it. At last she said, "That'd be all right, yes." And then, "I love you, Jock, don't you know that?"

"I know it now," he said. He bent over her, wrapping his arm around her body. The kitten on her stomach squealed protestingly as he began to draw her against him, and another chased down his back after the departing duvet, its little needle claws making themselves felt all the way.

Jock froze. "Is there some way of getting rid of all these cats, Sunny?" he asked. "I'd kind of like to make love to you without so much audience participation."

"Sure!" Sunny agreed. "Mousers!" she cried excitedly. *"Mousers!"*

*   *   *   *   *

This is the season of giving, and Silhouette proudly offers you its sixth annual Christmas collection.

SILHOUETTE

Christmas Stories

1991

Experience the joys of a holiday romance and treasure these heart-warming stories by four award-winning Silhouette authors:

Phyllis Halldorson—"A Memorable Noel"
Peggy Webb—"I Heard the Rabbits Singing"
Naomi Horton—"Dreaming of Angels"
Heather Graham Pozzessere—"The Christmas Bride"

Discover this yuletide celebration—sit back and enjoy Silhouette's Christmas gift of love.

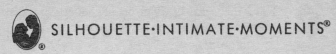

COMING NEXT MONTH

#409 TWILIGHT SHADOWS—Emilie Richards

When a friend's wedding party ended with bullets being exchanged instead of just ordinary vows, Griff Bryant discovered someone was out to get him, and he needed help—*fast*. However, capable *and* gorgeous private investigator Kelley O'Flynn Samuels gave "bodyguarding" a whole new meaning....

#410 NOWHERE TO RUN—Mary Anne Wilson

Psychiatrist R. J. Tyler had chosen to focus exclusively on the teaching side of his field. Yet, drawn by the vulnerability and fear in Lyndsey Cole's eyes, he made an exception. He had to help her remember who her attacker was, before it was too late. But was his heartfelt determination professional...or personal?

#411 LONG WHITE CLOUD—
Marilyn Cunningham

When Kiri MacKay inherited an island from the father who'd abandoned her as a child, she wanted nothing more than to sell the entire estate and be done with it. Then she met wildlife biologist Noel Trevorson, and her determination wavered. His arguments against the sale were persuasive, his kisses seductive. But was he after her—or her island?

#412 BAD MOON RISING—Kathleen Eagle

Schoolteacher Frankie Tracker thought she'd gotten over her adolescent crush on Trey Latimer. But the moment he returned to town, she knew trouble lay ahead. For Trey the man was twice as exciting as Trey the boy. And this time, *she* was a fully grown woman.

AVAILABLE NOW:

Angels Everywhere!

Everything's turning up angels at Silhouette. In November, Ann Williams's ANGEL ON MY SHOULDER (IM #408, $3.29) features a heroine who's absolutely heavenly—and we mean that literally! Her name is Cassandra, and once she comes down to earth, her whole picture of life—and love— undergoes a pretty radical change.

Then, in December, it's time for ANGEL FOR HIRE (D #680, $2.79) from Justine Davis. This time it's hero Michael Justice who brings a touch of out-of-this-world magic to the story. Talk about a match made in heaven . . . !

Look for both these spectacular stories wherever you buy books. But look soon—because they're going to be flying off the shelves as if they had wings!